★ "World Fantasy Award–winner Tidhar (*A Man Lies Dreaming*) magnificently blends literary and speculative elements in this streetwise mosaic novel set under the towering titular spaceport. In a future border town formed between Israeli Tel Aviv and Arab Jaffa, cyborg ex-soldiers deliver illicit drugs for psychic vampires, and robot priests give sermons and conduct circumcions. The Chong family struggles to save patriarch Vlad, lost in ble memory stream they all share, thanks to his of the Conversation, the collective unconscious. New children, born from back-alley genetic engineering, begin to experience actual and virtual reality simultaneo bring them all back and sustain them. Tidhar skilfully mixes classic SF concepts with prose styles and concepts that recall the best of world literature. The byways of Central Station ring with dusty life, like the bruising, depicted by Naguib Mahfouz. Characters wrestle with problems of identity forged under systems of oppression, much as displaced Easterners and Westerners do in the novels of Orhan Pamuk. And yet this is unmistakably SF. Readers of all persuasions will be entranced."
—*Publishers Weekly*, starred review

★ ". . . a fascinating future glimpsed through the lens of a tight-knit community. Verdict: Tidhar (*A Man Lies Dreaming; The Violent Century*) changes genres with every outing, but his astounding talents guarantee something new and compelling no matter the story he tells."
—*Library Journal*, starred review

"Beautiful, original, a shimmering tapestry of connections and images—I can't think of another SF novel quite like it. Lavie Tidhar is one of the most distinctive voices to enter the field in many years."
—Alastair Reynolds, author of the Revelation Space series

"A dazzling tale of complicated politics and even more complicated souls. Beautiful."
—Ken Liu, author of *The Grace of Kings*

"If Nalo Hopkinson and William Gibson held a séance to channel the spirit of Ray Bradbury, they might be inspired to produce a work as grimy, as gorgeous, and as downright sensual as *Central Station*."
—Peter Watts, author of *Blindsight* and *Echopraxia*

"*Central Station* is masterful: simultaneously spare and sweeping —a perfect combination of emotional sophistication and speculative vision. Tidhar always stuns me."
—Kij Johnson, author of *At the Mouth of the River of Bees*

"*Central Station* boasts complexity without complication, sharp prose, and a multi-dimensional world."
—Jeffrey Ford, author of *The Girl in the Glass*

"Lavie Tidhar weaves the threads of classic and modern science fiction tropes with the skills of a gene surgeon and creates a whole new landscape to portray a future both familiar and unsettling. A unique marriage of Philip K. Dick, William Gibson, C. L. Moore, China Miéville, and Larry Niven with 50 degrees of compassion and the bizarre added. An irresistible cocktail."

—Maxim Jakubowski, author of the *Sunday Times* bestselling Vina Jackson novels

"Like all good science fiction, the linked stories of *Central Station* are really about the here and now we live in. Most urgently, they are about just who 'we' might be, here on this overcrowded, contested, Anthropocene world that we all must share. Lavie Tidhar writes in generous detail and expansive vision of a New, and old Jerusalem, and of the many possible 'we's' who live there."

—Carter Scholz, author of *Radiance* and *The Amount to Carry*

"A mosaic of mind-blowing ideas and a dazzling look at a richly-imagined, textured future."

—Aliette de Bodard, author of *The House of Shattered Wings*

"Disturbingly strange, yet bizarrely familiar, like implanted memories from a future you have not yet lived. I loved it."

—Eileen Gunn, author of *Stable Strategies and Others*

"Tidhar weaves strands of faith and science fiction into a breathtaking and lush family history of the far future."

—Max Gladstone, author of *Three Parts Dead*

". . . a standout, absorbing, well realised sci-fi world, with characters who feel like they're about to stroll off the page and take you for a cup of *arak*."

—*Sci-Fi and Fantasy Reviews*

Also by Lavie Tidhar

Novels
Osama (2011)
The Violent Century (2013)
A Man Lies Dreaming (2014)

The Bookman Histories
The Bookman (2010)
Camera Obscura (2011)
The Great Game (2012)

Novellas
An Occupation of Angels (2010)
Cloud Permutations (2010)
Gorel and the Pot-Bellied God (2011)

Collections
HebrewPunk (2007)
Black Gods Kiss (2014)

Graphic Novels
Adolf Hitler's "I Dream of Ants!" (2012, with Neil Struthers)
Going to the Moon (2012, with Paul McCaffrey)
Adler (forthcoming, with Paul McCaffrey)

JAFFA-TEL AVIV /
JUDEA PALESTINA
FEDERAL UNION

MEDITERRANEAN SEA

8

THE GERMAN COLONY

OTHERS CORE ZONE
(AYODHYA PROTECTION

6

4

IBRAHIM AL-AJAMI ST.

JAFFA

DJEMAL PASHA AVENUE

LIOR TIROSH BIBLIO-
MUNICIALITY
SPECIAL ZONE

AJAMI

SOLAR HARVEST
FIELDS

PALACE OF
DISCARDED THINGS

7

DMZ

JAFFA ROAD

FLORENTIN

TRANSCENDENCE ZONE
(SEEKERS WELCOME)

SALAME ROAD

2

3

1

CENTRAL
STATION

5

ABANDONED

HIGHWAY

☆ ENTRANCE TO CENTRAL STATION

▢ TOP OF CENTRAL STATION

1. THE GREEN / ST. COHEN SHRINE

2. ROBOTNIK CAMP

3. NEVE SHA'ANAN ST.

4. OLD JAFFA

5. INTERCHANGE

6. CLOCK TOWER

7. ALLENBY STREET
   (TO CARMEL MARKET)

8. NEVE TZEDEK
   (CHRYOGENIC FACILITIES)

Central Station
Lavie Tidhar

CENTRAL STATION
LAVIE TIDHAR

TACHYON | SAN FRANCISCO

Tachyon Publications LLC
1459 18th Street #139
San Francisco, CA 94107
(415) 285-5615
tachyon@tachyonpublications.com

www.tachyonpublications.com
smart science fiction & fantasy

Series Editor: Jacob Weisman
Editor: Jill Roberts

ISBN 13: 978-1-61696-214-2
ISBN 10: 1-61696-214-3

Printed in the United States of America by Worzalla

9 8 7 6 5 4 3 2

PROLOGUE

I came first to Central Station on a day in winter. African refugees sat on the green, expressionless. They were waiting, but for what, I didn't know. Outside a butchery, two Filipino children played at being airplanes: arms spread wide they zoomed and circled, firing from imaginary under-wing machine guns. Behind the butcher's counter, a Filipino man was hitting a ribcage with his cleaver, separating meat and bones into individual chops. A little farther from it stood the Rosh Ha'ir shawarma stand, twice blown up by suicide bombers in the past but open for business as usual. The smell of lamb fat and cumin wafted across the noisy street and made me hungry.

Traffic lights blinked green, yellow, and red. Across the road a furniture store sprawled out onto the pavement in a profusion of garish sofas and chairs. A small gaggle of junkies sat on the burnt foundations of what had been the old bus station, chatting. I wore dark shades. The sun was high in the sky and though it was cold it was a Mediterranean winter, bright and at that moment dry.

I walked down the Neve Sha'anan pedestrian street. I found shelter in a small shebeen, a few wooden tables and chairs, a small counter serving Maccabee Beer and little else. A Nigerian man behind the counter regarded me without expression. I asked for a beer. I sat down and brought out my notebook and a pen and stared at the page.

Central Station, Tel Aviv. The present. Or a present. Another attack on Gaza, elections coming up, down south in the Arava desert they were building a massive separation wall to stop the refugees from coming in. The refugees were in Tel Aviv now, centred around the old bus station neighbourhood in the south of the city, some quarter million of them and the economic migrants here on sufferance, the Thai and Filipinos and Chinese. I sipped my beer. It was bad. I stared at the page. Rain fell.

I began to write:

Once, the world was young. The Exodus ships had only begun to leave the solar system then; the world of Heven had not been discovered; Dr. Novum had not yet come back from the stars. People still lived as they had always lived: in sun and rain, in and out of love, under a blue sky and in the Conversation, which is all about us, always.

This was in old Central Station, that vast space port which rises over the twin cityscapes of Arab Jaffa, Jewish Tel Aviv. It happened amidst the arches and the cobblestones, a stone-throw from the sea: you could still smell the salt and the tar in the air, and watch, at sunrise, the swoop and turn of solar kites and their winged surfers in the air.

This was a time of curious births, yes: you will read about that. You were no doubt wondering about the children of Central Station. Wondering, too, how a strigoi was allowed to come to Earth. This is the womb from which humanity crawled, tooth by bloody nail, towards the stars.

But it is an ancestral home, too, to the Others, those children of the digitality. In a way, this is as much their story.

There is death in here as well, of course: there always is. The Oracle is here, and Ibrahim, the alte-zachen man, and many others whose names may be familiar to you—

But you know all this already. You must have seen The Rise of Others. *It's all in there, though they made everyone look so handsome.*

This all happened long ago, but we still remember; and we whisper to each other the old tales across the aeons, here in our sojourn among the stars.

It begins with a little boy, waiting for an absent father.

One day, the old stories say, a man fell down to Earth from the stars. . . .

ONE:
THE INDIGNITY OF RAIN

The smell of rain caught them unprepared. It was spring, there was that smell of jasmine and it mixed with the hum of electric buses, and there were solar gliders in the sky, like flocks of birds. Ameliah Ko was doing a Kwasa-Kwasa remix of a Susan Wong cover of "Do You Wanna Dance." It had begun to rain in silver sheets, almost silently; the rain swallowed the sound of gunshots and it drenched the burning buggy down the street, and the old homeless man taking a shit by the dumpster, with his grey pants around his ankles, got caught in it, his one roll of toilet paper in his hand, and he cursed, but quietly. He was used to the indignity of rain.

The city had been called Tel Aviv. Central Station rose high into the atmosphere in the south of the city, bordered in by the webwork of silenced old highways. The station's roof rose too high to see, serving the stratospheric vehicles that rose from and landed onto its machine-smooth surface. Elevators like bullets shot up and down the station and, down below, in the fierce Mediterranean sun, around the space port a bustling market heaved with commerce, visitors and residents, and the usual assortment of pickpockets and identity thieves.

From orbit down to Central Station, from Central Station down to street level, and out from within the air-conditioned liminal space into the poverty of the neighbourhood around the port, where Mama Jones and the boy Kranki stood hand in hand, waiting.

The rain caught them by surprise. The space port, this great white whale, like a living mountain rising out of the urban bedrock, drew onto itself the formation of clouds, its very own miniature weather system. Like islands in the ocean, space ports saw localised rains, cloudy skies, and a growth industry of mini-farms growing like lichen on the side of their vast edifices.

The rain was warm and the drops fat and the boy reached out his hand and cupped a raindrop between his fingers.

Mama Jones, who had been born in this land, in this city that had been called many names, to a Nigerian father and a Filipina mother, in this very same neighbourhood, when the roads still thrummed to the sound of the internal combustion engine and the central station had served buses, not suborbitals, and could remember wars, and poverty, and being unwanted here, in this land fought over by Arab and Jew, looked at the boy with fierce protective pride. A thin, glittering membrane, like a soap bubble, appeared between his fingers, the boy secreting power and manipulating atoms to form this thing, this protective snow globe, capturing within it the single drop of rain. It hovered between his fingers, perfect and timeless.

Mama Jones waited, if a little impatiently. She ran a shebeen here, on the old Neve Sha'anan road, a pedestrianised zone from the old days, that ran right up to the side of the space port, and she needed to be back there.

"Let it go," she said, a little sadly. The boy turned deep blue eyes on her, a perfect blue that had been patented some decades earlier before finding its way to the gene clinics here, where it had been ripped, hacked and resold to the poor for a fraction of the cost.

They said south Tel Aviv had better clinics even than Chiba or Yunnan, though Mama Jones rather doubted it.

Cheaper, though, perhaps.

"Is he coming?" the boy said.

"I don't know," Mama Jones said. "Maybe. Maybe today he is coming."

The boy turned his head to her, and smiled. He looked very young when he smiled. He released the strange bubble in his hand and it floated upwards, through the rain, the single suspended raindrop inside rising towards the clouds that birthed it.

Mama Jones sighed, and she cast a worried glance at the boy. *Kranki* was not a name, as such. It was a word from Asteroid Pidgin, itself a product of Earth's old South Pacific contact languages, carried into space by the miners and engineers sent there as cheap labour by the Malay and Chinese companies. *Kranki*, from the old English *cranky*, it meant variously grumpy or crazy or . . .

Or a little odd.

Someone who did things that other people didn't.

What they called, in Asteroid Pidgin, *nakaimas.*

Black magic.

She was worried about Kranki.

"Is he coming? Is that him?"

There was a man coming towards them, a tall man with an aug behind his ear, and skin that showed the sort of tan one got from machines, and the uneasy steps of someone not used to this gravity. The boy pulled on her hand. "Is that him?"

"Maybe," she said, feeling the hopelessness of the situation as she did each time they repeated this little ritual, every Friday before the Shabbat entered, when the last load of disembarking passengers arrived at Tel Aviv from Lunar Port, or Tong Yun on Mars, or from the Belt, or from one of the other Earth cities like Newer Delhi or Amsterdam or São Paulo. Each week, because the boy's mother had told him, before she died, that his father would one day return, that his father was rich and was working far away, in space, and that one day he would return, return on a Friday so as not to be late for the Shabbat, and he would look after them.

Then she went and overdosed on Crucifixation, ascending to heaven on a blaze of white light, seeing God while they tried to pump her stomach but it was too late, and Mama Jones, somewhat reluctantly, had to look after the boy— because there was no one else.

In North Tel Aviv the Jews lived in their skyrises, and in Jaffa to the South the Arabs had reclaimed their old land by the sea. Here, in between, there were still those people of the land they had called variously Palestine or Israel and whose ancestors had come there as labourers from around the world, from the islands of the Philippines, and from the Sudan, from Nigeria, and from Thailand or China, whose children were born there, and their children's children, speaking Hebrew and Arabic and Asteroid Pidgin, that near-universal language of space. Mama Jones looked after the boy because there was no one else and the rule across this country was the same in whichever enclave of it you were. *We look after our own.*

Because there is no one else.

"It's him!" The boy pulled at her hand. The man was coming towards them, something familiar about his walk, his face, suddenly confusing Mama Jones. Could the boy really be right? But it was impossible, the boy wasn't even b—

"Kranki, stop!" The boy, pulling her by the hand, was running towards the man, who stopped, startled, seeing this boy and this woman bearing down on him. Kranki stopped before the man, breathing heavily. "Are you my dad?" he said.

"Kranki!" said Mama Jones.

The man went very still. He squatted down, to be level with the boy, and looked at him with a serious, intent expression.

"It's possible," he said. "I know that blue. It was popular for a while, I remember. We hacked an open source version out of the trademarked Armani code. . . ." He looked at the boy, then tapped the aug behind his ear—a Martian aug, Mama Jones noticed with alarm.

There had been life on Mars, not the ancient civilizations dreamed of in the past, but a dead, microscopic life. Then someone found a way to reverse engineer the genetic code, and made augmented units out of it. . . .

Alien symbionts no one understood, and few wanted to.

The boy froze, then smiled, and his smile was beatific. He beamed. "Stop it!" Mama Jones said. She shook the man until he almost lost his balance. "Stop it! What are you doing to him?"

"I'm . . ." The man shook his head. He tapped the aug and the boy unfroze, and looked around him, bewildered, as though he was suddenly lost. "You had no parents," the man told him. "You were labbed, right here, hacked together out of public property genomes and bits of black market nodes." He breathed. *"Nakaimas,"* he said, and took a step back.

"Stop it!" Mama Jones said again, feeling helpless. "He is not—"

"I know." The man had found his calm again. "I am sorry. He can speak to my aug. Without an interface. I must have done a better job than I thought, back then."

Something about the face, the voice, and suddenly she felt a tension in her chest, an old feeling, strange and unsettling now. "Boris?" she said. "Boris Chong?"

"What?" he raised his face, looking at her properly for the first time. She could see him so clearly now, the harsh Slavic features and the dark Chinese eyes, the whole assemblage of him, older now, changed by space and circumstances, but still him. . . .

"Miriam?"

She had been Miriam Jones, then. Miriam after her grandmother. She tried to smile, couldn't. "It's me," she said.

"But you—"

"I never left," she said. "You did."

The boy looked between them. Realisation, followed by disappointment, made his face crumble. Above his head the rain gathered, pulled out of the air, forming into a wavering sheet of water through which the sun broke into tiny rainbows.

"I have to go," Miriam said. It'd been a long time since she'd been Miriam to anybody.

"Where? Wait—" Boris Chong looked, for once, confused.

"Why did you come back?" Miriam said.

He shrugged. Behind his ear the Martian aug pulsed, a parasitic, living thing feeding off its host. "I . . ."

"I have to go," Mama Jones, Miriam, she had been a Miriam and that part of her, long buried, was awakening inside her, and it made her feel strange, and uncomfortable, and she tugged on the boy's hand and the shimmering sheet of water above his head burst, falling down on either side of him, forming a perfect, wet circle on the pavement.

Every week she had acquiesced to the boy's mute desire, had taken him to the space port, to this gleaming monstrosity in the heart of the city, to watch and to wait. The boy knew he had been labbed, knew no woman's womb had ever held him, that he had been birthed within the cheap labs where the paint peeled off the walls and the artificial wombs often malfunctioned—but there had been a market for disused foetuses too, there was a market for anything.

But like all children, he never *believed*. In his mind his mother really *had* gone up to heaven, Crucifixion her key to the gates, and in his mind his father would come back, just the way she'd told him, descend from the heavens of Central Station and come down, to this neighbourhood, stuck uncomfortably between North and South, Jew and Arab, and find him, and offer him love.

She pulled on Kranki's hand again and he came with her, and the wind like a scarf wound itself around him, and she knew what he was thinking.

Next week, perhaps, he would come.

"Miriam, wait!"

Boris Chong, who had once been beautiful, when she was beautiful, in the soft nights of spring long ago as they lay on top of the old building filled with domestic workers for the rich of the North, they had made themselves a nest there, between the solar panels and the wind traps, a little haven made of old discarded sofas and an awning of colourful calico from India with political slogans on it in a language neither of them spoke. They had lain there, and gloried in their naked bodies up on the roof, in spring, when the air was warm and scented with the lilacs and the bushes of jasmine down below, late-blooming jasmine, that released its smell at night, under the stars and the lights of the space port.

She kept moving, it was only a short walk to her shebeen, the boy came with her, and this man, a stranger now, who had once been young and beautiful, whispering to her in Hebrew his love, only to leave her, long ago, it was so long ago—

This man was following her, this man she no longer knew, and her heart beat fast inside her, her old, flesh heart, which had never been replaced. Still she marched on, passing fruit and vegetable stalls, the gene clinics, upload centres selling second-hand dreams, shoe shops (for people will always need shoes on their feet), the free clinic, a Sudanese restaurant, the rubbish bins, and finally she arrived at Mama Jones' Shebeen, a hole-in-the-wall nestled between an upholsterer's and a Church of Robot node, for people always need old sofas and armchairs reupholstered, and they always need faith, of whatever sort.

And drink, Miriam Jones thought as she entered the establishment, where the light was suitably dim, the tables made of wood, with cloth over each, and where the nearest node would have broadcast a selection of programming feeds had it not been stuck, some time back, on a South Sudanese channel showing a mixture of holy sermons, weather reports that never changed, and dubbed reruns of the long-running Martian soap *Chains of Assembly*, and nothing else.

A raised bar, offering Palestinian Taiba beer and Israeli Maccabee on tap, locally made Russian vodka, a selection of soft drinks and bottled lager, sheesha pipes for the customers and backgammon boards for use of same—it was a decent little place, it did not make much but it covered rent and food and looking after the boy, and she was proud of it. It was hers.

There were only a handful of regulars sitting inside, a couple of dockyard workers off-shift from the space port sharing a sheesha and drinking beer, chatting amiably, and a tentacle-junkie flopping in a bucket of water, drinking *arak*, and Isobel Chow, her friend Irena Chow's daughter, sitting there with a mint tea, looking deep in thought. Miriam touched her lightly on the shoulder as she came in but the girl did not even stir. She was deep in the virtuality, that is to say, in the Conversation.

Miriam went behind the bar. All around her the endless traffic of the Conversation surged and hummed and called, but she tuned the vast majority of it out of her consciousness.

"Kranki," Mama Jones said, "I think you should go up to the flat and do your school work."

"Finished," the boy said. He turned his attention to the sheesha pipe nearby and cupped blue smoke in his hand, turning it into a smooth round ball. He became intensely absorbed. Mama Jones, now standing behind her counter and feeling a lot more at ease, here, queen of her domain, heard the footsteps and saw the shadow pass and then the tall, thin frame of the man she last knew as Boris Chong came in, bending under the too-low doorframe.

"Miriam, can we talk?"

"What would you have?"

She gestured at the shelves behind her. Boris Chong's pupils dilated, and it made a shiver pass down Mama Jones' spine. He was communicating, silently, with his Martian aug.

"Well?" Her tone was sharper than she intended. Boris's eyes opened wider. He looked startled. "An arak," he said, and suddenly smiled, the smile transforming his face, making him younger, making him—

More human, she decided.

She nodded and pulled a bottle from the shelf and poured him a glass of arak, that anise drink so beloved in that land, and added ice, and brought it to him to a table, with chilled water to go beside it—when you poured the water in, the drink changed colour, the clear liquid becoming murky and pale like milk.

"Sit with me."

She stood with her arms crossed, then relented. She sat down and he, after a moment's hesitation, sat down also.

"Well?" she said.

"How have you been?" he said.

"Well."

"You know I had to leave. There was no work here anymore, no future—"

"I was here."

"Yes."

Her eyes softened. She knew what he meant, of course. Nor could she blame him. She had encouraged him to go and, once he was gone, there was nothing to it but for both of them to move on with life, and she, on the whole, did not regret the life she'd led.

"You own this place?"

"It pays the rent, the bills. I look after the boy."

"He is . . ."

She shrugged. "From the labs," she said. "It could be he was one of yours, like you said."

"There were so many . . ." he said. "Hacked together of whatever non-proprietary genetic code we could get our hands on. Are they all like him?"

Miriam shook her head. "I don't know . . . it's hard to keep track of all the kids. They don't stay kids, either. Not forever." She called out to the boy. "Kranki, could you bring me a coffee, please?"

The boy turned, his serious eyes trained on them both, the ball of smoke still in his hand. He tossed it in the air and it assumed its regular properties and dispersed. "Aww . . ." he said.

"*Now*, Kranki," Miriam said. "Thank you." The boy went to the bar and Miriam turned back to Boris.

"Where have you been all this time?" she said.

He shrugged. "Spent some time on Ceres, in the Belt, working for one of the Malay companies." He smiled. "No more babies. Just . . . fixing people. Then I did three years at Tong Yun, picked up this—" He gestured at the pulsating mass of biomatter behind his ear.

Miriam said, curious, "Did it hurt?"

"It grows with you," Boris said. "The . . . the seed of the thing is injected, it sits under the skin, then it starts to grow. It . . . can be uncomfortable. Not the physicality of it but when you start to communicate, to lay down a network."

It made Miriam feel strange, seeing it. "Can I touch it?" she said, surprising herself. Boris looked very self-conscious; he always did, she thought, and a fierce ray of pride, of affection, went through her, startling her.

"Sure," he said. "Go ahead."

She reached out, touched it, gingerly, with the tip of one finger. It felt like skin, she thought, surprised. Slightly warmer, perhaps. She pressed, it was like touching a boil. She removed her hand.

The boy, Kranki, came with her drink—a long-handled pot with black coffee inside it, brewed with cardamom seeds and cinnamon. She poured, into a small china cup, and held it between her fingers. Kranki said, "I can hear it."

"Hear what?"

"It," the boy said, insistent, pointing at the aug.

"Well, what does it say?" Miriam said, taking a sip of her coffee. She saw Boris was watching the boy intently.

"It's confused," Kranki said.

"How so?"

"It feels something strange from its host. A very strong emotion, or a mix of emotions. Love and lust and regret and hope, all tangled together . . . it's never experienced that before."

"Kranki!"

Miriam hid a shocked laugh as Boris reared back, turning red.

"That's quite enough for today," Miriam said. "Go play outside."

The boy brightened considerably. "Really? Can I?"

"Don't get too far. Stay where I can see you."

"I can always see *you*," the boy said, and ran out without a look back. She could see the faint echo of his passing through the digital sea of the Conversation, then he disappeared into the noise outside.

Miriam sighed. "Kids," she said.

"It's all right." Boris smiled, looking younger, reminding her of other days, another time. "I thought about you, often," he said.

"Boris, why are you here?"

He shrugged again. "After Tong Yun I got a job in the Galilean Republics. On Callisto. They're strange out there, in the Outer System. It's the view of Jupiter in the sky, or . . . they have strange technologies out there, and I did not understand their religions. Too close to Jettisoned, and Dragon's World . . . too far away from the sun."

"That's why you came back?" she said, a surprised laugh. "You missed the sun?"

"I missed home," he said. "I got a job in Lunar Port, it was incredible to be back, so close, to see Earthrise in the sky . . . the Inner System felt like home. Finally I took a holiday, and here I am." He spread his arms. She sensed unspoken words, a secret sorrow; but it wasn't in her to pry. Boris said, "I missed the sort of rain that falls from clouds."

"Your dad's still around," Miriam said. "I see him from time to time."

Boris smiled, though the web of lines at the corners of his eyes—they weren't there before, Miriam thought, suddenly touched—revealed old pain. "Yes, he's retired now," he said.

She remembered him, a big Sino-Russian man, wearing an exoskeleton with a crew of other builders, climbing like metallic spiders over the uncompleted walls of the space port. There had been something magnificent about seeing them like that, they were the size of insects high up there, the sun glinting off the metal, their pincers working, tearing down stone, erecting walls to hold up, it seemed, the world.

She saw him now, from time to time, sitting at the cafés, playing backgammon, drinking the bitter black coffee, endless cups of delicate china, throwing the dice again and again in repeating permutations, in the shadow of the edifice he had helped to build, and which had at last made him redundant.

"Are you going to see him?" she said.

Boris shrugged. "Maybe. Yes. Later—" He took a sip of his drink and grimaced and then smiled. "Arak," he said. "I forgot the taste."

Miriam smiled too. They smiled without reason or regret and, for now, it was enough.

It was quiet in the shebeen, the tentacle-junkie lay in his tub with his bulbous eyes closed, the two cargo workers were chatting in low voices, sitting back. Isobel sat motionless, still lost in the virtuality. Then Kranki was beside them. She hadn't seen him come in but he had the knack, all the children of the station had it, a way to both appear and disappear. He saw them smiling, and started smiling too.

Miriam took his hand. It was warm.

"We couldn't play," the boy complained. There was a halo above his head, rainbows breaking through the wet globules of water in his short, spiky hair. "It started to rain again." He looked at them with boyish suspicion. "Why are you smiling?"

Miriam looked at this man, Boris, this stranger who had been someone that the someone that she had been once loved.

"It must just be the rain," she said.

TWO:
UNDER THE EAVES

Isobel saw them talking, Mama Jones and the strange tall man who seemed somehow familiar, as though he were a distant relative she had once, distantly, glimpsed; but her mind was elsewhere. Will I see him again? Her heart beat a fast tattoo of an unfamiliar rhythm. She had not felt this way before and she was torn, so torn. It was easier in her other life; in the virtual you could make yourself anew. She saw how Mama Jones looked at the man, so strangely, as though . . .

But that was ridiculous. As though they were in love.

Love. Love was so confusing!

She gathered her things and left the shebeen. Will she see him again? Will he come? She passed Kranki on her way out, through the beaded curtain, and ruffled his hair. He looked up at her seriously, with those big blue eyes. Then she was out, and the station rose ahead, immense and familiar, gathering rain about itself like glitter on a dress.

It was madness, she thought. And yet her cheeks were flushed and she felt almost ill, giddy with anticipation.

Will he be there?

"Meet me tomorrow?" Isobel Chow said.

Motl the Robotnik looked from side to side, too quickly. Isobel took a step back.

"Tomorrow night. Under the eaves."

They were whispering. She gathered courage like cloth. Stepped up to him. Put her hand on his chest. His heart was beating fast, she could feel it through the metal. His smell was of machine oil and sweat.

"Go," he said. "You must—" the words died, unsaid. His heart was like a chick in her hand, so scared and helpless. She was suddenly aware of power. It excited her. To have power over someone else, like this.

His finger on her cheek, trailing. It was hot, metallic. She shivered. What if someone saw?

"I have to go," he said.

His hand left her. He pulled away and it rent her. "Tomorrow," she whispered. He said, "Under the eaves," and left, with quick steps, out of the shadow of the warehouse, in the direction of the sea.

She watched him go and then she, too, slipped away, into the night.

———————

In early morning the solitary shrine to St. Cohen of the Others, on the corner of Levinsky Street, sat untroubled and abandoned beside the green. Road cleaners crawled along the roads, sucking up dirt, spraying water and scrubbing, a low hum of gratitude filling the air as they gloried in this greatest of tasks, the momentary holding back of entropy.

By the shrine a solitary figure knelt. Miriam Jones, Mama Jones of Mama Jones' Shebeen, lighting a candle, laying down an offering, a broken electronics circuit as of an ancient television remote control, useless and obsolete.

"Guard us from the Blight and from the Worm, and from the attention of Others," Mama Jones whispered, "and give us the courage to make our own circuitous path in the world, St. Cohen."

The shrine did not reply. But then, Mama Jones did not expect it to, either.

She straightened up, slowly. It was becoming more difficult, with the knees. She still had her own kneecaps. She still had most of her original parts. It wasn't anything to be proud of, but it wasn't anything to be ashamed of, either. She stood there, taking in the morning air, the joyous hum of the road-cleaning machines, the imagined whistle of aircraft high above, suborbitals coming down from orbit, gliding down like parachuting spiders to land on the roof of Central Station.

Yesterday had been confusing, she thought. A holiday, Boris said. But she knew there was more unsaid, there were obligations, ties, there were *circumstances*.

But she did not want to think about all this. Not now.

It was a cool, fresh morning. The heat of summer did not yet lie heavy on the ground, choking the very air. She walked away from the shrine and stepped on the green, and it felt good to feel grass under her feet. She remembered the green when she was young, with the others like her, Somali and Sudanese refugees who found themselves in this strange country, having crossed desert and borders, seeking a semblance of peace, only to find themselves unwanted and isolated here, in this enclave of the Jews. She remembered her father waking every morning, and walking to the green and sitting there, with the others, the air of quiet desperation making them immobile. Waiting. Waiting for a man to come in a pickup truck and offer them a labourer's job, waiting for the UN agency bus—or, helplessly, for the Israeli police's special Oz Agency to come and check their papers, with a view towards arrest or deportation . . .

Oz meant "strength," in Hebrew. But the real strength, Miriam thought, wasn't in intimidating helpless people, who had nowhere else to turn. It was in surviving, the way her parents had, the way she had—learning Hebrew, working, making a small, quiet life as past turned to present and present to future, until one day there was only her, still living here, in Central Station.

Now the green was quiet, only a lone robotnik sitting with his back to a tree, asleep or awake she couldn't tell. Already traffic was growing on the roads, the sweepers, with little murmurs of disappointment, moving on. Small cars moved along the road, their solar panels spread like wings. There were solar panels everywhere, on rooftops and the sides of buildings, everyone trying to snatch away some free power in this sunniest of places. Tel Aviv. She knew there were sun farms beyond the city, vast tracts of land where panels stretched across the horizon, hungrily sucking in the sun's rays, converting them into energy that was then fed into central charging stations across the city. She liked the sight of them, and fashion-wise it was all the rage, Mama Jones' own clothes had tiny solar panes sewn in, and her wide-brimmed hat caught the sun, wasting nothing—it looked very stylish.

She left the green and crossed the road. As she did, she saw Isobel Chow passing by on her bicycle, heading to Central Station. Mama Jones waved, but Isobel didn't see her, and Mama Jones shrugged. It was time to open the shebeen, prepare the sheesha pipes, mix the drinks. There will be customers soon. There always were, in Central Station.

Isobel cycled along the Salame Road, her bicycle like a butterfly, wings open, sucking up sun, murmuring to her in a happy, sleepy voice, nodal connection mixed in with the broadcast of a hundred thousand other voices, channels, music, languages, the high-bandwidth indecipherable *toktok* of Others, weather reports, confessionals, off-world broadcasts time-lagged from Lunar Port and Tong Yun and the Belt, Isobel randomly tuning in and out of that deep and endless stream which was the Conversation.

The sounds and sights washed over her: deep space images from a lone spider crashing into a frozen rock in the Oort cloud, burrowing in to begin converting the asteroid into copies of itself; a rerun episode of *Chains of Assembly*; a Congolese station broadcasting Nuevo Kwasa-Kwasa music; from North Tel Aviv, a talk show on Torah studies, growing heated; from the side of the street, sudden and alarming, a repeated ping—*Please help. Please donate. Will work for spare parts.*

She slowed down. By the side of the road, on the Arab side, stood a robotnik. It was in bad shape—large patches of rust, a missing eye, one leg dangling uselessly—the robotnik's still-human single eye looked at her, but whether in mute appeal, or indifference, she couldn't tell. It was broadcasting on a wide band, mechanically, helplessly—on a blanket on the ground by its side was a small pile of spare parts, a near-empty gasoline can—solar didn't do much for robotniks.

No, she couldn't stop, she mustn't. It made her apprehensive. She cycled away but kept looking back, passersby ignoring the robotnik as though it wasn't there, the sun rising fast, it was going to be another hot day. She found his node, sent a small donation, more for her own ease than for him. Robotniks, the lost soldiers of the lost wars of the Jews—mechanized and sent to fight and then, later, when the wars ended, abandoned as they were, left to fend for themselves on the streets, begging for the parts that kept them alive. . . .

She knew many of them had emigrated off-world, gone to Tong Yun on Mars. Others were based in Jerusalem, living in the Russian Compound made theirs by long occupation. Beggars. You never paid much attention to them.

And they were old. Some of them had fought in wars that didn't even have names anymore.

She cycled away, up Salame, heading to the station.

Tonight, she thought. Under the eaves. Tonight, she thought; and her heart like a solar kite fluttered in anticipation, waiting to be set free.

Over the course of the day the sun rose behind the space port and traced an arc across it before landing at last in the sea.

Isobel worked inside Central Station and usually didn't see the sun at all.

The Level Three concourse offered a mixture of food courts, drone battle-zones, gamesworlds pod-hives and Louis Wu emporiums, *nakamals* and smoke bars, truflesh and virtual sex-work establishments, and a faith bazaar.

Isobel had heard the greatest faith bazaar was in Tong Yun City on Mars. The one they had on Level Three *here* was a low-key affair—a Church of Robot mission house, a Gorean temple, an Elronite Centre for the Advancement of Humankind, a Baha'i temple, a mosque, a synagogue, a Catholic church, an Armenian church, an Ogko shrine, and a Theravada Buddhist temple.

On her way to work Isobel went to church. She had been raised Catholic, her mother's family, themselves Chinese immigrants to the Philippines, having adopted that religion in another era, another time. Yet she could find no comfort in the hushed quietude of the spacious church, the smell of the candles, the dim light and the painted glass and the sorrowful look of the crucified Jesus.

The church forbids it, she thought, suddenly horrified. The quiet of the church seemed oppressive, the air too still. It was as if every item in the room was looking at her, was *aware* of her. She turned on her heels.

Outside, not looking, she almost bumped into Brother Patch-It.

"Daughter, you are *shaking*," R. Patch-It said, compassion in his voice. She knew R. Patch-It slightly, the robot had been a fixture of Central Station (both space port and neighbourhood) her entire life, and the part-time *moyel* for the Jewish residents in the event of the birth of a baby boy.

"I'm fine, really," Isobel said. The robot looked at her with his expressionless face. "Robot" was male in Hebrew, a gendered language. And most robots had been fashioned without genitalia or breasts, making them appear vaguely male. They had been a mistake, of sort. No one had produced robots for a very long time. They were a missing link, an awkward evolutionary step between human and Other.

"Would you like a cup of tea?" the robot said. "Perhaps cake? Sugar helps human distress, I am told." Somehow R. Patch-It managed to look abashed.

"I'm fine, really," Isobel said again. Then, on an impulse: "Do you believe that . . . can robots . . . I mean to say—"

She faltered. The robot regarded her with his old, expressionless face. A rust scar ran down one cheek, from his left eye to the corner of his mouth. "You can ask me anything," the robot said, gently. Isobel wondered what dead human's voice had been used to synthesise the robot's own.

"Do robots feel love?" she said.

The robot's mouth moved. Perhaps it was meant as a smile. "We feel nothing but love," the robot said.

"How can that be? How can you . . . how can you *feel*?" she was almost shouting. But this was Level Three, no one paid any attention.

"We're anthropomorphised," R. Patch-It said, gently. "We were fashioned human, given physicality, senses. It is the tin man's burden." His voice was sad. "Do you know that poem?"

"No," Isobel said. Then, "What about . . . what about Others?"

The robot shook his head. "Who can tell," he said. "For us, it is unimaginable, to exist as a pure digital entity, to not know physicality. And yet, at the same time, we seek to escape our physical existence, to achieve heaven, knowing it does not exist, that it must be built, the world fixed and patched . . . but what is it really that you ask me, Isobel daughter of Irena?"

"I don't know," she whispered, and she realised her face was wet. "The church—" her head inching, slightly, at the Catholic church behind them. The robot nodded, as if he understood.

"Youth feels so strongly," the robot said. His voice was gentle. "Don't be afraid, Isobel. Allow yourself to love."

"I don't know," Isobel said. "I don't know."

"Wait—"

But she had turned away from Brother Patch-It. Blinking back the tears—she didn't know where they came from—she walked away, she was late for work.

Tonight, she thought. Tonight, under the eaves. She wiped away the tears.

With dusk a welcome coolness settled over Central Station. In Mama Jones' Shebeen candles were lit and, across the road, the No-Name Nakamal was preparing the evening's kava, and the strong, earthy smell of it—the roots peeled and chopped, the flesh minced and mixed with water, squeezed repeatedly to release its very essence, the kavalactones in the plant—the smell filled the paved street that was the very heart of the neighbourhood.

On the green, robotniks huddled together around a makeshift fire in an upturned drum. Flames reflected in their faces, metal and human mixed artlessly, the still-living debris of long-gone wars. They spoke amidst themselves in that curious Battle Yiddish that had been imprinted on them by some well-meaning army developer—a hushed and secret language no one spoke anymore.

Inside Central Station the passengers dined and drank and played and worked and waited—Lunar traders, Martian Chinese on an Earth holiday package tour, Jews from the asteroid-kibbutzim in the Belt, the hurly burly of a humanity for whom Earth was no longer enough and yet was the centre of the universe, around which all planets and moons and habitats rotated, an Aristotelian model of the world superseding its one-time victor, Copernicus. On Level Three Isobel was embedded inside her work pod, existing simultaneously, like a Schrödinger's Cat, in physical space and the equally real virtuality of the Guilds of Ashkelon universe, where—

She was *the* Isobel Chow, captain of the *Nine-Tailed Cat*, a starship thousands of years old, upgraded and refashioned with each Universal Cycle, a salvage operation she, Isobel, was captain and commander of, hunting for precious gamesworld artefacts to sell on the Exchange—

Orbiting Black Betty, a Guilds of Ashkelon universal singularity, where a dead alien race had left behind enigmatic ruins, floating in space in broken rocks, airless asteroids of a once-great galactic empire—

Success there translating to food and water and rent *here*—

But what is here, what is *there*—

Isobel, Schrödingering, in the virtual and the real—or in the GoA and in what they call Universe-One—and she was working.

Night fell over Central Station. Lights came alive around the neighbourhood then, floating spheres casting a festive glow. Night was when Central Station came *alive*. . . .

Florists packing for the day in the wide sprawling market, and the boy Kranki playing by himself, stems on the ground and wilting dark Lunar roses, hydroponics grown, and none came too close to him, the boy was strange. . . .

Asteroid Pidgin around him as he played, making stems rise and dance before him, black rose heads opening and closing in a silent, graceless dance before the boy. The boy had nakaimas, he had the black magic, he had the quantum curse. Conversation flowing around him, traders closing for the day or opening for the night, the market changing faces, never shutting, people sleeping under their stands or having dinner, and from the food stalls the smells of frying fish, of chilli in vinegar, of soy and garlic frying, of cumin and turmeric and the fine purple powder of sumac, so called because it looks like a blush. The boy played, as boys would. The flowers danced, mutely.

———————

— Yu stap go wea? *Where are you going?*

— Mi stap go bak long haos. *I am going home.*

— Yu no save stap smoltaem, dring smolsmol bia? *Won't you stop for a small beer?*

Laughter. Then—

— Si, mi save stap smoltaem. *Yes, I could stop for a little while.*

Music playing, on numerous feeds and live, too—a young *kathoey* backpacker from Thailand on an old acoustic guitar, singing, while down the road a tentacle-junkie was beating time on multiple drums, adding distortions in real-time and broadcasting, a small voice weaving itself into the complex unending pattern of the Conversation.

— Mi lafem yu!

— Awo, yu drong!

Laughter, *I love you—You're drunk!*—a kiss, the two men walk away together, holding hands—

— Wan dei bae mi go long spes, bae mi go lukluk olbaot long ol star.

— Yu kranki we!

One day I will go to space, I will go look around all the planets—

You're crazy!

Laughter, and someone dropping in from the virtuality, blinking sleepy eyes, readjusting, someone turns a fish over on the grill, someone yawns, someone smiles, a fight breaks out, lovers meet, the moon on the horizon rises, the shadows of the moving spiders flicker on the surface of the moon.

———

Under the eaves. Under the eaves. Where it's always dry where it's always dark, under the eaves.

There, under the eaves of Central Station, around the great edifice, was a buffer zone, a separator between space port and neighbourhood. You could buy anything at Central Station and what you couldn't buy you could get there, in the shadows.

Isobel had finished work, she had come back to Universe-One, had left behind captainhood and ship and crew, climbed out of the pod, and on her feet, the sound of her blood in her ears, and when she touched her wrist she felt the blood pulsing there, too, the heart wants what the heart wants, reminding us that we are human, and frail, and weak.

Through a service tunnel she went, between floors, and came out on the northeast corner of the port, facing the Kibbutz Galuyot road and the old interchange.

It was quiet there, and dark, few shops, an unkosher pork butcher and a book binder and warehouses left from days gone by, now turned into sound-proofed clubs and gene clinics and synth emporiums. She waited in the shadow of the port, hugging the walls, they felt warm, the station always felt alive, on heat, the station like a heart, beating. She waited, her embedded node scanning for intruders, for digital signatures and heat, for motion—Isobel was a Central Station girl, she could take care of herself, she had a knife, she was cautious but not afraid of the shadows.

She waited, waited for him to come.

———

"You waited."

She pressed against him. He was warm, she didn't know where the metal of him finished and the organic of him began.

He said, "You came," and there was wonder in the words.

"I had to. I had to see you again."

"I was afraid." His voice was not above a whisper. His hand on her cheek, she turned her head, kissed it, tasting rust like blood.

"We are beggars," he said. "My kind. We are broken machines."

She looked at him, this old abandoned soldier. She knew he had died, that he had been remade, a human mind cyborged onto an alienated body, sent out to fight, and to die, again and again. That now he lived on scraps, depending on the charity of others. . . .

Robotnik. That old word, meaning *worker.*

But said like a curse.

She looked into his eyes. His eyes were almost human.

"I don't remember," he said. "I don't remember who I was, before."

"But you are . . . you are still . . . you are!" she said, as though finding truth, suddenly, and she laughed, she was giddy with laughter and happiness and he leaned in and kissed her, gently at first and then harder, their shared need melding them, joining them almost like a human is bonded to an Other.

In his strange obsolete Battle Yiddish he said, "Ich lieba dich."

In Asteroid Pidgin she replied.

— Mi lafem yu.

His finger on her cheek, hot, metallic, his smell of machine oil and gasoline and human sweat. She held him close, there against the wall of Central Station, in the shadows, as a plane high overhead, adorned in light, came in to land from some other and faraway place.

THREE:
THE SMELL OF
ORANGE GROVES

High overhead, on the rooftop, Boris was awake. He thought he saw, under the awnings of the station, two furtive figures break apart; but his mind was elsewhere.

It had been strange running into Miriam; she'd both changed and hadn't. She must have known why he'd come back, but she didn't pry, leaving him to his own secret sorrow.

On the roof the solar panels were folded in on themselves, still asleep, yet uneasily stirring, as though they could sense the imminent coming of the sun. The building's residents, his father's neighbours, had, over the years, planted and expanded an assortment of plants, in pots of clay and aluminium and wood, across the roof, turning it into a high-rise tropical garden.

It was quiet up there and, for the moment, still cool. He loved the smell of late-blooming jasmine, it crept along the walls of the building, climbing tenaciously high, spreading out all over the old neighbourhood that surrounded Central Station. He took a deep breath of night air and released it slowly, haltingly, watching the lights of the space port, moving stars tracing jewelled flight paths in the skies.

He loved the smell of this place, this city. The smell of the sea to the west, that wild scent of salt and open water, seaweed and tar, of suntan lotion and people. Loved the smell of cold conditioned air leaking out of windows, of basil when you rubbed it between your fingers, loved the smell of shawarma rising from street level with its heady mix of spices, loved the smell of vanished orange groves from far beyond the urban blocks of Tel Aviv or Jaffa.

Once it had all been orange groves. He stared out at the old neighbourhood, the peeling paint, boxlike apartment blocks in old-style Soviet architecture crowded in with magnificent early twentieth-century Bauhaus constructions, buildings made to look like ships, with long curving graceful balconies, small round windows, flat roofs like decks, like the one he stood on—

Mixed amongst the old buildings were newer constructions, Martian-style co-op buildings with drop-chutes for lifts, and small rooms divided and subdivided inside, many without any windows—

Laundry hanging as it had for hundreds of years, off wash lines and windows, faded blouses and shorts blowing in the wind, gently. Lanterns floated in the streets down below, dimming now, and Boris realised the night was receding, saw a blush of pink and red on the edge of the horizon, and he knew the sun was coming.

He had spent the night keeping vigil for his father. Vlad Chong, son of Weiwei Zhong (Zhong Weiwei in the Chinese manner) and of Yulia Chong, née Rabinovich. In the tradition of the family Boris, too, was given a Russian name. In another of the family's traditions, he was also given a second, Jewish name. He smiled wryly, thinking about it. Boris Aharon Chong, the heritage and weight of three shared and ancient histories pressing down heavily on his slim, no longer young shoulders.

It had not been an easy night.

Once it had all been orange groves . . . he took a deep breath, that smell of old asphalt and combustion-engine exhaust fumes, gone now like the oranges yet still, somehow, lingering, a memory-scent.

He'd tried to leave it behind. The family's memory, what they sometimes called the Curse of the Family Chong: what they called Weiwei's Folly.

He could still remember it. Of course he could. A day so long ago, that Boris Aharon Chong himself was not yet an idea, an I-loop that hadn't yet been formed. . . .

It was in Jaffa, in the Old City on top of the hill, above the harbour. The home of the Others.

Zhong Weiwei cycled up the hill, sweating in the heat. He mistrusted these narrow winding streets, both of the Old City itself and of Ajami, the neighbourhood that had at last reclaimed its heritage. Weiwei understood this place's conflicts very well.

There were Arabs and Jews and they wanted the same land and so they fought. Weiwei understood land, and how you were willing to die for it.

But he also knew the concept of land had changed. That land was a concept less of a physicality now, and more of the mind. Recently, he had invested some of his money in an entire planetary system in the Guilds of Ashkelon gamesworld. Soon he would have children—Yulia was in her third trimester already—and then grandchildren, and great-grandchildren, and so on down the generations, and they would remember Weiwei, their progenitor. They would thank him for what he'd done, for the real estate both real and virtual, and for what he was hoping to achieve today.

He, Zhong Weiwei, would begin a dynasty, here in this divided land. For he had understood the most basic of aspects, he alone saw the relevance of that foreign enclave that was Central Station. Jews to the north (and his children, too, would be Jewish, which was a strange and unsettling thought), Arabs to the south, now they have returned, reclaimed Ajami and Menashiya, and were building New Jaffa, a city towering into the sky in steel and stone and glass. Divided cities, like Akko, and Haifa, in the north, and the new cities sprouting in the desert, in the Negev and the Arava.

Arab or Jew, they needed their immigrants, their foreign workers, their Thai and Filipino and Chinese, Somali and Nigerian. And they needed their buffer, that in-between-zone that was Central Station, old South Tel Aviv, a poor place, a vibrant place—most of all, a liminal place.

A border town.

And he would make it his home. His, and his children's, and his children's children. The Jews and the Arabs understood family, at least. In that they were like the Chinese—so different to the Anglos, with their nuclear families, strained relations, all living separately, alone. . . . This, Weiwei swore, would not happen to his children.

At the top of the hill he stopped, and wiped the sweat from his brow with the cloth handkerchief he kept for that purpose. Cars went past him, and the sound of construction was everywhere. He himself worked on one of the buildings they were erecting here, a diasporic construction crew, small Vietnamese and tall Nigerians and pale, solid Transylvanians, communicating by hand signals and Asteroid Pidgin (though that had not yet been in widespread use at that time) and automatic translators through their nodes. Weiwei himself worked the exoskeleton suits, climbing up the tower blocks with spiderlike grips, watching the city far down below and looking out to sea, and distant ships. . . .

But today was his day off. He had saved money—some to send, every month, to his family back in Chengdu, some for his soon to be growing family here. And the rest for this, for the favour to be asked of the Others.

Folding the handkerchief neatly away, he pushed the bike along the road and into the maze of alleyways that was the Old City of Jaffa. The remains of an ancient Egyptian fort could still be seen there, the gate had been refashioned a century before, and an orange tree still hung by chains, planted within a heavy, egg-shaped stone basket, in the shade of the walls, an art installation. Weiwei didn't stop, but kept going until he reached, at last, the place where the Oracle dwelt.

―――――――

Boris looked at the rising sun. He felt tired, drained. He kept his father company throughout the night. His father, Vlad, hardly slept anymore. He sat for hours in his armchair, a thing worn and full of holes, dragged one day, years ago (the memory crystal-clear in Boris's mind) with great effort and pride from Jaffa's flea market. Vlad's hands moved through the air, moving and rearranging invisible objects. He would not give Boris access to his visual feed. He barely communicated anymore. Boris suspected the objects were memories, that Vlad was trying to somehow fit them back together again.

But he couldn't tell for sure.

Like Weiwei, Vlad had been a construction worker. He had been one of the people who had built Central Station, climbing up the unfinished gigantic structure, this space port that was now an entity unto itself, a miniature mall-nation to which neither Tel Aviv nor Jaffa could lay complete claim.

But that had been long ago. Humans lived longer now, but the mind grew old just the same, and Vlad's mind was older than his body. Boris, on the roof, went to the corner by the door. It was shaded by a miniature palm tree, and now the solar panels, too, were opening out, extending delicate wings, the better to catch the rising sun and provide shade and shelter to the plants.

Long ago, the resident association had installed a communal table and a samovar there, and each week a different flat took turns to supply the tea and the coffee and the sugar. Boris gently plucked leaves off the potted mint plant nearby, and made himself a cup of tea. The sound of boiling water pouring into the mug was soothing, and the smell of the mint spread in the air, fresh and clean, waking him up. He waited as the mint brewed; took the mug with him back to the edge of the roof. Looking down, Central Station—never truly asleep—was noisily waking up.

He sipped his tea, and thought of the Oracle.

The Oracle's name had once been Cohen, and rumour had it that she was a relation of St. Cohen of the Others, though no one could tell for certain. Few people today knew this. For three generations she had resided in the Old City, in that dark and quiet stone house, her and her Other alone.

The Other's name, or ident tag, was not known, which was not unusual, with Others.

Regardless of possible familial links, outside the stone house there stood a small shrine to St. Cohen. It was a modest thing, with random items of golden colour placed on it, and old, broken circuits and the like, and candles burning at all hours. Weiwei, when he came to the door, paused for a moment before the shrine, and lit a candle, and placed an offering—a defunct computer chip from the old days, purchased at great expense in the flea market down the hill.

Help me achieve my goal today, he thought, help me unify my family and let them share my mind when I am gone.

There was no wind in the Old City, but the old stone walls radiated a comforting coolness. Weiwei, who had only recently had a node installed, pinged the door and, a moment later, it opened. He went inside.

Boris remembered that moment as a stillness and at the same time, paradoxically, as a *shifting*, a sudden inexplicable change of perspective. His grandfather's memory glinted in the mind. For all his posturing, Weiwei was like an explorer in an unknown land, feeling his way by touch and instinct. He had not grown up with a node; he found it difficult to follow the Conversation, that endless chatter of human and machine feeds a modern human would feel deaf and blind without; yet he was a man who could sense the future as instinctively as a chrysalis can sense adulthood. He knew his children would be different, and their children different in their turn, but he equally knew there can be no future without a past—

"Zhong Weiwei," the Oracle said. Weiwei bowed. The Oracle was surprisingly young, or young-looking at any rate. She had short black hair and unremarkable features and pale skin and a golden prosthetic for a thumb, which made Weiwei shiver without warning: it was her Other.

"I seek a boon," Weiwei said. He hesitated, then extended forward the small box. "Chocolates," he said, and—or was it just his imagination?—the Oracle smiled.

It was quiet in the room. It took him a moment to realise it was the Conversation, ceasing. The Oracle took the box from him and opened it, selecting one particular piece with care and putting it in her mouth. She chewed thoughtfully for a moment and indicated approval by inching her head. Weiwei bowed again.

"Please," the Oracle said. "Sit down."

Weiwei sat down. The chair was high-backed and old and worn—from the flea market, he thought, and the thought made him feel strange, the idea of the Oracle shopping in the stalls, almost as though she were human. But of course, she was human. It should have made him feel more at ease, but somehow it didn't.

Then the Oracle's eyes subtly changed colour, and her voice, when it came, was different, rougher, a little lower than it had been, and Weiwei swallowed again. "What is it you wish to ask of us, Zhong Weiwei?"

It was her Other, speaking now. The Other, shotgun-riding on the human body, Joined with the Oracle, quantum processors running within that golden thumb . . . Weiwei, gathering his courage, said, "I seek a bridge."

The Other nodded, indicating for him to proceed.

"A bridge between past and future," Weiwei said. "A . . . continuity."

"Immortality," the Other said. It sighed. Its hand rose and scratched its chin, the golden thumb digging into the woman's pale flesh. "All humans want is immortality."

Weiwei shook his head, though he could not deny it. The idea of death, of dying, terrified him. He lacked faith, he knew. Many believed, belief was what kept humanity going. Reincarnation or the afterlife, or the mythical Upload, what they called being Translated—they were the same, they required a belief he did not possess, much as he may long for it. He knew that when he died, that would be it. The I-loop with the ident tag of Zhong Weiwei would cease to exist, simply and without fuss, and the universe would continue just as it always had. It was a terrible thing to contemplate, one's insignificance. For human I-loops, they were the universe's focal point, the object around which everything revolved. Reality was subjective. And yet that was an illusion, just as an "I" was, the human personality a composite machine compiled out of billions of neurons, delicate networks operating semi-independently in the grey matter of a human brain. Machines augmented it, but they could not preserve it, not forever. So: yes, Weiwei thought. The thing that he was seeking was a vain thing, but it was also a practical thing. He took a deep breath and said, "I want my children to remember me"

Boris watched Central Station. The sun was rising now behind the space port, and down below robotniks moved into position, spreading out blankets and crude, handwritten signs asking for donations of spare parts or gasoline or vodka.

He saw R. Brother Patch-It, of the Church of Robot, doing his rounds—the Church tried to look after the robotniks, as it did after its small flock of humans. Robots were a strange missing link between human and Other, not fitting in either world—digital beings shaped by physicality, by bodies, many refusing the Upload in favour of their own, strange faith. . . . Boris remembered Brother Patch-It, from childhood—he had done Boris's circumcision, his father's too. The question of Who Is a Jew had been asked not just about the Chong family, but of the robots too, and was settled long ago. Boris had fragmented memories, from the matrilineal side, predating Weiwei—the protests in Jerusalem, Matt Cohen's labs and the first, primitive Breeding Grounds, where digital entities evolved in ruthless evolutionary cycles:

Plaques waving on King George Street, a mass demonstration: *No To Slavery!* And *Destroy the Concentration Camp!* and so on, an angry mass of humanity coming together to protest the perceived enslavement of those first, fragile Others in their locked-down networks, Matt Cohen's laboratories under siege, his rag-tag team of scientists, kicked out from one country after another before settling, at long last, in Jerusalem—

St. Cohen of the Others, they called him now. Boris lifted the mug to his lips and discovered it was empty. He put it down, rubbed his eyes. He should have slept. He was no longer young, could not go days without sleep, powered by stimulants and restless, youthful energy. The days when he and Miriam hid on this very same roof, holding each other, making promises they knew, even then, they couldn't keep. . . .

He thought of her now, trying to catch a glimpse of her walking down the paved street to her shebeen. It was hard to think of her, to *ache* like this, like a, like a *boy*. He had not come back because of her but, somewhere in the back of his mind, it must have been, the thought. . . .

On his neck the aug breathed softly. He had picked it up in Tong Yun City in a backstreet off Arafat Avenue, in a no-name clinic run by a third-generation Martian Chinese, a Mr. Wong, who installed it for him.

It was supposed to have been bred out of the fossilised remains of micro-bacterial Martian life forms, but whether that was true no one knew for sure. It was strange, having the aug. It was a parasite, it fed off of Boris, it pulsated gently against his neck, a part of him now, another appendage,

feeding him alien thoughts, alien feelings, taking in turn
Boris's human perspective and subtly *shifting* it, it was like
watching your ideas filtered through a kaleidoscope.

He put his hand against the aug and felt its warm surface.
It moved under his fingers, breathing gently. Sometimes the
aug synthesised strange substances, they acted as drugs on
Boris's system, catching him by surprise. At other times it
shifted visual perspective, or even interfaced with Boris's
node, the digital networking component of his brain,
installed shortly after birth, without which one was worse
than blind, worse than deaf: one was disconnected from the
Conversation.

He had tried to run away, he knew. He had left home,
had left Weiwei's memory, or tried to, for a while. He went
into Central Station, and he rode the elevators to the very
top, and beyond. He had left the Earth, beyond orbit, gone
to Mars and the Belt, to the Up and Out, but the memories
followed him, Weiwei's bridge, linking forever future and
past. . . .

"I wish my memory to live on, when I am gone."

"So do all humans," the Other said.

*"I wish . . ." Gathering courage, he continued. "I wish for
my family to remember," he said. "To learn from the past, to
plan for the future. I wish my children to have my memories,
and for their memories, in turn, to be passed on. I want my
grandchildren and their grandchildren and onwards, down the
ages, into the future, to remember this moment."*

"And so it shall be," the Other said.

And so it was, Boris thought. The memory was clear in his mind, suspended like a dew drop, perfect and unchanged. Weiwei had gotten what he asked for, and his memories were Boris's now, as were Vlad's, as were his grandmother Yulia's and his mother's, and all the rest of them—cousins and nieces and uncles, nephews and aunts, all sharing the Chong family's central reservoir of memory, each able to dip, instantaneously, into that deep pool of memories, into the ocean of the past.

Weiwei's Folly, as they still called it, in the family. It worked in strange ways, sometimes, even far away, when he was working in the birthing clinics on Ceres, or walking down an avenue in Tong Yun City on Mars, a sudden memory would form in his head, a new memory—Cousin Oksana's memories of giving birth for the first time, to little Yan—pain and joy mixing in with random thoughts, wondering if anyone had fed the dog, the midwife's voice saying, "Push! Push!," the smell of sweat and the beeping of monitors, the low chatter of people outside the door, and that indescribable feeling as the baby slowly emerged out of her. . . .

He put down the mug. Down below Central Station was awake now, the neighbourhood stalls set with fresh produce, the market alive with sounds, the smell of smoke and chickens roasting slowly on a grill, the shouts of children as they went to school—

He thought of Miriam, and how they had loved each other, when the world was young, loved in the Hebrew that was their childhood tongue, but were separated, not by flood or war but simple life, and the things it did to people. Boris worked the birthing clinics of Central Station, but there were too many memories here, memories like ghosts, and at last he rebelled, and had gone into Central Station and then into orbit, to the place they called Gateway, and from there, first, to Lunar Port.

He was young, he had wanted adventure. He had tried to get away. Lunar Port, Ceres, Tong Yun . . . but the memories pursued him, and worst amongst them were his father's. They followed him through the chatter of the Conversation, compressed memories bouncing from one Mirror to the other, across space, at the speed of light, and so they remembered him here on Earth just as he remembered them there, and at last the weight of it became such that he returned.

He had been back in Lunar Port when it happened. He had been brushing his teeth, watching his face—not young, not old, a common enough face, the eyes Chinese, the facial features Slavic, his hair thinning a little—when the memory attacked him, suffused him—he dropped the toothbrush.

Not his father's memory, his cousin's, Yan, and recent: Vlad sitting in the chair, in his apartment, his father older than Boris remembered, thinner, and something that hurt him obscurely, that reached across space and made his chest tighten with pain—that clouded look in his father's eyes. Vlad sat without speaking, without acknowledging his cousin or the rest of them, who had come to visit him.

He sat there and his hands moved through the air, arranging and rearranging objects none could see.

––––––––––

"Boris!"

"Yan."

His cousin's shy smile. "I didn't think you were real."

Time-delay, moon-to-Earth round-trip, node-to-node. "You've grown."

"Yes, well. . . ."

Yan worked inside Central Station. A lab on Level Five where they manufactured viral ads, airborne microscopic agents that transferred themselves from person to person, thriving in a closed-environment, air-conditioned system like Central Station, coded to deliver person-specific offers, organics interfacing with nodal equipment, all to shout *Buy. Buy. Buy.* He was seeing a boy now, Youssou, but they were going through a rough patch.

"It's your father."

"What happened?"

"We don't know."

That admission must have hurt Yan. Boris waited, silence eating bandwidth, silence on an Earth-moon return trip.

"Did you take him to the doctors?"

"You know we did."

"And?"

"They don't know."

Silence between them, silence at the speed of light, travelling through space.

"Come home, Boris," Yan said, and Boris marvelled at how the boy had grown, the man coming out, this stranger he did not know and yet whose life he could so clearly remember.

Come home.

That same day he packed his meagre belongings, checked out of the Libra Hotel on Armstrong Boulevard, and took the shuttle to lunar orbit, and from there a ship to Gateway, and down, at last, to Central Station.

Memory like a cancer growing. Boris was a doctor, he had seen Weiwei's Bridge for himself—that strange semi-organic growth that wove itself into the Chongs' cerebral cortexes and into the grey matter of their brains, interfacing with their nodes, growing, strange delicate spirals of alien matter, an evolved technology, *verboten*, Other. It was overgrowing his father's mind, somehow it had gotten out of control, it was growing like a cancer, and Vlad could not move for the memories.

Boris suspected but he couldn't know, just as he did not know what Weiwei had paid for this boon, what terrible fee had been extracted from him—that memory, and that alone, had been wiped clean—only the Other, saying, *And so it shall be*, and then, the next moment, Weiwei was standing outside and the door was closed and he blinked, there amidst the old stone walls, wondering if it had worked.

Once it had all been orange groves . . . he remembered thinking that, as he went out of the doors of Central Station, on his arrival, back on Earth, the gravity confusing and uncomfortable, into the hot and humid air outside. Standing under the eaves, he breathed in deeply, gravity pulled him down but he didn't care. It smelled just like he remembered, and the oranges, vanished or not, were still there, the famed Jaffa oranges that grew here when all this, not Tel Aviv, not Central Station, existed, when it was all orange groves, and sand, and sea. . . .

He crossed the road, his feet leading him, they had their own memory, crossing the road from the grand doors of Central Station to the pedestrian street, the heart of the old neighbourhood, and it was so much smaller than he remembered, as a child it was a world and now it had shrunk—

Crowds of people, solar tuk-tuks buzzing along the road, tourists gawking, a memcordist checking her feed stats as everything she saw and felt and smelled was broadcast live across the networks, capturing Boris in a glance that went out to millions of indifferent viewers across the solar system—

Pickpockets, bored CS Security keeping an eye out, a begging robotnik with a missing eye and bad patches of rust on his chest, dark-suited Mormons sweating in the heat, handing out leaflets, while on the other side of the road Elronites did the same—

Light rain, falling.

From the nearby market the shouts of sellers promising the freshest pomegranates, melons, grapes, bananas, in a café ahead old men playing backgammon—R. Patch-It walking slowly amidst the chaos, the robot an oasis of calm in the mass of noisy, sweaty humanity—

Looking, smelling, listening, *remembering*, so intensely he didn't at first see them, the woman and the child, on the other side of the road, until he almost ran into them—

Miriam, and the boy.

He wanted to go to her now. The world was awake, and Boris was alone on the roof of the old apartment building, alone and free, but for the memories. He saw the old alte-zachen man, Ibrahim, go past on his cart in the street below; the Lord of Discarded Things, they used to call him; and Boris marvelled that he was still among the living. A boy sat beside him, a boy not unlike Kranki. Their patient horse pulled the cart along the road, and Boris followed their path until they went out of sight.

He didn't know what he would do about his father. He remembered holding his hand, once, when he was small, and Vlad had seemed so big, so confident and sure, and full of life. They had gone to the beach that day, it was a summer's day and in Menashiya, Jews and Arabs and Filipinos all mingled together, the Muslim women in their long dark clothes and the children running shrieking in their underwear; Tel Aviv girls in tiny bikinis, sunbathing placidly; someone smoking a joint, and the strong smell of it wafting in the sea air; Ibrahim, the alte-zachen man, he was there then, too, passing along the road with his horse (a different one, then); the life guard in his tower calling out trilingual instructions—"Keep to the marked areas! Did anyone lose a child? Please come to the lifeguards *now*! You with the boat, head towards the Tel Aviv harbour and away from the swimming area!"—the words getting lost in the chatter, someone had parked their car and was blaring out beats from the stereo, Somali refugees were cooking a barbeque on the promenade's grassy part, a dreadlocked white guy was playing a guitar; and Vlad held

Boris's hand as they went into the water, strong and safe, and Boris knew nothing would ever happen to him; that his father would always be there to protect him, no matter what happened.

FOUR:
THE LORD OF
DISCARDED THINGS

There were still alte-zachen men in Jaffa and Central Station in those days, as there always were, and chief amongst them was Ibrahim, he who was sometimes called the Lord of Discarded Things.

There were still alte-zachen men in Jaffa in those days. There had always been junk gypsies, part Jew, part Arab, part something else again. It was not long after the Messiah Murder, of which you must have heard, of which the historian Elezra (himself a progenitor of Miriam Elezra, who with the Golda Meir automaton journeyed to ancient Mars-That-Never-Was, and changed the course of a planet) has written, "It was a time of fervour and uncertainty, a time of hate and peace, in which the messiah's appearance and subsequent execution were almost incidental."

You must have seen him approach a thousand times. He

appears in the background, always in the background, of tourist-taken images, of numerous feeds. The cart, first: a flat top carried on the four wheels of a liberated, ancient car. In Jaffa's junkyards combustion engine-era vehicles proliferated, towers of them making a town of junk in which hid the city's unfortunates. The cart pulled by one or two horses, city-bred and born: mismatched grey and white, these Palestinian horses, an intermingling of breeds, distant cousins to the noble Arabian strains. Small, strong and patient, they carried the cart overloaded with broken-down things, without complaint, on the weekends putting on bells and colourful garb and carrying small children along the seaside promenade for a price.

The alte-zachen, like the ancient port's porters in their days, had a *lijana*, a secret board of rulers—a legion chosen by dint of age and experience—of which the most prominent member was Ibrahim.

Who was Ibrahim and how had he come to the city of Jaffa, by the blue sparkling waters of the Mediterranean Sea?

The truth was, no one knew. He had always been there. The once and future king of the discarded. Rumour had it he was Other-cousin to the Oracle on the hill, for Ibrahim, too, was Joined, his thumb a golden prosthetic, an Other bonded into his node, human and digital minds commingled. No one knew the name of the Other. Perhaps both were called Ibrahim.

His route seldom varied. Down the narrow passageways of ancient Ajami, the stone houses overlooking the sea and the harbour, away from the new high-rises of the returnees; down the hill to the ancient clock tower, right along Salame Road, calling out as he went: "Alte-zachen! Alte-zachen!"

Junk accumulating on the cart. The discarded waste of

centuries. People knew to wait for Ibrahim. Torn, stained mattresses, tables with broken legs, ancient Chinese mass-produced grandfather clocks of a sort popular in some nameless gone-by decade. Discarded automatons, Vietnamese battle-dolls used in some long-ago war. Paintings. Print books, moulding, shedding pages like leaves. Engines for giant fish refrigeration units. Faded Turkish rugs.

Once, a baby.

He had found the little thing on his rounds. It was early, the sun had barely risen yet. Ibrahim had travelled up Salame and turned to Central Station.

Adaptoplant neighbourhoods high above moved in the breeze. They sprouted around Central Station like weeds. On the outskirts of the old neighbourhood, along the old abandoned highways of Tel Aviv they grew, ringing the immense structure of the space port rising high into the sky. Houses sprouted like trees, blooming, adaptoplant weeds feeding on rain and sun and digging roots into the sandy ground, breaking ancient asphalt. Adaptoplant neighbourhoods, seasonal, unstable, sprouting walls and doors and windows, half-open sewers hanging in the air, exposed bamboo pipes, apartments growing over and into each other, growing without order or sense, creating pavements suspended in midair, houses at crazy angles, shacks and huts with half-formed doors, windows like eyes—

In autumn the neighbourhoods shed, doors drying, windows shrinking slowly, pipes drooping. Houses fell like leaves to the ground below and the road-cleaning machines murmured happily, eating up the shrunken leaves of former residencies. Above ground the tenants of those seasonal buoyant suburbs stepped cautiously, testing the ground with each step taken, to see if it would hold, migrating nervously across the skyline to other, fresher spurts of growth, new adaptoplant blooming delicately, windows opening like fruit—

Discarded metal and plastic on the road down below. Ibrahim couldn't tell what it had once been: cars and water bottles turned into abandoned sculpture, perhaps. Art sprouted like wildtech in Central Station.

It lay nearby. It was a small package, he had not noticed it until it moved. Ibrahim went to it warily, things sometimes got loose in Central Station. Sometimes amidst the junk there had been snakes, still-living battle-dolls, adaptoplant furniture with hostile programming, old guns and ammunition, uberuser-created, virtual religious artefacts of uncertain powers—

Ibrahim approached the package and it made a sound. The sound made him freeze. It was that kind of sound. Once there had been a wolf pup, smuggled in from Mongolia. It died in captivity. It had made that kind of sound.

Ibrahim came closer nonetheless. Looked.

A baby looked up at him. An ordinary baby such as one saw every day, everywhere: Jaffa and Central Station were filled with children. This one, however, was inside a shoebox.

Ibrahim knelt next to the baby. The shoebox was for a cheap brand. The baby had clear sparkling green eyes, his skin was dark, his head was hairless. Ibrahim stared at the baby. There was no one around. The baby burped.

Ibrahim reached for the boy—it was a boy—carefully, still wary. One never knew, in Central Station. The boy's hand rose to meet his. Older than his years. As if he were shaking hands. Their fingers touched. A current, like high-bandwidth data, hit Ibrahim. Images crowded his mind. Impossible things. Views from the rings of Saturn. A battle of four-armed, red-skinned Martian Re-Born in their virtual empire. A rabbi on a spaceship travelling to the Belt, praying in the field of asteroids, in a small dank room inside an ancient mining craft.

In the touch of the boy there was the toktok blong narawan, the language of Others.

Ibrahim's Other woke up. Said, *What the—*

Ibrahim's mind couldn't face the onslaught. The data-storm raged, diverting to his Other, which shut down as it tried to cope—

One word hovering clear out of the maelstrom, making him cringe—

Messiah—

Pull your hand away!

The light touch of the child imprisoned him. He fought—

The baby burped and laughed. The contact broke.

Ibrahim: *Did you get all that?*

Nothing from his Other.

Ibrahim: *??*

His Other, at last: *!*

Ibrahim stared at the baby, and his Other, through Ibrahim's eyes, did likewise.

One thought in both of their minds:

Not another one.

Ibrahim could have put out a distress call. An alarm broadcast from his node, bouncing across the endless networks that crisscrossed this city, its planet, the human-inhabited space around it, planets and moons and rings and Exodus ships. Peace-keeping machines would have materialised, spiderlike, mecha-CSIs double-coded, for this was the buffer zone, Central Station separating Arab Jaffa from Jewish Tel Aviv. A high-encryption digital dispute over territory, analysis of the boy's DNA—though with just the eye-colour (Bose trademark, hacked, several decades old but still fiercely protected by licensing laws) Ibrahim knew. The boy was vat-grown, it was a Central Station specialty.

Messiah breeding programme? the Other inquired, recovering.

"I don't know."

He spoke aloud, but softly. The boy gurgled.

Is this wise?

"Do you have another idea?"

I don't like this.

Communication speeding up, speech giving way to image codes, clouds of meanings. Ibrahim, cutting it off midflow, picked up the baby.

"The boy," he said, to no one in particular, memories of the Jerusalem killing still fresh in the mind, "deserves a different fate."

That had been years before. They named the boy Ismail. They brought him up as best they could.

Ibrahim lived in the vast junkyard that straddled the border of Jaffa and what used to be the Jewish suburb of Bat Yam. Tiny semi-sentient machines lived there, and robotniks, all the homeless and the lost.

The junkyard.

The Palace of Discarded Things.

It seemed appropriate for the boy.

And so Ismail grew up speaking the Arabic of Ajami and the Battle Yiddish of the robotniks. He spoke Asteroid Pidgin, that *Toktok blong Spes*. He spoke the neighbouring city's Hebrew. When he grew older he sometimes helped Ibrahim on his rounds.

Through Ajami down to the clock tower, down Salame to Central Station . . . Ibrahim picked up wounded things, his robotniks had been discarded on the streets of Central Station, he had picked them up and fixed them and they gave him their loyalty, it was the only thing they had left to give. There were synth-flesh dolls, patched up, with mismatched organs, child-sized, their faces crudely drawn, some were refugees from the flesh pits, some were miniature soldiers in urban wars, all had been mass-imported from far-off factories and discarded when their usefulness ran out.

Modified animals, Frankensteined by home-lab kid enthusiasts with a gene kit and an incubator. Ismail's pet dragon, a sad creature adapted from a Canary Islands *Lagarto Gigante de la Gomera*, part-meched with fire-breathing apparatus; the poor thing, coughing fire, had been nicknamed "Chamudi" by the boy, despite all evidence to the contrary, for there was nothing cute about it.

The whole tribe of them living in the vast junkyard, centuries of buried layers, an archaeological site in which everything could be found, the remnants of the ages.

The boy had . . . some disturbing habits.

When he slept, his dreams materialised sometimes, above

his head, cowboys and Indians chasing each other in a hazy grey bubble of dreamstuff forming out of condensation in the air, evaporating as REM sleep gave way to the deeper states of NREM.

He had an affinity with machines. He had been, like all children, noded at birth. He was not Other Joined, not bonded, and yet, sometimes, Ibrahim and his Other had the distinct sense that the boy could hear them speak.

You know what it is, of course, the Other said.

Ibrahim nodded.

They had been standing in the yard. The sun beat down, and beyond the stone houses of Ajami the sea lay flat as a mirror, solar surfers diving and rising on the winds above it.

There are others, the Other said. *Children born in the vat-labs of Central Station.*

"I know."

We should speak to the Oracle—

Ibrahim knew her of old. Knew, even, her real name. No one was born an oracle . . . and they were blood-related, as well as Other-ken. He said, "No."

Ibrahim. . . .

"No."

We are making a mistake.

"The children will make their own way. In time."

"Baba!" the boy came running up to Ibrahim. "Can I come with you on the cart today?"

"Not today," Ibrahim said. "Maybe tomorrow."

The boy's face crumpled in disappointment. "You always say tomorrow," he accused.

It's safe here, the Other said, silently. *Here he is protected.*

"But he needs to be with children his own age."

"What's that, Baba?"

"Nothing, Ismail," Ibrahim said. "It's nothing."

But it was not nothing.

Chamudi, the dragon, died a few months later. There had been a funeral, the grandest ever held at the Palace of Discarded Things. The dragon had an honour guard of patched-up battle-dolls and robotniks, people from the neighbourhood had turned out in solemn clothes despite the heat. Junkmen dug a hole in the ground, dislodging buried treasures, a rusting bicycle and a box of hand-carved chess pieces made of dark wood, and a metal skull. Noah the blind beggar, Ibrahim's friend, stood beside him as the small coffin was lowered. A priest, a Martian Re-Born, follower of the Way, officiated, red skin glistening with sweat in the sun, four arms moving in complex forms as she wove words of bereavement and comfort, speaking of the Emperor of Time and his acceptance of this gift. Ismail stood to one side, his eyes dry now from tears.

Noah the blind beggar, whose eyes were precious stones, watched the ceremony unfold through multiple nodal transmissions. Pym, the famous memcordist, was there, the funeral joined like a strand into his life-long Narrative. It was going out to Pym's subscribers, their numbers fluctuated in the millions across the solar system. All in all it was a moving and dignified occasion.

"Who is the boy beside Ismail?" Noah asked. Ibrahim looked and said, "What boy?"

"The small, quiet one," Noah said. Ibrahim frowned. His Other whispered in his mind. Ibrahim shifted, eyes could be deceiving. He looked at the scene the way Noah did, through the Conversation.

He could see the boy now, but fragmented. In some of the feeds he was missing entirely, in some he was just a shade. It was only Noah's multifaceted view that gave, at last, the entire picture. The boy and Ismail didn't speak and yet he got the sense that they were communicating rapidly.

The boy had deep blue eyes. Armani, those eyes. Ibrahim wondered if he'd seen him before. One of the Central Station kids. The boy raised his eyes, seeming to somehow, impossibly, sense their attention. A smile tugged at the corners of his mouth.

Earth covered the miniature dragon. The Re-Born priest intoned the final words of farewell. The guests sighed. Robotniks saluted, lethargically. It was a hot day.

"Who is your friend?" Ibrahim said, later, when they were drinking cool lemonade in the shade of piled cars. The two boys smiled, mischievously, and the boy said, "Nem blong mi Kranki."

My name is Kranki.

It was hard to see the boy. He kept shifting through visual feeds, a ghost in the crisscrossed networks.

"Hello, Kranki," Ibrahim said.

"Mama is calling me," the boy said, suddenly. His voice came from everywhere and nowhere. "I'd better go."

He faded away, and Ibrahim was troubled.

———

"The messianic impulse is strongest when concentrated," Noah said, philosophically. The funeral was over and Ismail was nowhere in sight. Ibrahim knew the boy had gone to the beach with some of the other children. Corporeal, this time. "This land of ours has always been a lode-stone for seekers of faith."

A lot remained unsaid between them. Ibrahim, speaking carefully, said, "I wanted for the boy a normal life."

Noah shrugged, and the precious stones that were his eyes glinted in the faint light. "What is normal?" he said. "You and I are relics of a distant past. Fossilised shells buried in the sands of time."

Ibrahim was forced to laugh. "You sound like a Re-Born," he said. Noah grinned, then shrugged. "The Re-Born believe in a past that never was," he said. "They dig for virtual fossils."

Ibrahim had lost his smile. "Whereas?" he said, prompting.

"Whereas what the children represent is a future," Noah said. "Not, perhaps, *the* future, but *a* future. The present fragments. We can both feel it. Futures branch out like the growths from a tree."

"How many?" Ibrahim said, uneasily. Noah shrugged. "Children?"

Ibrahim nodded. Noah said, "Ask the man in the birthing clinics," and stood up, stiffly. "I'd better go," he said. "Ophelia will be waiting for me."

Ibrahim remained alone in the junkyard. It felt as though the city was preparing for a crusade. He still remembered the messiah, a genuine descendant of King David, genetically certified, arriving in Jerusalem on a white donkey, all the portents there and present. Not *the* End of Days, but *an* End of Days. Then someone took him out with a sniper rifle.

One messiah down.

This part of the world had always needed a messiah. So did others. There had been rumours . . . the Singularity Jesus project in Laos. The Black Monks. On Mars, they said, on New Israel, they were preparing a vast virtuality in which the Holocaust never took place. Six million ghosts multiplying. They said the Zion asteroid was heading out of the solar system altogether, following the beamed dream of an alien god. Ibrahim was old. He had been around when there were still oranges. Steamers once docked at Jaffa and camels brought the *shamouti* oranges to the harbour, and small boats carried them to the waiting ships. It had always been a hub in a global network. The oranges went to England, to the ports of Manchester and Southampton and Plymouth, people there still remembered the Jaffa orange.

But Central Station was new, he thought. It was a new hub on a new network. Somewhere in that microcosm of alienation new religions were born, messiahs hatched. He wanted normality for the boy. But normality had never been a given, it was a consensus illusion and the boy with the trademarked eyes could see clear through most.

The children had been birthed. Someone had planned their emergence. One day the boy would change, but what he would grow into Ibrahim did not yet know.

That night, after the funeral, as he was sitting in the Palace of Discarded Things, Ismail came back from the beach. His small wiry body still glistened from the saltwater, and his eyes were bright, and he was laughing. Ibrahim, who never had children of his own, hugged the boy. "Baba!" the boy said. "Look what I found!"

Love was anxiety and pride, intermingled. Ibrahim watched as the boy went out of the yard and came back with a puppy, a small black dog with a white nose who licked the back of his hand. "I'm going to call him Suleiman," he said.

Ibrahim laughed. "You'll have to feed him," he warned.

"I know," the boy said, "I'll look after him. You'll see."

Ismail ran across the junkyard and the dog ran behind him, tongue lolling. Ibrahim watched them both go, and worried.

That night he had a dream. In the dream the two boys stood by the fire burning in an open drum nearby. Even though he knew Ismail was asleep, and his friend, Kranki, was far away in Central Station, nevertheless he felt that the dream had a strange reality about it. The two boys spoke; their lips moved; but no sound emerged, and Ibrahim could not understand what they were saying. He woke abruptly, his heart racing, his Other awake in his mind.

She's coming, the Other said. *She's coming.*

He sensed the Other's confusion. The words must have come from the dream.

But who was coming, and why, and for what purpose, they didn't know.

FIVE: STRIGOI

On a day in spring, a Strigoi came to Central Station. A *Shambleau*. Her hair was done in a style then popular in Tong Yun: long dreadlocks woven with thin, flexible metal wires that corresponded to an invisible charge, and moved like water snakes, in the air about the girl's head, extending lazily from her skull.

She had vat-grown violet eyes, her hair was reddish-brown and woven with gold that caught the sun.

Her name was Carmel.

A patch of new skin on the soft lower flesh of her left arm could have once been a tattoo. That tattoo could have testified that she had been previously captured and accordingly marked. She stepped out of the general transport suborbital on the rooftop of Central Station, disembarking with the other passengers, and stopped, and breathed in the rare air of Earth.

You who have never been to Manhome! Remember the words of the poet Bashō, who wrote:

Sip blong Spes
Planet Es hemia!
Ea blong hem i no semak
Ol narafala ples

Translated roughly as "ship of space / Earth it is! / Its air is unlike / that of any other place."

Though the term *Manhome* has fallen from favour, and a more proper designation would have been Humanity Prime or, as the Others sometimes called it, the Core.

Regardless.

The Shambleau called Carmel came to Central Station in spring, when the smell in the air truly is intoxicating. It is a smell of the sea, and of the sweat of so many bodies, their heat and their warmth, and it is the smell of humanity's spices and the cool scent of its many machines; and it is the scent of the resin or sap that sometimes drips from a cut in the eternally renewing adaptoplant neighbourhoods, and of ancient asphalt heating in the sun, and of vanished oranges, and of freshly cut lemongrass: it is the smell of Humanity Prime, that richest and most concentrated of smells; there is nothing like it in the outer worlds.

And on the roof of Central Station the girl, Carmel, stood, for a long moment, her eyes closed, taking it all in: the strange and unfamiliar gravity, the relentless push of the sun, the gentle, modulated pulling of the wind, the whole thing surprising, unpredictable, a planet-wide atmospheric system that wasn't even *digital.*

The pulse and surf of the Conversation hit her then. On the way over—on those slow months from Tong Yun on Mars, all the way at last to Gateway, there in Earth orbit—she had done well filtering the Conversation to a minimum, near starving herself. She had travelled on the *Gel Blong Mota*, that most ancient of cargo craft traversing the solar system. Quiet was what she had wanted.

But now the Conversation exploded around her, almost overwhelming her. Ever more concentrated, here on Earth. Different, too. Odd, archaic protocols intermingled with the intensity of the toktok blong narawan. Here, the part of the Conversation to come from the Outer System—from Jettisoned and the Oort cloud and Titan and the Galilean Republics—was faint, diluted. The Belt twinkled with dozens of loose strands. Mars was a quiet murmur. Lunar Port was a cry in the night. But Earth!

She had never imagined the Conversation as she experienced it just then—the *nearness* and yet the *distance* of it, the *compressedness* of it all. Billions of humans, uncounted billions of digitals and machines, all talking, chattering, sharing at once. Images, text, voice, recordings, all-immersive memcordist media, gamesworlds spill-over—it came on her at once, and she reeled against it.

"Are you all right, dear?" a kindly voice said. It was a Chinese-Martian woman, with bright, alive green (natural?—a quick scan did not reveal a patented signature) eyes. "Is it the gravity? It can be hard to adjust, the first time."

She lent Carmel her arm, to lean on. Carmel gratefully accepted, though she was afraid. She shielded the woman out as much as she could. Being this close to a human's node was a temptation she was afraid to follow. Her hunger, her weakened state, did not help. She needed to feed, and soon.

And Earth was like an all-you-can-eat Tong Yun City twenty-four-hour buffet.

"Thank you," she said. The woman smiled and they walked down the marked path, to Disembarkation. Carmel tensed, but only a little, as the gateway systems scanned her. Her internal networks pretending she was something she was not.

A ping on her internal node: Approved. She let out a breath. Carmel and the woman rode the elevators down to the lower levels.

"This is my third time on Earth," the woman said. She spoke easily, taking Carmel into her confidence as if she did that every day of her life. Red Chinese, but not Tong Yun; one of the innumerable communes that had sprouted up over the centuries in the Valles Marineris, in the shadow of Olympus Mons. "This is my third time on Earth, isn't it wonderful? Of course it is an expensive trip but my ancestors are here, in Central Station." She smiled a quick delighted smile. "Yes, isn't it strange? They came from China and from the Philippines, to work for the Jews of Tel Aviv at that time, and stayed. Here. The old neighbourhood. I still have relatives here. My name's Magdalena Wu, but I am of the Chongs of Central Station. It is strange . . . I grew up on Mars. We farm tomatoes, water melons, medical marijuana, *waetbun kabij* . . . our greenhouses spread out for miles underground, there is a joy you don't expect, perhaps, in tending to all that greenery. They say Mars is red but when I think of it, when I think of home, I always think of it as green. Is that strange?"

Carmel, perhaps overwhelmed, perhaps at ease with this chatty, older woman, said nothing. Magdalena nodded.

"So much demand for *waetbun*," she said. Waetbun kabij—Asteroid Pidgin for garden-variety cabbage. "My family emigrated in the Century of Dragon—" That meant, Carmel knew, the century when Dragon first established his/their/its strange colony on Hydra. Momentary images, by reflex, poured over her: public images of Dragon's World, the endless, termite-built warrens, the thousands of disposable dolls moving through it on their unknown purposes, each a node linking the whole into something greater than its parts, the Other known as Dragon, a digital entity with a strange fascination with the *physicality*, with Universe-One. "We grew—not rich, but comfortable, on the cabbage trade. Such a useful plant! It is a great source of vitamin C and indole-three-carbinol. It is used in nearly every kitchen. A neighbour started a kimchi factory, then married into the family." She shrugged. "We make do," she said. "Enough for me to travel here twice before. To see where it began. From Central Station, we went to the stars. Isn't that something? It's strange, their outdoors don't feel quite real, don't you think? Oh, you haven't felt them, yet. But their outside feels smaller than the inside of our greenhouses. All those miles . . . I love to walk them."

They had reached a level within the giant space port. The doors opened. They both stepped out. "Level Three," the woman said. "It's like a miniature version of the Level Three concourse of Tong Yun City, don't you think? It's so quaint."

Carmel remembered Level Three. The Multifaith Bazaar. The gamesworlds nodes. The droid arenas. She had . . . she had roamed there, for a time. So many churches, and so many of the righteous took it upon themselves to hunt Strigoi.

They had almost caught her once. A crowd had gathered. She had been drunk on feed. *Shambleau!* they cried. Pointed. Jeered. Awed and repulsed. Then casting stones. Worse. Denial of Service attacks, crude, but effective. Blocking her from the Conversation. Cutting her off from her feed.

"Do you go to Tel Aviv?" Magdalena said. Seeing Carmel's confused expression—"Jaffa? No? Farther away?"

"Here," Carmel said. Speaking felt strange. She had not spoken in all her time on the ship. "Just . . . here," she said.

"Outside?"

Carmel just shrugged. She didn't know.

As if taking pity on her, Magdalena nodded, took her hand, gently, in hers. "There is a small shrine here," she said. "It's for Ogko, but . . . we could go there together, if you like. Where do you need to go? Do you know?"

"I . . ." The thing that drove her across space and to this foreign, alienating place, for a moment eluded her.

"You don't talk much, do you," Magdalena said. Carmel smiled; she hadn't expected to. Magdalena smiled back. "Let's go see Ogko," she said. "Then we'll see what we can do about you."

Arm in arm, they walked across the vast concourse, towards the Multifaith Bazaar.

There is a shrine to Ogko in most places nowadays. Though Ogko did not approve of shrines. He was the most cantankerous of deities, a reluctant messiah. If you subscribe to the Alien Theory of Spiritual Beings, which was briefly popular around the time of the Shangri-La Affair, Ogko would be considered, alongside Jesus, Mohammed, Uri Geller, and L. Ron Hubbard, as an alien entity. It was the answer to Fermi's famous paradox. The reason we don't see aliens *out there*, reasoned the proponents of the AToSB, is because they're *here*. They walk—and preach—among us.

In *The Book of Ogko*, a man tells the story of having encountered an alien being, an energy creature called Ogko. "I made him up," he wrote. "I took his shape and form from water and leaf, from the damp earth of the Mekong and from the flight patterns of the wild battle drones of the Golden Triangle. He isn't real. Neither am I."

Ogko, he cheerfully admitted, was a liar. Yet his philosophy-of-no-philosophy, his strangely delighted view of an insignificant humanity, "A shower of bright sparks against a vast darkness," as he once put it, in one of his more flowery moments of language, somehow took hold.

He endured. His message—"We don't matter—only to ourselves"—strangely resonated. And little shrines, to this fictive, playful entity, if it had existed at all, kept springing up in odd places, on street corners and plantations, in the Exodus ships and in the underground warrens of Mars, on the lone mining ships of the asteroids and in the gamesworlds and virtualities of the Conversation.

In Central Station, tucked alongside an Elronite Temple and a Catholic church, there was indeed a small shrine. Potted plants were left there, in a profusion of colours and scents, flowers and vines, and on a small pedestal sticks of incense burned, and candles in various stages of depletion stood, some burning, some extinguished. Magdalena lit a small candle, then called to her hand-luggage. A suitcase promptly appeared in the distance, racing on tiny wheels towards the shrine. When it arrived, Magdalena patted it absent-mindedly before extracting from it a small parcel. She left it alongside a pot of geraniums and a half-starved Venusian Fly Trap. Growing in Magdalena's pot was, of course, a small, white bone-coloured cabbage.

Carmel watched the Venusian Fly Trap in horrified fascination. It was like staring at a mirror. The thing was starved of feed. And thinking of feed, which it was impossible not to, the presence of this Martian woman, Magdalena, was becoming increasingly more difficult: her node's pathetic protection meant nothing to Carmel, she kept getting snatches of images, data packets, random noise coming off from the woman, like the scent of baking bread, making her mouth water. It would be so easy to. . . .

Unthinkingly, she took a step back. Magdalena, turning round, said, "Are you all right?"

"I should go," Carmel said. Speaking quickly. Panic rose through her like tiny bubbles. All the noise, the sound of the Conversation she had been keeping out, burst in on her. "I have to—" She didn't finish the thought.

"Wait!" the older woman said—but Carmel was already turning, running, across the vast hall of Level Three, seeking a way out; seeking escape.

Nighttime in Polyport, Titan. Beyond the dome, purples fought with reds as a storm raged. Inside Polyphemus Port itself the air felt hot, humid. She walked down the narrow, twisting streets, avoiding the entrances into the underworld as she stalked the shadows.

Feed on Titan was more diffuse. The local networks thronged and signals were broadcast and captured through the strings of hubs floating out in solar space, but they were fainter here. And anyway what she needed was more immediate. What she needed was a lot more *intimate*.

Polyport built of ragged stone, foreign flora everywhere, thick vines climbing the one and two storey buildings. She had come here a runaway, hitchhiking on a cargo ship that passed through the Belt, on its way to the Outer System. That's when it had happened to her.

No one is born Shambleau.

It was a dirty old ship, the *Emaciated Saviour*: a mile-long, rock-and-metal, trans-solar transport, hacked out of space rock in the docks of Mars orbit, centuries before, its hull pockmarked with countless impacts, its corridors dank; the lights often didn't work, the recycled air never smelled fresh, the hydroponics gardens were fitfully maintained.

A jungle grew in the belly of the ship. Ancient servitors tried and failed to control its growth. There were rats there, too, an Earth breed that had since spread everywhere, and fire ants, tiny organisms whose bite burned like a flame and could not be eased.

Cargo came from everywhere. In space, cargo was a religion all by itself. It came from Earth, shipped up to orbit, to the massive habitat called Gateway. It came from Lunar Port, and it came from the Belt, from Ceres and Vesta where the wealth of the Belt poured. It came from Tong Yun City and from across Mars: Inner System cargo, en route to the outer worlds.

Everything had been fine until that long voyage, that crossing of space. After the Belt, stopping only at a few undistinguished rings and habitats, they made the long journey to Jupiter's moons, and from there the even longer crossing to the second gas giant, Saturn. When they had arrived at Ganymede she had been too frightened to get off, the Galilean Republics had tight immigration controls and she was already infected.

They finally booted her off the ship on Titan.

She had hitchhiked the ride on the *Emaciated Saviour*. Room there was aplenty, and the crewman who picked her up was decent enough, he was a Martian Re-Born, four-armed in the manner of the followers of the Way, and did not demand she follow his faith. His name was Moses. She had gotten used to his smell, oil and soil and sweat, to his soft voice, his gentle manners. He was sexually undemanding. Most of the time she wandered the ship, explored the maze of corridors, ventured into the hydroponics jungle. After a Belt childhood the ship felt immense: a whole self-contained world.

The attack came without warning, once they were deep into the crossing. Carmel was, of course, noded. The background hum of the Conversation was all about her, wherever she went. Like most people her age she had experimented with memcording but found that not only did she value her privacy, but that few were apparently interested in watching a continuous feed of her life. Like most people her age she had ventured into one of the gamesworlds at some point, and for a time worked as a liaison-entertainment officer at a lunar base in the Guilds of Ashkelon universe, converting her gamesworld-earned currency into Universe-One cash. There were a lot of alien species in the GoA universe and the role of a liaison-entertainment officer could sometimes be demanding, if educational.

Apart from this, Carmel's node and the resultant network filaments growing out of it were filled with the usual data, no more, probably, than a few exabytes in total.

All this was to change.

Carmel was walking through a service corridor. It felt disused. The atmosphere felt cooler here, dust hung motionless in the air. It was dark and the light ahead flashed brokenly on and off, as if spelling out a secret message.

The woman came at her from a door that wasn't there. The wall opened like a mesh of spider silk pulled sideways, smooth metal somehow torn aside like a bead curtain. Carmel couldn't see the woman clearly. She was short, slight of build. Smaller than her. Hardly a threat. The woman said, "Shambleau." Something terrified and terrifying in equal measures in her voice. The word coursed through Carmel's mind, through her node. It multiplied like a virus. It broke up into fragments that mutated and mated with each other, multiplied, grew, split, spread, crawling through her node, her wires, her mind. Carmel was frozen. Somehow, she couldn't move. The woman came close to her. Held her. Her mouth was on Carmel's neck. She bit her. The bite did not hurt. It felt cold, then hot. Carmel swayed. The woman held her as she fell, gently, to the floor. The woman knelt beside her, her mouth on Carmel's neck.

A terrible, exhilarating sensation. As if the woman had somehow pulled a Louis Wu on her, a low electric current stimulating the pleasure centres of the brain, releasing high quantities of dopamine. Carmel swooned as her mind was being devoured, data, all her most secret intimate trivial recall sucked up, devoured:

In the mining ship with her father, who lets her use the controls, for just a moment—

Visiting the Ceres Botanical Gardens and being amazed by the flowers, that there could be so many—

Watching an episode of *Chains of Assembly* where Johnny Novum kisses Tempest Teapot-Jones as Count Victor, unseen by either, watches in hatred—

First sexual experience with a boy her own age in the "sea"—it's what they call the saltwater pool on their little home world, the asteroid Ng. Merurun, the tips of his fingers feel rough on her chest, an unfamiliar heat inside her—

And in the Guilds of Ashkelon universe welcoming her first alien, assuming an abstract avatar for the guest, an ambassador from a powerful guild in galactic north, an insectoid thing, but his pinchers on her are the touch of a frightened boy, her age, and she guides him, feeling power—

Trying to learn to play the guitar, and failing—

Floating in zero gravity on the mining ship and singing to herself, a Sivan Shoshanim song that is popular that year—

Cooking, for the family, in the small kitchen off their quarters on the long corridor of the longhouse, a rare feast, for the birth of her sister's firstborn they slaughter a pig—

Strigoi.

The word rose like a bubble in her paralysed mind. She was losing the memories, losing her own self, awash in the joy, the unbearable *pleasure* of the woman's touch, that current of electricity in the brain as her node was raided, her data sucked away by this . . . *thing* that had an ancient, terrible name, a word she once heard her sister use, and her mother shushed her angrily—

Shambleau.

The word evoked in her a sudden repulsion, a horror even the dopamine could not counter. She struggled against the woman, her limbs suddenly free. She could no longer recall who she was, who she had been. But the woman was surprisingly strong, she pressed her back, and Carmel could smell her then, the fear and the hunger and the arousal that wafted off of this human-shaped creature, and she tried to cry out but her voice didn't work.

The Strigoi's teeth left Carmel's neck. Then, as if reaching a difficult decision, which Carmel only later, much later, realised, the Strigoi bit her again.

This time it was different. Carmel subsided against the cold hard floor of the service corridor. The rush of data flowed over her, *into* her, a sensory outpouring that left her numb, gasping for virtual air. Not only herself, but bits of other people, entities, all intermingled, memories without anchor, and for fleeting moments she was like a slideshow of humans, she was a Lunar shopkeeper and a Martian field worker, she was a Re-Born in the ancient Mars-That-Never-Was, four-armed and bronze-red, standing on the shimmering canals. She was a human with an Other flesh-surfing him, she was a robot priest at a shrine for St. Cohen, she was a Hagiratech hunter on Jettisoned, she was an Exodus ship departing the solar system, she was a human from Manhome itself, swimming in a vast and alien ocean. . . .

She came to in the dark. The Strigoi was gone. She was alone. Her head hurt. When she touched her mouth it felt delicate, raw. When she opened it against her skin she hurt herself. Her teeth had grown, she had two canines that lengthened. She was frightened.

She had a new awareness of herself. It came and went, it grew on her in the days to come. She knew herself from the inside, the whispering of the filaments spreading like a cancer from her node, filling her, invading her. Her node grew, spread, it was become her. She had returned to the cabin, where Moses was asleep. She lay beside him. She fell asleep and, when she woke up, he was gone. She ran a shower and watched herself in the mirror but she no longer needed a mirror. She could see herself reflected in the virtuality, every part of her, and she was filled with other people's ghosts.

Nighttime in Polyport, and she was hungry, the words of a poem running endlessly on a loop through her head.

The poet Bashō, who had once encountered a Shambleau on his slow voyage through the solar system, reputedly at a lonely outpost on Mars, wrote:

Oli saksakem save blong yumi
Oli saksakem maen blong yumi
Oli haed long sado

Awo!

Olgeta kakai faea blong yumi
Olgeta kakai save blong yumi
Oli go wokabaot long sado

Awo!

Sambelu. Sambelu. Sambelu.
Oli kakai faea. Oli haed long sado.
Olgeta Sambelu.

Which, translated, reads something like: "They suck our knowledge / they suck our mind / they hide in the shadow / oh! / they eat our fire / they eat our knowledge / they walk in shadow / oh! / Shambleau. / Shambleau. / Shambleau. / They eat fire. They hide in shadow. / They are Shambleau."

She was hungry, on Polyport. She had hid on the *Emaciated Saviour* for months, Moses had avoided her, the crew shunned her, but the ship was haunted by more than one presence and she was not persecuted. There were Shambleau on that ship, there were ghosts in the digitality, there were bloodied rituals in the bowels of the ship, acts of dread nakaimas.

They booted her out on Titan, at last, spreading across the ship, driving away the dark presences, she amongst them.

They were released on Polyphemus Port, and she was a long way from home, the sun cold and distant in the sky.

She hunted. Confused. A Carmel with others' memories, others' knowledge behind her eyes. She saw him walk down the street, weaving drunkenly, his node open, vulnerable, low-level broadcasting to anyone who would listen. She approached him, her hands shaking, her legs felt weak. He turned, smiled at her. "Beautiful young thing," he said, fondly. "What are you doing on this desolate moon?"

She reached for him. Her hand touched his shoulder and he froze, his system compromised, and she came closer to him and sunk her new fangs into his neck, draining him.

His mind was rich, so rich! He was an artist, a weather hacker, his mind full of swirling storms, of rain, of wind and power. His name was Stolly—"Like the vodka"—and he was a Polyporter, a Titanite born and bred. She gained arcane weather-hacking routines, memories of a party he had once attended, where the Memcordist Pym had been, bits of poems, agalmatophilia, which was the sexual impulse strongest in Stolly—an attraction to dolls, mannequins and statues—a modest talent for gardening, a love of the powerful red wine made from the grapes of subterranean Titan.

She was feeding, too much, she suddenly realised. She was draining him. She pulled away, out, putting a barrier between her node and his, her teeth withdrew. "Wait," he said. He sounded drugged. "I . . ." He blinked. "I need you," he said.

Then came a time of interdependence. She moved in with Stolly. He was pliable to her, addicted. "Shambleau," he'd say, his voice a mixture of wonder and desire. They would lie in his bed, the white sheets stained with sweat, and he would stroke her hair, worship her, and she fed on him, trying to control her need, to measure it out, in dribs and drabs, to give as much as take, so that he existed still, but faded.

It was a crime. Made worse by the fact that she could *not* control it. The filaments had spread through her body, she had been turned. Perhaps the one who turned her, the one on the ship, did it out of spite, wanting to pass on the dark curse of Strigoi. But Carmel came to realise that a more likely explanation was that the nameless Shambleau had drained her too much, and could only save her by turning her. Now she, too, was a mirror, reflecting others yet casting no reflection herself. She fed on others' minds, on others' data, the hunger always in her. Who first developed Strigoi? She never learned. Some ancient Earth weapon, released into the wild. Strigoi could be valuable, if held in captivity. Bounty hunters sought them out, military factions sometimes made cruel use of them. In her mind, images of mobs, rending Shambleau limb from limb. Whether it was a real memory or an amalgamation of data gleaned from the Conversation she didn't know; but people frightened her.

There were stories of Shambleau acting as muses for the people they fed on. Inspiring their work. Certainly there was something strange, perhaps unique, about that sort of intimate sharing of data. And Stolly seemed happy, adoring. He was working on a new installation, *Stillness within a Storm*, and yet. . . .

He was fading before her eyes.

She was draining him and she couldn't stop. The only

answer would be to turn him, she knew, and she was unwilling to do that, to make copies of herself would be an obscene act. She was old before she was young. Her escape from home brought with it no freedom, only a new kind of imprisonment.

Her life on Titan came to an end on the eve of Stolly's unveiling of his new installation. . . .

Carmel blinked. She was alone on the Level Three concourse. Bright lights, sounds of explosions and cheering from the battle droid arenas. Masses of people, so many, moving to and fro, food courts with unfamiliar smells, in the distance the Multifaith Bazaar, that Martian woman, Magdalena Wu, lost to sight. . . .

Central Station.

It felt like an alien world.

She was not sure what was outside. An alien planet, and she a landing explorer, hesitant before setting foot down on the planet's surface, in its alien air. She would plant no flag here. Already she could discern in the Conversation around her hints, clues to the one she sought. Outside was another world, an old neighbourhood, older than anything humanity had ever put up in space. The very age of it was terrifying to her. She was a creature of a different age, a different sky. Almost blindly, she groped her way along a virtual map interposed before her eyes, the Level Three concourse spread out, until she found the gamesworlds pods.

Dark nooks along a narrow corridor, tens of full-immersion pods in each, only half of them occupied. People worked in the gamesworlds, people lived and dreamed and made love in them.

A solitary, human, attendant. Young, thin, nervous looking, he wouldn't look at her directly, though Carmel's hair, moving of its own volition, kept creeping up on him. She paid for a night and, exhausted, slid into a pod.

It closed over her, sealing her in silence and in darkness, and she slept, plugged in and yet unplugged.

Polyport, at dusk. . . .

The unveiling ceremony took place against the membrane of the dome, on the designated eastern side, at the end of a maze of narrow streets.

Later, her memory remained hazy—

Stolly standing there, his image, smiling faintly, pale, broadcast across the networks, across Polyphemus Port and the other few Titanic settlements and beyond, into Saturn space and, gradually, across the space hubs, everywhere, to anyone who cared to watch, data moving at the speed of light, so slowly. . . .

Stolly standing there, giving a little speech—something something "My Muse"—that capital letter—Stolly's hands shaking, he moved them through the air, summoning the last of the subroutines and embedded protocols, bringing to life his creation—

The explosion took off his head, showered blood over the assembled guests.

Screams, intensifying with the second explosion, and a breach in the wall of the dome sucking in poisonous atmosphere, Titan being allowed into the port—the panic, screaming, the sudden network traffic increasing a thousandfold as all over Polyport and near-space people tuned in to watch—

To watch Stolly's last, greatest masterpiece.

Stillness within a Storm can still be viewed on the east side of Polyport, though special permission must be obtained. Tickets are on sale through the regular channels. The breach in the hull has never been repaired, but somehow, Stolichnaya Birú, the artist, had formulated a kind of localised storm in which outdoor and indoor pressure cancelled each other out.

The storm is roughly globular in structure. It seems to contract and expand periodically, and a security corridor has been established around the site, as well as emergency filters ready to be activated at the first sign of danger.

But the weather hacker had known what he was doing.

The storm combines both internal atmosphere and the atmosphere of Titan itself, merging them into a complex, always-raging ball of storm, in hues of purple and white, inside which—

Pressure cancels pressure, but filaments of gas and dust weave themselves, within that stillness, into something resembling a face. Much has been made of that face, and efforts to interpret it have failed. It is humanoid, possibly feminine. Its eyes are explosions in violet. Its mouth opens, white streaks like canines slide out, gradually, and it seems the image grimaces, or grins. It rotates slowly, dissipates, returns. For months on end it remains perfectly still, frozen. Then it disintegrates and is reborn, again and again, a stillness captured in a storm.

The image of the artist's head exploding as the breach

first occurred has since become a minor meme in the Conversation. The artist's blood and brain matter itself became incorporated into the installation, helping to form part of the enigmatic face.

As for Carmel, she made her way to the embarkation field and took transport on the first available ship, never to be seen on Titan again.

She tore open the pod. Blinked in the sudden glare of electric light. Sat up. Her head ached, her mouth was filled with saliva. The machine had otherwise taken care of her bodily functions, her human waste. She felt ravenous. Strigoi-hungry. Human-hungry. She pulled herself out of the pod. Stood on shaking legs. The gravity pressed down on her. Remembered where she was. Earth. Central Station.

She stumbled out of the pod-room and found a burger bar and devoured a double helping, red meat, deep-fried potatoes, starch and salt and fats. Strigoi still ate food, their hunger was something else, a craving not of the physical.

It made her think again of Mars, and of the reason she came here, and a feeling stole over her, suddenly, of a terrible loneliness, like a cosmic wind blowing, cold and forlorn, between the stars.

The space port, this Central Station, felt to her like a womb, or a prison—anyhow, somewhere from which she had to escape. Wiping away ketchup and mustard stains and crumpling the cheap paper napkin into a ball, she stood up, walked, almost running, to the giant elevators, and descended down to street level.

The doors opened. Hot air blew in, fighting the internal air-conditioning units. Carmel felt moisture form on her lips, licked it away. She walked through the doors and found herself, at last, outside.

The Mediterranean sun was hot, its light fell in sheets, like glass, it suffused the world, picking objects and people in sharp relief, casting halos, obliterating shade. Carmel blinked, thin cataract-like growths of radiation-filtering transparent material formed over her eyes, shielding them from the sun. She blinked again, sneezed. The reaction took her by surprise and for a moment she hovered, uncertain, before bursting into a sudden, rare, natural laugh.

People stared, but she didn't mind. She crossed the road and it was like being in another world, this old neighbourhood of rundown buildings out there in the open, the space port receding behind her back to insignificance. This is where people lived, it was like Titan, or Mars, or the asteroids, only the dome above her head was higher, and circled an entire world. There was something comforting, she thought, about domes. About barriers. The space port was a violation of that.

She entered an old, pleasant pedestrian street. Neve Sha'anan, the sign said. It was shaded here by the old buildings rising on both sides of it, shops on the ground level, flats overhead. She passed old men sitting playing backgammon and *bao* outside, puffing on sweet-smelling water pipes, drinking coffee. She passed a greengrocers' where watermelons spilled beside oranges and *narafika*, that small, sweet, South Pacific fruit they sometimes called Malay Apple or *Syzygium ricchi*. She passed a shoe shop and allowed herself a moment to stop, and browse, and try on a pair that particularly captivated her.

She did not know where she would find him, but she knew she was close. She didn't know what she would say, or how she could explain why she had come, all this way, when she herself hardly knew.

She had met him in Tong Yun.

"Hello!" The voice startled her, coming at her unexpected and loud. She turned, shielding her eyes, and saw the Martian woman, Magdalena, waving from the doorway of a small shop with a sign above it that said, simply, *Shebeen*.

Magdalena came up to her, she was a soft filled-in woman, she put out warmth like a warhead or a sun. "You never told me your name," she said, almost accusingly.

"It's Carmel," Carmel said, and the other woman beamed, and said, "What a beautiful name!"

"Thank you," Carmel said, awkwardly. She was uncomfortable next to regular humans. Always feeling they should see her for what she was, what she had become. Always afraid of being discovered. But already Magdalena was pulling her with her, as if she, Carmel, were a loose space rock, caught in the gravitational force of a planet. Before she knew it she was at the entrance to the shebeen and then inside.

It was cool there and dark, a small, sparsely furnished room. Dusty bottles on shelves on the wall. Magdalena Wu pulled a chair for Carmel and sat down across from her. A third woman came over, from behind the bar, and she smiled, wiping her hands with a towel.

"Miriam," Magdalena said, "this is Carmel."

"Nice to meet you," the woman said. Carmel said, "Likewise—" Liking this small, compact person, without quite knowing why.

"What can I get you?" Miriam said.

"Let's have some lemonade," Magdalena said. "It's a hot day."

"Yes," Miriam agreed. She went around the bar, came back with a glass jug, frosted with ice. Miriam put down three glasses on the table and sat down, joining them.

"What brings you to Earth, Carmel?" she said. "I like your hair."

Carmel's dreads moved slowly in the air above her head, like snakes drugged by the heat. "Thank you. I'm . . . I hoped to find someone I used to know," Carmel said.

"Here?" Miriam said. "In Central Station? Or . . ." she smiled. "Most people only pass through here," she said. "Are you?"

"No. I mean, yes. Or, I don't know." Carmel took a sip from her lemonade, feeling exposed. Someone came into the shebeen then; a quiet, tall form passed around them, laid a hand on Miriam's shoulder, a gesture of affection, of closeness, and Miriam squeezed the man's hand, said, "Boris."

At the sound of the name Carmel felt her hands shake and she put down the glass with exaggerated care. She did not look up.

"Hello, Magda," Boris said.

The Martian woman said, "Cousin," warmth in her voice. "I'd like you to meet a friend of mine, Ca—"

"Carmel," Boris said. Shock in his voice. Carmel raised her head at last. Her hair moved, agitated, a dark halo surrounding her face. "Boris," she said. He was tall, thin, the Martian aug that was so much a part of him pulsated gently.

"Carmel, what are you *doing* here?"

She saw them all looking at her. Magdalena, and Miriam, and Boris, a range of emotions, concern, suspicion, mistrust, fear, bemusement, their nodes were broadcasting, Magdalena said, "Boris, you know this girl?" and Boris said, flatly, the words like blades cutting Carmel up, "She is no girl. She is Strigoi."

She had met Boris Aharon Chong two months after returning to Tong Yun.

Tong Yun City, Mars: the streets dirty and crowded together under the dome, but most of the city was underground, level under level leading at last to the Dark Sea, the Ocean of Refuge—*Solwota blong Dak*, or *Solwota blong Doti*. Carmel had been living in a hostel of sorts on Level Five, a dark, vast region of caves and tunnels where rent was cheap and questions were few. But she had gone up to the surface, on Julius Nyerere Avenue she had a milkshake in the shade and watched the trams go past and a robotnik, rusted with age, begging for spare parts on the street—his kind were ubiquitous on Mars.

Mars was not as she had expected it to be. She was afraid to leave the city, beyond Tong Yun and its space elevator the planet was a wild unknown, the Red Soviet and New Israel and the Chinese tunnel networks and the isolated homesteads and kibbutzim, places too small, where a Strigoi would be all too easy to detect. She remained in the city, hiding in the crowd, feeding flittingly, at risk, though down in the lower levels people disappeared, and she was not the only hunter stalking the shadows. . . .

She just wasn't very *good* at it, she thought. She had often wished that nameless Shambleau on board the *Emaciated Saviour* had picked someone—anyone—else. She, Carmel, had just wanted to leave home. She wanted to see what the rest of the worlds looked like. Instead she became sick before she ever got off the ship. And it was a sickness without a cure, an affliction the only way out of which was death.

There was a man sitting at a nearby table, sipping coconut juice, and she felt her eyes drawn to him, more and more, as she sat there. He was alone, he was a tall, pale man and wore an aug, a Martian lab-bred parasite. She could not look away. He turned, then, and saw her looking, and smiled, a small, private smile that made her like him. He did not come over. Neither did she. But when he paid and left she did the same, and she followed him that day through the streets of Tong Yun, down Nyerere and Ho Chi Minh and Mandela and down the smaller streets where forgotten rulers and leaders out of dusty history intermingled uneasily. The man she was following lived in a co-op building, common to Tong Yun, a town where housing came at a premium. She had watched him go in and followed, the building's meagre security no match to her cancerous internal network. She followed him up to the fourth floor of the building and entered his room after him, picking the lock.

He had turned. She remembered it vividly. He had turned, that look of quiet surprise on his face. He said nothing. Took her in, and there was pity in his eyes, somehow that was the worst thing about it. Her hair was cut short then, she did not have the dreads. He said, "Shambleau . . ." softly. She approached him. He did not back away. Her mind, her node, her senses went for him. The hunger welling inside her, so severely she imagined filaments pushing out of her skin like worms, wriggling in their eagerness to feed. He did not resist her. She sank her teeth into his neck, ready to feed, and—

Something rotten but not unpleasant, something dark without having shape. She could not understand it. She could not break into his mind, it was a locked prison surrounded by alien matter, no dopamine response, no wash of precious data over her, it was like biting cardboard rather than a man.

Almost gently, he pushed her away. Held her arms. She stared into his eyes, confused, shaking with the hunger. The Martian aug was pulsating on his neck. "I already have one parasite," he said—almost, it seemed, apologetic.

"You know her," Miriam said. Boris wouldn't meet her eyes. Carmel looked from one to the other, afraid, angry. Miriam said, "You never told me . . ." There was wounded hurt in her voice.

"I have a past," Boris said. Almost angry, Carmel thought. "We all do."

"But your past followed you here," Miriam said. Then, looking at Carmel. "Look at the poor girl. She's shaking!"

"Shambleau?" Magdalena Wu looked at Carmel, looked at Boris, her cousin. "How could you—?" And seeing Miriam approach Carmel she said, in horror, "No! Don't go near her, she could—"

"It's a sickness, Magda," Boris said. His voice was flat. "It's not her fault."

"No," Magdalena said, "no . . ." She shook her head, pushed back the chair: it came crashing down on the floor with a bang. "I can't. You must—"

"Then go," Miriam said. "But don't—" A look passed between them. Carmel could not decipher it. Then Magdalena was gone.

"She was nice to me," Carmel said. Miriam put her hand on Carmel's brow. It felt warm there, comforting. Miriam's node was wide open, Carmel could have devoured her in an instant. "How could you?" Miriam said, angry. "She is only a girl!"

They had gone to bed together, that first night. It felt so strange, to be this close, this physical, with someone, and yet be unable to get into their mind, to share who, what, they were. In that tiny apartment in Tong Yun, on Boris's narrow bed, they made love.

She had to learn him from the outside, to piece together clues, hints, things he told her, things he didn't. She could not read him, the aug was always between them. He was a doctor, he told her. He used to work in the birthing clinics, he had specialised in Progeny Design, but he wasn't doing that anymore. He was from Earth, originally. From that region called the Middle East (but east of what? middle of where?), a place called Central Station. He was as exotic to her as she must have seemed to him, she studied him the old-fashioned way, with fingers, tongue, with taste and smell. They explored each other, fashioning maps. But he could not ease her hunger.

He sat opposite her now. His fingers on her jawline, lifting up her head, gently. "What am I going to do with you, Carmel?" he said. He sounded exasperated. He was patronising. She watched him silently, watched Miriam, that small compact woman, owner of this shebeen, could almost see, visually, the lines of affection and shared history that bound her and Boris together. And she felt jealous.

"Why did you *come* here?"

Wonder in his voice.

"Leave her be," Miriam, like a mother, fussing over her. Made Carmel want to hiss, like a comical Strigoi, like something out of that classic Phobos Studios production, *Shambleau*, where Elvis Mandela played the fearless Strigoi hunter who ends up falling for the parasite he catches. There had been several sequels, and knockoffs and copies, but the films always ended the same way.

The Strigoi had to die.

"Why?" the Shambleau says. This is the penultimate scene of the film. An unlikely set of circumstances sees Elvis Mandela first stalk and then capture the Shambleau, become addicted, flee from a group of silent assassins (headed by Shirkan Goodbye, who always played the villain in the Phobos productions), find shelter in a Church of Robot node, escape again, run into a group of Martian Re-Born and finally ubicked into the virtuality of ancient Mars-That-Never-Was, where the scene is set.

Mars-That-Never-Was. An ancient land of canals and steamy jungles, ruled over by the Emperor of Time; a construct of the Re-Born faith, facilitated by Others, a sophisticated digital universe, some said; a reality of which our own is but a shadow, the Re-Born said. In that penultimate scene, on the Grand Canal, Elvis Mandela holds the Shambleau in his arms as they watch the dying sun. "Why?" the Shambleau says.

Elvis Mandela draws the katana blade from its sheath. He strokes the Shambleau's head, the protruding nodal filaments of her hair. "Because I have to," he says.

Their affair was doomed, Carmel knew. She knew Boris was fascinated by her. Aroused by her difference. And his aug somehow protected him, it was an alien buffer her own cancerous nodal growths could not penetrate. Boris wanted to help her. To remake her. To *study* her. All the while knowing his own weakness, admitting to his sexual infatuation with her, this human kink that made them lust for Strigoi, for the thing that could harm them.

It did not last long. Three, four months, always in his apartment, Carmel afraid of going out, Boris making love to her and drawing her blood and running diagnostics, until even he had to admit the wrong of what he was doing, this playing of doctor and patient, unethical, corrupting, wrong.

He never gave her up. Never betrayed her. But she left him, because she had to, because it was wrong, and because she was hungry.

She returned to Level Five and to hunting in the tunnels.

Sometimes she even met other Strigoi, but something in them mutually repelled each other, some glitch or built-in effect that ensured they did not hunt together, that they would remain always alone.

What prompted her to go to Earth? To undertake another space voyage, on board a ship where she might be discovered, past the network verification systems of old Earth, and to that strange land Boris had once come from? She knew he had gone home. She kept track of him, on and off, through the Conversation. Knew he had left Tong Yun, later, heard he had gone back to Earth.

But what was home? For her, that asteroid she came from? The longhouse, the multitude of relatives, the lone mine-ships, and watching endless reruns of *Chains of Assembly*?

"Perhaps I just wanted to see Earth," she said. "I don't know anyone else on this planet."

"How did you even get *through*?" he said. "The immigration systems should have picked you up, arrested you!"

"I bought an ident tag, a whole new being," she said. "From a Conch called Shemesh, back in Tong Yun."

Boris stood up. Paced. Miriam sat opposite Carmel. Looked at her. "So you're . . . Shambleau?" she said. "I never met. . . ."

"We don't belong here," Carmel said. Squirmed. Miriam made her feel both welcome and uncomfortable. "We're creatures of the spaceways." A line from that Elvis Mandela picture. Even to her ears it sounded ridiculous.

"She can't stay here," Boris said. The aug pulsed on his

neck. At that moment, Carmel hated him. It. *Them*. There was no man without the Martian growth. They were one, a single being, Joined.

Miriam said nothing. Just looked at Boris. And he turned back. No words between them. No data transfer, either. Just a look, speaking more than an encrypted message ever could.

"She's dangerous," Boris said. Already defeated.

"There are other ways of knowing," Miriam said. "This is Manhome, they say, but they are wrong. This is Womanhome, the womb of humanity, and there are older, stranger powers here, Boris."

"Like what?" he said. Bitter, suddenly. "God? Always your God!"

"You need to have faith," Miriam said. But gently. "It is hard enough just being alive. You have to have a little faith."

Boris shook his head. But Miriam had already dismissed him. She turned to Carmel, a wordless question in her eyes.

Would you like to stay?

Carmel didn't know what to say.

The poet Bashō, who, it was rumoured, had met and fallen in love with a Shambleau near an Ogko shrine below Olympus Mons, had never told the tale of that affair. Did it end as it does in the film franchise from Phobos Studios? Or had it ended differently, with mutual love, with a recognition that a Strigoi is no more predator than man is? Had Bashō fled, or was he propelled onwards, a restless spirit on a quest that had no goal beyond the road itself?

We do not, cannot, know. But this is Womanhome, Earth

Prime, and there are other ways of knowing and of seeing, and greater mysteries, as we are yet to see. As for Bashō, our only clue is one final poem he wrote, though never published. It runs like this:

Sambelu.
Taem yu save lafem hem, hemi kilim yu. Sambelu. Awo! Sambelu,
Sambelu blong mi. Mi lafem yu. Mi lukluk yu. Yu kilim mi,
Mi kilim yu. Yu lafem mi, mi lafem yu. Sambelu. Sambelu. Sambelu.

And translates, roughly, so: "Shambleau. / When you love her, she hurts you. Shambleau. Oh! Shambleau, / my Shambleau. I love you, I look at you. You hurt me / I hurt you. You love me, and I love you. Shambleau. Shambleau. / Shambleau."

"Yes," Carmel said.

SIX:
FILAMENTS

"Reality," said the robo-priest, "is a thin and fragile thing."

R. Brother Patch-It watched its small congregation. Level Three Concourse, Central Station: this Church of Robot node. Few followed the true faith anymore. Robots alone, it sometimes seemed to R. Patch-It, still believed. Others, those strange, bodyless digital intelligences, had absconded belief for worlds of pure mathematics, an infinity of virtual possibilities. Whereas humans needed, sometimes craved, faith, but seldom knew which path to choose, and competition was fierce when one had Judaism alongside Roman Catholicism, Buddhism against Elronism, the Martian Re-Born alongside Islam.

And the Church of Robot was austere, robots saw

themselves as metal shepherds, the awkward link between human physicality and Other transcendence. R. Brother Patch-It coughed with the voice of a long-dead man and resumed the sermon. "Reality," it said, and faltered. The congregation watched attentively. Missus Chong the Elder at the pews at the back, and her friend Esther, they were religion-shoppers, sampling each faith like connoisseurs, covering their bets the closer they got to old age. A group of disgruntled house appliances watched the sermon in the virtuality—coffee makers, cooling units, a couple of toilets—appliances, more than anyone else, needed the robots' guidance, yet they were often wilful, bitter, prone to petty arguments, both with their owners and with themselves. There had never been that many robots. Humanoid, awkward, they belonged in neither world, the real or the irreal, and none had been made for a century or more. To make ends meet, R. Brother Patch-It doubled as a moyel for the Jews of Central Station. In that, at least, he was valued. He was a good moyel, and had been ordained, and could perform the delicate surgery of removing the foreskin, expertly, there had never been complaints. In his younger days R. Brother Patch-It had toyed with the idea of conversion. Becoming a robot Jew was not that far-fetched, there was a famous rabbi on Mars who was one of the first robots ever made. But it was not easy becoming a Jew. It was a faith that discouraged strangers.

"Consensus reality is like a cloth," it started again. The congregation listened, there was the sound of dry rustling in the small, dark church, the smell of metal and pine resin. "It is made of many individual strands, each of which is a reality upon itself, a self-encoded world. We each have our own reality, a world made by our senses and our minds. The tapestry of consensus reality is therefore a group effort. It requires enough of us to agree on what reality *is*. To determine the shape of the tapestry, if you will."

R. Brother Patch-It liked that last addition. *If you will.* It lent a certain weight to arguments. "If you will," it said, savouring the words. "For reality to exist we must all will it into being. We dream—"

It hesitated again. Robots didn't dream, not as such. And the thrust of the argument was becoming positively Buddhist. R. Patch-It had often contemplated reincarnation. Many digitals were practicing Buddhists. The digital being born in the Breeding Grounds as a piece of specialised I-loop responsible for animating a coffee maker could, in its next cycle, become a mind calculating the diffusion of distant nebulas, or a submarine shuttle riding to and from the underwater cities of the humans, or it could even transcend, become a true Other, disembodied, constantly mutating and changing, seeking that which was truth, and therefore beautiful, in the irreal.

But robots seldom changed, R. Brother Patch-It thought, a little sadly. Like humans, they merely became more themselves.

"We dream a consensus of a reality," it said now. It coughed again. It had a range of carefully selected coughs. "Imagine the world is a vast network, all living things are nodes connected together by delicate threads. Without the network we would each be alone, isolated nodes, pinpricks of light in a vast intergalactic darkness. The Way of Robot is the way of seeking to be Joined with all things. It is not an easy road. Often, it is a lonely road. The living and the ur-living both make reality. Let me guide you, now . . ."

R. Brother Patch-It lowered its head and the congregation did likewise, the humans and the digitals who followed. "Our maker who art in the zero point field, hallowed be thy nine billion names . . ."

The congregation murmured after the robo-priest. Then, one by one, they lined up to receive the sacrament. The digital wafer contained high-encryption Crucifixation routines. The humans put it on their tongues, where it slowly melted and was absorbed into the bloodstream and into the biological-nodal interface. The digitals received it directly. For a short moment, the small congregation of this Church of Robot node was truly Joined, forming one I-loop, agreeing on a consensus reality; however short-lived.

The *bris* went well, R. Patch-It felt. It was the youngest Chong boy, Levi. R. Patch-It had known the Chongs for generations, from Zhong Weiwei, the founder of the family, down to all the cousins and nephews and nieces and aunts that spread all around Central Station. Vlad sat in the seat of honour, the *sandak*, or godfather, to the child. The old man held the baby, but his face was blank, unseeing. A sickness of memory afflicted Vlad Chong. R. Patch-It worried for him.

But this was a time for joy. Carefully, the robot separated the foreskin from the infant's penis with his special knife, the *izmel*, while making the first blessing. Then it performed the *pria*, the revealing of the infant's glans by separating the inner preputial epithelium, again with the knife. The proud father made the second and third blessings. Then, watched by the attendant audience in the small synagogue, the robot performed the *metzitza ba'peh*, sucking at the wound until drawing blood.

The baby was crying. Carefully pouring the wine for blessing into its cup, which the robot held in its right hand, he announced the child's name—Levi Chong—and the name of his father, Elad. The robot drank from the wine. The child was now, by the ancient laws, a Jew. At last, R. Brother Patch-It dipped a metal finger in the wine and put it into the infant's mouth. The boy suckled on the finger and stopped crying. Everyone cheered. Ancient Missus Chong the Elder, cyborged but sharp, cried saltwater tears.

The ceremony ending at last, the baby admired by his relatives, the crowd moved to the next room for the breakfast spread. Pastries and breads, *shakshuka*—fried eggs over a thick, slowly cooked tomato and capsicum sauce—coffee from a samovar, a cheese platter, *burekas* pastries filled with cheese or potatoes or mushrooms, omelettes, jams—hungry Chongs swarming over the breakfast buffet as though starved beyond belief. The robot moved amongst the family and friends, shaking hands, chatting—it held a cup of black coffee, which it sipped from time to time.

R. Patch-It stopped a moment before a man who looked familiar. He had the Chong look, but for a moment the robot could not place him. The man seemed quiet, comfortable in his surroundings, but there was something shy, perhaps reserved, about him, too. He stood next to a woman the robo-priest knew well: Mama Jones, and her boy, Kranki.

"Miriam," R. Patch-It said to the woman. "It is lovely to see you, as always."

"You, too, R. Patch-It," she said, smiling.

They knew each other of old. The robot turned to look downwards. The boy's hacked eyes stared at him, a mischievous smile turning the corners of his mouth. "Hello, Kranki," R. Patch-It said. The boy made the robot feel clumsy, somehow. He unsettled R. Patch-It.

"Hey, tin man," the boy said.

Miriam, shocked, said, "Kranki!"

"It's all right," the robot said. He noticed the Chong man beside Miriam couldn't quite hide a smile. "How are you, Kranki? Do you remember me?"

The robo-priest had been the moyel in Kranki's own bris, of course. The boy said, "I went to the beach yesterday with Ismail. We caught a fish!" He made a shape with his hands. "It was *this* big."

Miriam put her hand on the boy's head. The robo-priest was about to speak when the boy said, "Let me show you!" His small hand went to the robo-priest's own metal one, trustingly. The robot reached out automatically—

The boy's pointing finger touched the metal of the robot's palm, lightly.

What is the real?

The words whispered in the robot's brain. Billions of cycles, uncounted millions of branches on a quantum binary tree, shifting and merging, an Aristocratic Small-World network like a planet or a human brain, billions of disparate elements making up a single, precious I-loop, an illusion of being.

What is real?

The words whispered in the robot's old brain, auto-translated into a dozen languages, chief amongst them Hebrew and Asteroid Pidgin: *Ma amiti? Wanem ia i tru?*

The images swarmed through the robot's mind, a high-level onslaught of data in which a single image permeated: the boy, Kranki, and a seeming twin, a boy whose eyes were a green Bose trademark for Kranki's Armani blue. The two boys at the Jaffa beach, walking on water, fishing with their small hands, reaching into the clear blue of the Mediterranean Sea. . . .

Which exploded into stars, galaxies swirling, planets orbiting yellow suns like baleful eyes, vast black-hulled spaceships moving like specks of dust amidst the planets, the view focuses, shifts, rings spinning in the space beyond Titan, killer drones fighting soundlessly in the Galilean Republics, intelligent mines tracking in orbit around Callisto, in the space beyond beyond, the song of spiders as they seed the Oort cloud with new nodes, on Dragon's World, a frozen moon off Pluto, the dragon's millions of bodies moving in the tunnels on their mysterious rounds, the whole ice-moon a vast extensive ant warren—

Wanem ia i tru?

On Mars, in Tong Yun City, at a wooded shrine under the great dome, the poet Bashō translating Shakespeare into Pidgin:

Blong stap o no blong stap
Hemi wan gudfala kwesjen ia

And across space, away from moving Mars and its twin
moons burning with human-made lights, across *solwota blong
Spes*, images dancing, *solwota blong wori*, the sea of worry and
these slings and *bunaro* of outrageous fortune—

On the Earth's moon the vast terraforming spiders moved,
dull silver metal silent, two boys standing on the surface,
helmetless, laughing, as at a secret joke shared, with their
hands signing:

Wanem ia i ril?

R. Patch-It was shocked out of the data-storm. It stood there,
looking at the boy, the storm slowly receding.

"Brother Patch-It?" Miriam Jones said. "Are you feeling all
right?"

The I-loop tagged R. Patch-It came back to life, or online,
or into being. "I am a robot," it said. "I seldom get sick."

Mama Jones smiled, politely. The man beside her said,
"I don't know if you remember me, Brother." He extended
his hand for a shake. "Boris," he said, seeming suddenly
embarrassed. "Boris Chong."

R. Patch-It looked at him. "*Boris* Chong?" it said—
marvelled. Perfect images in its recall—a shy boy, tall, gangly,
with a smile, he always had a smile, quiet child, before that
the baby, R. Patch-It had been the moyel at that bris, too—
"But you had left, it was—"

The robot stopped, it could recite it to the day, the hour, the minute, had it wanted to. How had it not recognised him? But Boris had left a boy, returned a man, the Up and Out changed him, the robot saw.

R. Patch-It itself had been to space, of course. Once, a century past, it had undertaken pilgrimage, the robot's *hajj*, to Mars, to Tong Yun City, to the Level Three Concourse deep under the Martian sands, where the greatest of all multifaith bazaars lies, there to meet the Robo-Pope itself, in the robot's Vatican. It had been a glorious occasion! Hundreds of robots, some former battle drones, some scrap-heap refugees, all congregating together, from every habitable moon and planet they came, from Polyport on Titan and from the deserts of the Martian kibbutzim; from Lunar Port and Moscow, Newer Delhi to the Baha'i rings in orbit around Saturn. And one from Central Station. *Hajji* R. Patch-It, ordained in that great communion of physicality and the digital.

Then, too, at that meeting, some had chosen to go farther still. To accompany the Exodus ships, on their slow, one-way journeys out of the solar system. And some had chosen to remain, and in the depths of Mars to fashion new of their kind, to create children. . . .

Children!

Perhaps it all came back to that, R. Patch-It thought, the data-surge fading, the image of these two Central Station boys on the moon, Kranki and his friend.

Children. The robot had circumcised hundreds of children, but never had one of its own.

"Brother?"

The human's voice brought it back to itself. "Boris Chong," the robot said, marvelling. "Where have you been all these years?"

The man shrugged. His hand, the robot noticed, went to Miriam's, the tips of his fingers touching hers. R. Patch-It remembered them, together, the boy and the girl they had been. Love made humans shine, as though they were metal filaments heated by an electrical current.

The human said, "I went to Mars, the Belt, I . . . I came back recently. My father—"

Yes, R. Patch-It wanted to say. Vlad Chong sat across the room, vacant eyes staring into space. Some humans suffered a gradual loss of memory, but for Vlad, the robot thought, it was the other way around. Vlad's mind was literally swarming with memory, perfect and enduring like diamond, memories stored since Weiwei's time. Vladimir Chong could not see, for his gaze was turned, terribly, inside himself.

The robot nodded, shook Boris's hand, touched Miriam lightly on the shoulder. The boy, Kranki, had gone to play with the other kids. Boris had worked in the birthing clinics, R. Patch-It remembered. What manner of children had they made there, hacked out of rogue genomes and stolen code?

The robot felt—if robots could be said to feel, it thought— weary. Its body was running at less than optimum capacity. Its body was old, patched, the old parts were hard to come by, no one had manufactured robots in decades. R. Patch-It wanted to simply plug itself into a current, like a human wire-head at a Louis Wu emporium. The humans had found a way to stimulate the brain's pleasure centres with a low current of electricity. Sometimes R. Patch-It longed for Body, for sensation. The humans were sensation-addicts.

"Brother?"

The coffee had turned cold in the cup. R. Patch-It deposited it on a table and went to take another. Coffee was energy, a robot could convert food and drink into energy as efficiently as any human. But could it derive *pleasure* from it?

Pleasure was a difficult and bewildering concept. R. Patch-It thought it might make it the subject of next week's sermon.

"Brother?"

The voice came again and this time it registered. R. Patch-It turned. The two smiling men, holding hands, stood before him. "Yan," R. Patch-It said. "Youssou!"

They, too, made a handsome couple, he thought. Yan was a Chong; Youssou was of the Joneses of Central Station. "Is it official?" R. Patch-It said.

The two men beamed even more. "It is," Youssou said.

"We had a fight—" Yan said—shy, proud. So much like his cousin Boris, R. Patch-It thought.

"He was going to do it that night—" from Youssou.

"I had it all ready. We were at the Grand Lounge—"

"I wasn't ready," Youssou said. "I didn't think I was ready."

"He walked away, we didn't speak for a month. But . . ."

"I missed him." They both said it together, then laughed.

"Mazal tov!" the robot said. It clasped them on the arms. So much love, both young and old, in that room. It must be spring again, R. Patch-It thought. It almost hadn't noticed. Spring had that effect on humans.

"We made up, I couldn't sleep, I was living in the adaptoplant tenements," Youssou said.

"I was sleeping in the lab," Yan said. "I was working all the time."

"We got together, and—"

"Mazal tov," the robot said again.

Yan said, "Brother. We wanted to ask you something."

"Anything," R. Patch-It said. Meaning it.

"We'd like you to marry us," Youssou said.

They both looked at him, expectantly. The robot looked at them both. "I would be honoured," R. Patch-It said.

Weddings it had officiated over before. Weddings and circumcisions, and funerals, too. A robot, R. Patch-It thought, more than anything a robot needed *purpose*. Shaking hands all around, metal against flesh. "Thank you, Brother!" Relatives gathering around to congratulate the young couple.

"Brother Patch-It," a voice said. It was Missus Chong the Elder, coming over. They looked at each other. She was more than half-machine. She smiled. "It will be an honour for my family to have you officiate," she said.

The ceremony would be conducted in the manner of the Church of Robot. Central Station was an amalgamation of faiths. The Jewish Chongs were a mix of Chinese and Israeli Jew; the Chows were Roman Catholic; the Joneses were, well, he wasn't sure: though Miriam Jones could often be found at the shrine for St. Cohen of the Others.

"Thank you," the robot said. "Thank you for asking me."

Could a robot feel? If you pricked a robot, it did not bleed. But *if* it felt, then it felt, right then—overwhelmed, it thought. Tired, elated—suddenly the room full of humans felt oppressive, it needed space, solitude, time to withdraw from the physicality. Some of the robots left the Church, they abandoned physicality entire, went into the digitality, incorporeality, the realm of Others. Some went on the Exodus ships, some transformed, reincarnated themselves into humbler vessels, one could sometimes encounter an ancient coffee maker that had once been a robot, seeking a different path to enlightenment in service.

"Brother?"

"Please, Missus Chong," the robot said. "I must retire."

She looked at him and her eyes were inhuman, understanding. One day Missus Chong the Elder would shed the last of her humanity and become a seeker like itself. It had hopes for Missus Chong, she was the most promising of Brother Patch-It's novices.

She nodded, a small, barely perceptible gesture. The robo-priest made its way out of the room. It was still uncertain as to what happened with the boy, Kranki. The boy was not entirely human, it realised. Perhaps, somehow, he was part-Other: and the mystery of it puzzled R. Patch-It.

The robot made its way to the elevators and rose to Level Four where, for countless years, it had rented small accommodation for itself. Service tunnels, storage lockers, corridors leading ever deeper into the station, where warehouses vast beyond recall sat and where the station's heart beat a steady rhythm—the robot felt it in its joints.

R. Patch-It opened the door to his own private space: it was a small, dark closet, one in a row of identical such habitats. Here it could truly be alone.

It was home.

It shut itself inside and opened its mind to the Conversation, the endless wash of talk moving between worlds, and the words floated again in its mind, unanswered: *Wanem ia i tru?*

Brother R. Patch-It floated through space, watching multiple feeds through multiple nodes. A child was born on a Martian kibbutz, in the space around Io an ancient mine exploded itself, committing suicide, on Titan a muezzin was calling the faithful to prayer. Space was full of questions, life was a sentence always ending in an ellipsis or a question mark. You couldn't answer everything. You could only believe there were answers at all.

To be a robot, you needed faith, R. Patch-It thought.

To be a human, too.

SEVEN: ROBOTNIK

Motl needed faith. He needed it bad.

How had he come to be at Central Station?

Motl glanced around him. His body itched, one arm was rusted, and the joints squeaked when he moved it. He needed vodka, to power himself, and he needed oil, to take care of the rust in the joints, but most of all, what he needed was religion. He needed a pill, something to ease back the pain. . . .

Earlier, he had met Isobel again, under the eaves. It had been dark and quiet there. They had. . . .

He knew she loved him.

Love was dangerous. Love was a dark drug and it was addictive and, for a long time, forbidden to him. He was, paradoxically, both all past and without a past. Once he had a name, a body. Once he was alive.

113

———————

"I love you."

"I . . . I too."

That one word, missing. Her body was against his. She was warm, human. She smelled of rice vinegar and soy and garlic, of the sweaty faux-leather of an immersion pod, of a perfume he couldn't put a name to, of pheromones and hormones and salt. She looked up, into his eyes. "I'm old," he said.

"I don't care!"

Fiercely. Protectively. It made him feel strange inside. Vulnerable. Ancient programming kicked in, trying to stop it. Trying to flood his body with hormone suppressants, though the equipment had run dry long before. He was free now, to feel as he liked.

"I'm . . ." He didn't know what to say. "Isobel." He whispered her name. She had a real name, a name that belonged to her. "Ich lieba dich," he said, in that ancient, obsolete Battle Yiddish they had given him. Like the Navajo of Code Talkers in another long-gone war. He could no longer remember the wars he'd been in, he assumed they were given names, that in some historical record they were placed down reverently, dated, placed into context. All he remembered was the pain.

The Sinai desert, the Red Sea shimmering in the heat. Their platoon had encamped in the ruins of Sharm el-Sheikh. No humans in sight, they were robotniks, the best of the best, and they were waiting for an attack that didn't come.

Motl could no longer recall what the war had been about, or who they were fighting, exactly. The other side had semi-sentient fliers, they were predatory things that came from the sky, silently, that had talons that could tear through armour. Jubjub Birds. Earlier they had watched a Leviathan rise from the depths, organic gun turrets shining wetly in the sunlight, eye stalks scanning the horizon for heat signatures, infrared—

Another platoon had gone underwater, armoured humanoids communicating subvocally in Battle Yiddish as they targeted the Leviathan. They attached themselves to the enemy creature like barnacles. They strapped themselves to the glistening flesh, in the depths, their charges tied to their exoskeletons. Motl and the others watched the explosion, the slow death of Leviathan, the huge body thrashing helplessly in the water. Its death cry made their ears bleed. The Leviathan's death cloud of spores rose above the water, drifting in the wind. Motl prayed they would not be sent on egg duty. Leviathan spores would hatch in the water and new machines would be born to continue the fighting. Motl was jealous of the others, the ones who had blown themselves up. At least they were allowed true death. . . .

It was quiet there, in the ruins of Sharm. It had once been a minor fishing village then, during Israel's short-lived occupation, it was a city called Ofira. Now, Motl wasn't even sure who occupied it. The Bedouins kept well away.

He was a sleek death machine in those days, but that didn't stop the backwash. That's what they called it. The backwash was the flow of thoughts and emotions stemming from who you once were, the human you had been, the one they took off the battlefield and cyborged, the dead thing you were before they made you robotnik. Dead man's memories, you weren't supposed to have them, but sometimes. . . .

Beyond the shore the Leviathan died, slowly. In the distance a convoy of Jubjubs hunted above the shore line of the Arabian Peninsula.

Motl rested under a palm tree. Made sure his weapons—a part of him—were charged and loaded, that everything worked, that he was primed, ready . . . but the backwash came on him then and it was suddenly hard to think, a memory—

A palm tree very much like this one, a desert oasis, an armed convoy approaching, he and the others lying in wait—

Flares lighting up the sky, he could see rockets, something slammed into the ground nearby sending up a cloud of sand, he heard screams—

Pain erupting, all over, at once. The air was full of things like midges, they crawled over his skin, they got into his mouth, into his nose, his ears, his rectum, they crawled inside him and outside him, dissolving him, hurting him—

Motl blinked. He was trying to fight it, his internal systems (fully operational then) were mainlining sedatives, but it wasn't enough, it wasn't enough to stop the backwash—

He writhed in the sand, screaming, but no sound came. There had been a full moon and it looked down on him. The air was thick with blood and the reek of guts and urine. They wouldn't let him die. They were everywhere, violating him, they were laying eggs in his bloodstream, they were crawling inside his brain—

Then something changed—minutes or hours or days later. He

saw them. He could see. A platoon, desert-coloured uniforms. He didn't know which side he'd been on, and which side they were.

"We've got a live one here," one of them said.

"Take him."

The other grinned. He had a—was that a sword? Something so archaic . . . the blade came down, swiftly, and the pain and all sensory perception stopped.

How could he explain all that to Isobel? he thought. Central Station, the stars above, a sliver blade moon. His hands were shaking. He walked down Neve Sha'anan, past Mama Jones' Shebeen, the Church of Robot node beside it, went towards the core of the old bus station, the abandoned tunnels where once passengers boarded buses, long ago, when buses and robotniks still ran on petrol.

How could he explain the *craving*?

In the Sinai, in that long-ago campaign, he had gone and sought the priest. The priest was like him, he was a robotnik, but he was also different, he had the offerings of God and the comfort of religion entrusted in his hands.

The priest was standing on a sand dune beyond the ruined city. The sky was darkening, and the priest spoke, preaching into the desert.

And he said: "Let the day perish wherein I was born, and the night in which it was said, There is a man-child conceived."

And he said: "Let that day be darkness; let not God regard it from above, neither let the light shine upon it."

"Let darkness and the shadow of death stain it," Motl whispered. "Let a cloud dwell upon it; let the blackness of the day terrify it."

He watched the priest, longingly, the need burning in him. The priest said, "Because it shut not up the doors of my mother's womb, nor hid sorrow from mine eyes."

And Motl replied: "Why died I not from the womb? Why did I not give up the ghost when I came out of the belly?"

The unanswered question of the robotnik, the sermon of Job delivered there, on a sand dune, with Leviathan dying in the warm waters of the Red Sea. "Please," Motl said. "I need it."

The priest descended the dune. They were of the same height, but now Motl knelt down, for the priest to bless him. He opened his mouth and felt the priest's metal fingers, warmed from the sun, on his still-organic tongue. "God," the priest said, and Motl closed his mouth, and swallowed, the small pill on his tongue melting into his bloodstream.

Crucifixation.

It hit him like a bullet, and the heavens opened.

Walking alone with Central Station at his back . . . west was the sea, the smell of brine and tar, that brought back half-remembered memories. He walked through the night market and the smell of jasmine and deep-fried *nambaeit gato* and grilled kebabs, but he was not interested in the food.

Isobel could not understand. She had not yet died, had not been reborn.

"For now should I have lain still and been quiet, I should have slept: then had I been at rest," he whispered. His hands were shaking. The need was on him, driving him. His left leg clanged as he walked. He drew stares but then they looked away. Just another broken-down robotnik, just another beggar haunting the night streets looking for a handout or a fix or both.

He came to the tunnels. From above, waste lying on the ground, the black ring of an old fire, the crumbling remnants of bus platforms. There, a grate in an old ventilation shaft. He pulled it out and slid inside, down the rusting ladder and into the tunnels.

Along an abandoned platform stood three figures. They had lit a fire in an open metal drum and stood around it, motionless, the flames reflecting in their metal skin. Motl approached, his heavy footsteps and that clanking noise the only sound in that underground cavern.

"Motl."

"Ezekiel. Samuel. Jedediah."

Motionless. A rat scuttled down below. The flames reflected in expressionless metal faces.

Sending him back. . . .

He was kneeling by the water's edge. The Red Sea, at sunrise. The sun reflected off the water and off Motl's body, suffusing him. Faith came in little pills that dissolved on one's tongue, God's own flesh cannibalized by humanity's child. He had spent the night praying, *believing*—God, manufactured and produced in the Jerusalem labs, was all-encompassing, it made the backwash recede into the background, become irrelevant—God said, You are doing God's work, there is a purpose to your being, you are loved, you may be a tool but a tool that is *needed*—

The effects of Crucifixation were wearing off now. The world still shone, but not as brightly. Just the memory of being needed, and of being loved, and that would have to be enough—

Sand exploded upwards, he half-turned, weapons at the ready—

The Leviathan had died in the night and its giant corpse floated, half-sunk, drifting towards Aqaba.

Ordered, terse commands in Battle Yiddish, and Motl was rising, firing—

*The thing erupted out of the sand, bullet-shaped head glistening with slime—*vermes arenae sinaitici gigantes, *the giant sandworms of the Sinai—it snatched up Ebenezer, teeth crunching metal as though it were dough, then it burrowed into the sand again.*

Silence. Robotniks spreading out across the ruined town, tense, waiting. No one spoke now. God's lingering presence still suffused Motl's being, but overriding it was fear, and the smell of spilled coolant and gunpowder.

He didn't know who had first introduced the giant sand-worms to the Sinai, they had been used in the same way one planted mines, for future conflicts, but unlike mines they had multiplied, they thrived. The Bedouins hunted them, they made medicines from their poison.

"*It's coming!*"

A sandworm erupted ahead of Motl, one of his fellow robotniks, Isidore, jumped on it, blades flashing, but when you sliced a Sinaiticus Gigans it didn't die, it split—

And now, from the air—they must have hidden nearby, waiting—a convoy of Jubjub Birds came swooping down, red-eyed, with talons extended, and their smell was the smell of garbage and excrement, and it mixed with the sickly sweet stench of the sandworms—

Someone threw a firebomb, it caught the lead Jubjub and the bird screamed, became a phoenix in flames—

Hell, Motl thought, running, guns firing, hell was a place right here on Earth, a special place God couldn't go—

A sandworm blasted out of the sand, knocking him off his feet. Dimly he saw Ishmael open up with the flamethrower, and the giant creature burst into flames, keening a high-pitched sound as it thrashed in the sand, unable to burrow under to save itself. Motl rolled, his left leg was unresponsive. He rose stiffly, fired at a Jubjub which came diving at him. Sharm el-Sheikh was burning all around him now, and he placed a sniper shot straight into the bird's brain and watched it fall into the flames. Whatever the old writers knew about hell, he thought, they got it right about the fire.

Silence in the abandoned tunnels of the old bus station, abandoned but for the robotniks. Derelicts, Motl thought with sudden vehemence. Beggars, homeless, worthless, infidels . . . their only fidelity was to themselves.

Robotniks looked after their own.

There was no one else to do so.

How had he come to be in this place? How had he come to Central Station?

His hands were shaking. He needed a fix.

After that last battle they had patched him up and upgraded him, and sent him out again, and then again, and then again. There was always one last battle, one final war. Then for a long time there weren't any more engagements and they stayed on the base, waiting, mainlining faith because it kept you from going all *heretic*, and one day, there wasn't even *word*, as such, it was just that the gate opened and the human staff all left and that was that: they'd become, it appeared, obsolete.

After a while, in ones and twos, they had simply wandered off. The world outside the base was strange and uncomfortable, it was hostile in a way the battlefield never was. Motl did odd jobs. It had been good at first, freedom. He'd even laid off the dope.

Then parts started to fail. . . .

"Motl."

It was Ezekiel. In Central Station, he ruled. He was their captain here.

There were robotniks in Jerusalem, drawn there like leeches to a vein. And some made it off-world, gone to Tong Yun City or Lunar Port. But he, Motl, ended up here.

Backwash, hitting him: memories that shouldn't be, of times that never were. A woman with dark hair, smiling up at him, a pencil behind one delicate ear; a small girl laughing, chubby pink fingers reaching for him to lift her; the sound of a bicycle bell; the smell of freshly cut grass.

His hands shook.

"Motl."

"I need it, Ezekiel. I need it."

"I heard you were with a girl."

The silence around the fire became more pronounced. Motl, too, was still.

"A human girl, Motl?"

The silence from the others was like sheathed blades.

Motl thought of Isobel, under the eaves of Central Station. Her body radiating warmth, her small hand touching his face, and something must have broken in his lacrimal apparatus, it must have done, because his eyes were wet, and he saw her through a film, through mist.

He'd met her in Central Station, on Level Three where she worked, captain in the virtuality of the Guilds of Ashkelon. They had got to talking, he had a job, now, he was a sweeper, moving slowly across the floors of that busiest of levels. Plenty all around to clean. Good steady work.

She'd been unsteady on her feet, she'd just spent eight hours in a pod, in the virtual. She'd stumbled and he went to her, he gave her balance. It made him feel strange, her hands, her skin on his own metal arm, and as she straightened she smiled at him, with brown eyes, white teeth a little crooked, smiled without any self-consciousness or unease, as if, already, they were good friends.

"Sorry," Motl mumbled, releasing her, but she stopped him.

"Wait!" He stopped and looked at her, he was taller than her. She was so alive. She said, "I've seen you around."

He didn't know what to say to that; stayed poised for flight. "I don't know your name," she said.

"It's Motl."

"Motl . . ." The name, when she said it, hit him with its strangeness.

"I like it," she said. Then—"I'm Isobel."

"I . . . I know."

She had dark hair, pale skin. She smiled easily. She was still young. "How do you know?"

"I've seen you around."

They laughed, together. And suddenly it wasn't awkward at all. Suddenly it was the most natural thing in the world to talk together, it was something he had never experienced, or rather, he had, he must have had, in another life; another, lost time.

It scared him. His internal systems were breaking down, they couldn't stop him feeling. His hands shook. "I need it, Ezekiel," he said. His own voice grated on him.

"What do you think you're doing, Motl?"

That voice, cool and calm. There were no lone soldiers. Military form kept order. Ezekiel got his share from Motl's work, just as he got his share from the Crucifixation trade, and the occasional mugging, and what protection racket was going, and from anything else he could get his metal fingers into. Motl respected him for it. Ezekiel looked after his troops.

There was no one else to do it.

"I didn't mean for it to happen, Ezekiel," he said. "It wasn't something I—"

He fell silent. How did he really feel? Before, he did not have to *feel*, not this much. Feeling was something they had taken out of you when they remade you, when the old you, the one who had a name and a life, that human died and you were reborn in his place. Emotion was regulated, back when all his internal systems worked, back when there was maintenance—fear and anger were good, within reason, but love and affection made you soft. Worse, they made you vulnerable.

He looked at his fellow soldiers now, and saw them new, the reflection of the fire in their metal exoskeletons casting them in a new light. He saw them new, then old, he saw their tarnished rusting skin, and heard the soft clanking sound of despair from broken joints and ill-repaired appendages. They had always been weak, he thought. They had always been vulnerable.

"Do you love the girl?" Ezekiel said, and now Motl heard his question with new ears, a new understanding. They were his brothers, his kin.

"I . . ." he said, and then he thought, courage. It was a thing he had almost forgotten.

"I love her," he said, simply.

Around the fire the mute robotniks stirred. Ezekiel nodded his heavy head, once.

"Then go to her," he said.

In the Sinai that time under a waning moon, he had knelt in the sand and dipped his hands in the warm waters of the Red Sea and watched the dying Leviathan in the distance. The drug, Crucifixation, had taken hold of him, and a beam of light came down from the heavens and lifted him, and his spirit hovered on the waters. Faith, he'd needed faith, they all did, faith to go on.

He would find Isobel, he thought. Right now, he'd go to her, he didn't care who would see them together. His hands were still shaking and the craving was still there but he ignored it; he tried to. Sometimes you needed to believe you could believe, sometimes you had to figure heaven could come from another human being and not just in a pill.

Sometimes.

EIGHT:
THE BOOKSELLER

Early morning light suffused Central Station as Ibrahim, the alte-zachen man, came along Neve Sha'anan with his horse and cart. He stopped when he saw Achimwene, who was standing outside the tiny alcove which passed for his shop, and raised his hand in greeting.

Nothing pleased Achimwene Haile Selassie Jones as much as the sight of the sun rising behind Central Station. It highlighted exhausted sex workers and street-sweeping machines, and the bobbing floating lanterns that, with dawn coming, were slowly drifting away, to their own habitats, there to wait until next nightfall. On the rooftops solar panels unfurled themselves, welcoming the sun. The air was still cool at this time. Soon it would be hot, the sun beating down, the aircon units turning on with a roar of cold air in shops and restaurants and crowded apartments all over the old neighbourhood.

127

"Ibrahim," Achimwene said, acknowledging the alte-zachen man as he approached. Ibrahim was perched on top of his cart, the boy Ismail by his side. The cart was already filled, with adaptoplant furniture, scrap plastic and metal, boxes of discarded housewares and, lying carelessly on its side, a discarded stone bust of Albert Einstein.

"Achimwene," Ibrahim said, smiling. "How is the weather?"

"Fair to middling," Achimwene said, and they both laughed, comfortable in the near-daily ritual.

This is Achimwene: he was not the most imposing of people, did not draw the eye in a crowd. He was slight of frame, and somewhat stooped, and wore old-fashioned glasses to correct a minor fault of vision. His hair was once thickly curled, but not much of it was left now, and he was mostly, sad to say, bald. He had a soft mouth and patient, trusting eyes, with fine lines of disappointment at their corners. His name meant "brother" in Chichewa, a language dominant in Malawi, though he was of the Joneses of Central Station, and the brother, indeed, of Miriam Jones, of Mama Jones' Shebeen. Every morning he rose early, bathed hurriedly, and went out into the streets in time to catch the rising sun and the alte-zachen man. Now he rubbed his hands together, as if cold, and said, in his soft, quiet voice, "Do you have anything for me today, Ibrahim?"

Ibrahim ran his hand over his own bald pate and smiled. Sometimes the answer was a simple "No." Sometimes it came with a hesitant "Perhaps . . ."

Today it was a "Yes," Ibrahim said, and Achimwene raised his eyes, to him or to the heavens, and said, "Show me?"

"Ismail," Ibrahim said, and the boy, who sat beside him

wordless until then, climbed down from the cart with a quick, confident grin, and went to the back of the cart. "It's heavy!" he complained. Achimwene hurried to his side and helped him carry down a box that was, indeed, heavy.

He looked at it wordlessly, in anticipation.

"Open it," Ibrahim said. "Are these any good to you?"

Achimwene knelt by the side of the box. His fingers reached for it, traced an opening. Slowly, he pulled the flaps of the box apart. Savouring the moment that light would fall upon the box's contents, and the smell of those precious, fragile things inside would rise, released, into the air, and tickle his nose. There was no other smell like it in the world, the smell of old and weathered paper.

The box opened. He looked inside.

Books. No wonder the box was heavy. It had the weight of paper.

Not the endless scrolls of text and images, moving and static, nor full-immersion narratives he understood other people to experience, in what he called, in his obsolete tongue, the networks, and others called, simply, the Conversation. Not those, to which he, anyway, had no access. Nor were they books as decorations, physical objects handcrafted by artisans, vellum-bound, gold-tooled, typeset by hand and sold at a premium.

No.

He looked at the things in the box, these fragile, worn, faded, thin, cheap paper-bound books. They smelled of dust, and mould, and age. They smelled, faintly, of pee, and tobacco, and spilled coffee. They smelled like things which had *lived*.

They smelled like history.

With careful fingers he took a book out and held it, gently turning the pages. It was all but priceless. His breath, as they often said in those very same books, caught in his throat.

It was a *Ringo*.

A genuine Ringo.

The cover of this fragile paperback showed a leather-faced gunman against a desert-red background. RINGO, it said, in giant letters, and below, the fictitious author's name, Jeff McNamara. Finally, the individual title of the book, one of many in that long-running Western series. This one was *On the Road to Kansas City*.

Were they all like this?

Of course, there had never been a "Jeff McNamara." Ringo was a series of Hebrew-language Westerns, all written pseudonymously by starving young writers in a bygone Tel Aviv, who also contributed similar tales of space adventure, sexual titillation or soppy romance, as the occasion (and the publisher's pocket) had called for. Achimwene rifled carefully through the rest of the books. All paperbacks, printed on cheap, thin pulp paper centuries before. How had they been preserved? Some of these he had only ever seen mentioned in auction catalogues, their existence, here, now, was nothing short of a miracle. There was a nurse romance; a murder mystery; a World War Two adventure; an erotic tale whose lurid cover made Achimwene blush. They were impossible, they could not possibly exist. "Where did you *find* them?" he said.

Ibrahim shrugged. "An opened Century Vault," he said.

Achimwene exhaled a sigh. He had heard of such things—subterranean safe-rooms, built in some long-ago war of the Jews, pockets of reinforced concrete shelters caught like bubbles all under the city surface. But he had never expected. . . .

"Are there . . . many of them?" he said.

Ibrahim smiled. "Many," he said. Then, taking pity on Achimwene, said, "Many vaults, but most are inaccessible. Every now and then, construction work uncovers one . . . the owners called me, for they viewed much of it as rubbish. What, after all, would a modern person want with one of these?" and he gestured at the box, saying, "I saved them for you. The rest of the kipple is back in the junkyard, but this was the only box of books."

"I can pay," Achimwene said. "I mean, I will work something out, I will borrow—" The thought stuck like a bone in his throat (as they said in those books)—"I will borrow from my sister."

But Ibrahim, to Achimwene's delight and incomprehension, waved him aside with a laugh. "Pay me the usual," he said. "After all, it is only a box, and this is mere paper. It cost me nothing, and I have made my profit already. What extra value you place on it surely is a value of your own."

"But they are precious!" Achimwene said, shocked. "Collectors would pay—" Imagination failed him.

Ibrahim smiled, and his smile was gentle. "You are the only collector I know," he said. "Can you afford what you think they're worth?"

"No," Achimwene said—whispered.

"Then pay only what I ask," Ibrahim said and, with a shake of his head, as at the folly of his fellow man, steered the horse into action. The patient beast beat its flank with its tail, shooing away flies, and ambled onwards. The boy, Ismail, remained there a moment longer, staring at the books. "Lots of old junk in the vaults!" he said. He spread his arms wide to describe them. "I was there, I saw it! These . . . books?" He shot an uncertain look at Achimwene, then ploughed on—"And big flat square things called televisions that we took for plastic scrap, and old guns, lots of old guns! But the police took those—why do you think they buried those things to begin with?" the boy said. His eyes, vat-grown haunting greens, stared at Achimwene. "So much kipple," the boy said, at last, with a note of finality, and then, laughing, ran after the cart, jumping up on it with youthful ease.

Achimwene stared at the cart until it disappeared around the bend. Then, with the tenderness of a father picking up a newborn infant, he picked up the box of books and carried them the short way to his alcove.

Achimwene's life was about to change, but he did not yet know it. He spent the rest of the morning happily cataloguing, preserving and shelving the ancient books. Each lurid cover delighted him. He handled the books with only the tips of his fingers, turning the pages carefully, reverently. There were many faiths in Central Station, but only Achimwene's called for this. The worship of old, obsolete books. The worship, he liked to think, of history itself.

He spent the morning quite happily, therefore, with only one customer. For Achimwene was not alone in his— obsession? Fervour?

Others were like him. Mostly men, and mostly, like himself, broken in some fundamental fashion. They came from all over, pilgrims taking hesitant steps through the unfamiliar streets of the old neighbourhood, reaching at last Achimwene's alcove, a shop which had no name. They needed no sign. They simply knew.

There was an Armenian priest from Jerusalem who came once a month, a devotee of Hebrew pulps so obscure even Achimwene struggled with the conversation—romance chapbooks printed in twenty or thirty stapled pages at a time, filled with Zionist fervour and lovers' longings, so rare and fragile few remained in the world. There was a rare woman, whose name was Nur, who came from Damascus once a year, and whose speciality was the works of obscure poet and science fiction writer Lior Tirosh. There was a man from Haifa who collected erotica, and a man from the Galilee who collected mysteries.

"Achimwene? *Shalom!*"

Achimwene straightened in his chair. He had sat at his desk for some half an hour, typing, on what was his pride and joy, a rare collector's item: a genuine, Hebrew typewriter. It was his peace and his escape, in the quiet times, to sit at his desk and pen, in the words of those old, vanished pulp writers, similarly exciting narratives of derring-do, rescues, and escapes.

"Shalom, Gideon," he said, sighing a little. The man, who hovered at the door, now came fully inside. He was a stooped figure, with long, white hair, twinkling eyes, and a bottle of cheap arak held, as an offering, in one hand.

"Got glasses?"

"Sure. . . ."

Achimwene brought out two glasses, neither too clean, and put them on the desk. The man, Gideon, motioned with his head at the typewriter. "Writing again?" he said.

"You know," Achimwene said.

Hebrew was the language of his birth. The Joneses were once Nigerian immigrants. Some said they had come over on work visas, and stayed. Others that they had escaped some long-forgotten civil war, had crossed the border illegally from Egypt, and stayed. One way or the other, the Joneses, like the Chongs, had lived in Central Station for generations.

Gideon opened the bottle, poured them both a drink. "Water?" Achimwene said.

Gideon shook his head. Achimwene sighed again and Gideon raised the glass, the liquid clear. "*L'chaim*," he said.

They clinked glasses. Achimwene drank, the arak burning his throat, the anise flavour tickling his nose. Made him think of his sister's shebeen. Said, "So, *nu*? What's new with you, Gideon?"

He'd decided, suddenly and with aching clarity, that he won't share the new haul with Gideon. Will keep the books to himself, a private secret, for just a little while longer. Later, perhaps, he'd sell one or two. But not yet. For the moment, they were his, and his alone.

They chatted, whiling away an hour or two. Two men old before their time, in a dark alcove, sipping arak, reminiscing of books found and lost, of bargains struck and the ones that got away. At last Gideon left, having purchased a minor Western, in what is termed, in those circles, Good condition—that is, it was falling apart. Achimwene breathed out a sigh of relief, his head swimming from the arak, and returned to his typewriter. He punched an experimental *heh*, then a *nun*. He began to type.

The g.
The girl.
The girl was in trouble.
A crowd surrounded her. Excitable, their faces twisted in the light of their torches. They held stones, blades. They shouted a word, a name, like a curse. The girl looked at them, her delicate face frightened.

"Won't someone save me?" she cried. "A hero, a—"

Achimwene frowned in irritation for, from the outside, a commotion was rising, the noise disturbing his concentration. He listened, but the noise only grew louder and, with a sigh of irritation, he pulled himself up and went to the door.

Perhaps this is how lives change. A momentary decision, the toss of a coin. He could have returned to his desk, completed his sentence, or chosen to tidy up the shelves, or make a cup of coffee. He chose to open the door instead.

They are dangerous things, doors, Ogko had once said. You never knew what you'd find on the other side of one.

Achimwene opened the door and stepped outside.

The g.
The girl.

The girl was in trouble.

This much Achimwene saw, though for the moment, the *why* of it escaped him.

This is what he saw:

The crowd was composed of people Achimwene knew. Neighbours, cousins, acquaintances. He thought he saw young Yan there, and his fiancé, Youssou (Achimwene's second cousin); the greengrocer from around the corner; some adaptoplant dwellers he knew by sight if not name; and others. They were just people. They were of Central Station.

The girl wasn't.

Achimwene had never seen her before. She was slight of frame. She walked with a strange gait, as though unaccustomed to the gravity. Her face was narrow, indeed delicate. Her hair had been done in some other-worldly fashion, it was woven into dreadlocks that moved slowly, even sluggishly, above her head, and an ancient name rose in Achimwene's mind.

Medusa.

The girl's panicked eyes turned, looking. For just a moment, they found his. But her look did not (as Medusa's was said to) turn him to stone.

She turned away.

The crowd surrounded her in a semicircle. Her back was to Achimwene. The crowd—the word *mob* flashed through Achimwene's mind uneasily—was excited, restless. Some held stones in their hands, but uncertainly, as though they were not sure why, or what they were meant to do with them. A mood of ugly energy animated them. And now Achimwene could hear a shouted word, a name, rising and falling in different intonations as the girl turned and turned, helplessly seeking escape.

"Shambleau!"

The word sent a shiver down Achimwene's back (a sensation he had often read about in the pulps, yet seldom if ever experienced in real life). It arose in him vague, menacing images, desolate Martian landscapes, isolated kibbutzim on the Martian tundra, red sunsets the colour of blood.

"Strigoi!"

And there it was, that other word, a word conjuring, as though from thin air, images of brooding mountains, dark castles, bat-shaped shadows fleeting on the winds against a blood-red, setting sun . . . images of an ageless Count, of teeth elongating in a hungry skull, sinking to touch skin, to drain blood. . . .

"Shambleau!"

"Get back! Get back to where you came from!"

"Leave her alone!"

The cry pierced the night. The mob milled, confused. The voice like a blade had cut through the day and the girl, startled and surprised, turned this way and that, searching for the source of that voice.

Who said it?

Who dared the wrath of the mob?

With a sense of reality cleaving in half, Achimwene, almost with a slight *frisson*, a delicious shiver of recognition, realised that it was he, himself, who had spoken.

Had, indeed, stepped forward from his door, a little hunched figure facing this mob of relatives and acquaintances and, even, perhaps, a few friends. "Leave her alone," he said again, savouring the words, and for once, perhaps for the first time in his life, people listened to him. A silence had descended. The girl, caught between her tormentors and this mysterious new figure, seemed uncertain.

"Oh, it's Achimwene," someone said, and somebody else suddenly, crudely laughed, breaking the silence.

"She's Shambleau," someone else said, and the first speaker (he couldn't quite see who it was) said, "Well, she'd be no harm to *him*."

That crude laughter again and then, as if by some unspoken agreement, or command, the crowd began, slowly, to disperse.

Achimwene found that his heart was beating fast; that his palms sweated; that his eyes developed a sudden itch. He felt like sneezing. The girl, slowly, floated over to him. They were of the same height. She looked into his eyes. Her eyes were violet. They regarded each other as the rest of the mob dispersed. Soon they were left alone, in that quiet street, with Achimwene's back to the door of his shop.

She regarded him quizzically; her lips moved without sound, her eyes flicked up and down, scanning him. She looked confused, then shocked. She took a step back.

"No, wait!" he said.

"You are . . . you are not. . . ."

He realised she had been trying to communicate with him. His silence had baffled her. Repelled her, most likely. He was a cripple. He said, "I have no node."

"How is that . . . possible?"

He laughed, though there was no humour in it. "It is not that unusual, here, on Earth," he said.

"You know I am not—" she said, and hesitated, and he said, "From here? I guessed. You are from Mars?"

A smile twisted her lips, for just a moment. "The asteroids," she admitted.

"What is it like, in space?" Excitement animated him.

She shrugged. "Olsem difren," she said, in the pidgin of the asteroids.

The same, but different.

They stared at each other, two strangers, her vat-grown eyes against his natural-birth ones. "My name is Achimwene," he said.

"Oh."

"And you are?"

That same half-smile twisting her lips. He could tell she was bewildered by him. Repelled. Something inside him fluttered, like a caged bird, dying of a lack of oxygen.

"Carmel," she said, softly. "My name is Carmel."

He nodded. The bird was free, it was beating its wings inside him. "Would you like to come in?" he said. He gestured at his shop. The door, still standing half open.

Decisions splitting quantum universes . . . she bit her lip. There was no blood. He noticed her canines, then. Long and sharp. Unease took him again. Truth in the old stories? A Shambleau? Here?

"A cup of tea?" he said, desperately.

She nodded, distractedly. She was still trying to speak to him, he realised. She could not understand why he wasn't replying.

"I am unnoded," he said again. Shrugged. "It is—"

"Yes," she said.

"Yes?"

"Yes, I would like to come in. For . . . tea." She stepped closer to him. He could not read the look in her eyes. "Thank you," she said, in her soft voice, that strange accent. "For . . . you know."

"Yes." He grinned, suddenly, feeling bold, almost invincible. "It's nothing."

"Not . . . nothing." Her hand touched his shoulder, briefly, a light touch. Then she went past him and disappeared through the half-open door.

The shelves inside were arranged by genre.

Romance.

Mystery.

Detection.

Adventure.

And so on.

Life wasn't like that neat classification system, Achimwene had come to realise. Life was half-completed plots abandoned, heroes dying halfway along their quests, loves requited and un-, some fading inexplicably, some burning short and bright. There was a story of a man who fell in love with a vampire. . . .

Carmel was fascinated by him, but increasingly distant. She did not understand him. He had no taste to him, nothing she could sink her teeth into. She was a predator, she needed *feed*, and Achimwene could not provide it to her.

That first time, when she had come into his shop, had run her fingers along the spines of ancient books, fascinated, shy: "We had books, on the asteroid," she admitted, embarrassed, it seemed, by the confession of a shared history. "On Nungai Merurun, we had a library of physical books, they had come in one of the ships, once, a great-uncle traded something for them—" leaving Achimwene with dreams of going into space, of visiting this Ng. Merurun, discovering a priceless treasure hidden away.

Lamely, he had offered her tea. He brewed it on the small primus stove, in a dented saucepan, with fresh mint leaves in the water. Stirred sugar into the glasses. She had looked at the tea in incomprehension, concentrating. It was only later he realised she was trying to communicate with him again.

She frowned, shook her head. She was shaking a little, he realised. "Please," he said. "Drink."

"I don't," she said. "You're not." She gave up.

Achimwene often wondered what the Conversation was like. He knew that, wherever he passed, nearly anything he saw or touched was noded. Humans, yes, but also plants, robots, appliances, walls, solar panels—nearly everything was connected, in an ever-expanding, organically growing Aristocratic Small-World network, that spread out, across Central Station, across Tel Aviv and Jaffa, across the interwoven entity that was Palestine/Israel, across that region called the Middle East, across Earth, across trans-solar space and beyond, where the lone spiders sang to each other as they built more nodes and hubs, expanded farther and farther their intricate web. He knew a human was surrounded, every living moment, by the constant hum of other humans, other minds, an endless conversation going on in ways Achimwene could not conceive of. His own life was silent. He was a node of one. He moved his lips. Voice came. That was all. He said, "You are Strigoi."

"Yes." Her lips twisted in that half-smile. "I am a monster."

"Don't say that." His heart beat fast. He said, "You're beautiful."

Her smile disappeared. She came closer to him, the tea forgotten. She leaned into him. Put her lips against his skin, against his neck, he felt her breath, the lightness of her lips on his hot skin. Sudden pain bit into him. She had fastened her lips over the wound, her teeth piercing his skin. He sighed. "Nothing!" she said. She pulled away from him abruptly. "It is like . . . I don't know!" She shook. He realised she was frightened. He touched the wound on his neck. He felt nothing now. "Always, to buy love, to buy obedience, to buy worship, I must feed," she said, matter-of-factly. "I drain them of their precious data, bleed them for it, and pay them in dopamine, in ecstasy. But you have no storage, no broadcast, no firewall . . . *there is nothing there.* You are like a simulacra," she said. The word pleased her. "A *simulacra*," she repeated, softly. "You have the appearance of a man but there is nothing behind your eyes. You do not broadcast."

"That's ridiculous," Achimwene said, anger flaring, suddenly. "I speak. You can hear me. I have a mind. I can express my—"

But she was only shaking her head, and shivering. "I'm hungry," she said. "I need to feed."

———————

"Where do you come from?" he once asked her, as they lay on his narrow bed, the window open and the heat making them sweat, and she told him of Ng. Merurun, the tiny asteroid where she grew up, and how she ran away.

"And how did you come to be here?" he said, and sensed, almost before he spoke, her unease, her reluctance to answer. Jealousy flared in him then, and he could not say why.

His sister came to visit him. She walked into the bookshop as he sat behind the desk, typing. He was writing less and less, now; his new life seemed to him a kind of novel.

"Achimwene," she said.

He raised his head. "Miriam," he said, heavily.

They did not get along.

"The girl, Carmel. She is with you?"

"I let her stay," he said, carefully.

"Oh, Achimwene, you are a fool!" she said.

Her boy was with her. "Hey, Kranki," Achimwene said.

"Anggkel," the boy said—*uncle*, in the pidgin. "Yu olsem wanem?"

"I gud," Achimwene said.

How are you? I am well.

"Fren blong mi Ismail I stap aotside," Kranki said. "I stret hemi kam insaed?"

My friend Ismail is outside. Is it ok if he comes in?

"I stret," Achimwene said.

Miriam blinked. "Ismail," she said. "Where did you come from?"

Kranki had turned, appeared, to all intents and purposes,

to play with an invisible playmate. Achimwene said, carefully, "There is no one there."

"Of course there is," his sister snapped. "It's Ismail, the Jaffa boy."

Achimwene shook his head.

"Listen, Achimwene. The girl. Do you know why she came here?"

"No."

"She followed Boris."

"Boris," Achimwene said. "Your Boris?"

"My Boris," she said.

"She knew him before?"

"She knew him on Mars. In Tong Yun City."

"I . . . see."

"You see nothing, Achi. You are blind like a worm."

Old words, still with the power to hurt him. They had never been close, somehow. He said, "What do you want, Miriam?"

Her face softened. "I do not want . . . I do not want her to hurt you."

"I am a grown-up," he said. "I can take care of myself."

"Achi, like you ever could!"

Could that be affection in her voice? It sounded like frustration. Miriam said, "Is she here?"

"Kranki," Achimwene said, "Who are you playing with?"

"Ismail," Kranki said, pausing in the middle of telling a story to someone only he could see.

"He's not here," Achimwene said.

"Sure he is. He's right there."

Achimwene formed his lips into an O of understanding. "Is he virtual?" he said.

Kranki shrugged. "I guess," he said. He clearly felt uncomfortable with—or didn't understand—the question. Achimwene let it go.

His sister said, "I like the girl, Achi."

It took him by surprise. "You've met her?"

"She has a sickness. She needs help."

"I *am* helping her! I'm trying to!"

But his sister only shook her head.

"Go away, Miriam," he said, feeling suddenly tired, depressed.

His sister said, "Is she here?"

"She is resting."

Above his shop there was a tiny flat, accessible by narrow, twisting stairs. It wasn't much but it was home. "Carmel?" his sister called. "Carmel!"

There was a sound above, as of someone moving. Then a lack of sound. Achimwene watched his sister standing impassively. Realised she was talking, in the way of other people, with Carmel. Communicating in a way that was barred to him. Then normal sound again, feet on the stairs, and Carmel came into the room.

"Hi," she said, awkwardly. She came and stood closer to Achimwene, then took his hands in hers. The feel of her small, cold fingers in between his hands startled him and made pleasure spread throughout his body, like warmth in the blood. Nothing more was said. The physical action was itself an act of speaking.

Miriam nodded.

Then Kranki startled them all.

Carmel had spent the previous night feeding. There were willing victims, in Central Station. Being fed on gave pleasure. . . .

Achimwene told himself he didn't mind. When Carmel came back she moved lethargically, and he knew she was drunk on data. She had tried to describe it to him once, but he didn't really understand it, what it was like.

He had lain there on the narrow bed with her and watched the moon outside, and the floating lanterns with their rudimentary intelligence. He had his arm around the sleeping Carmel, and he had never felt happier.

Kranki turned and regarded Carmel. He whispered something to the air—to the place Ismail was standing, Achimwene guessed. He giggled at the reply and turned to Carmel.

"Are you a *vampire*?" he said.

"Kranki!"

At the horrified look on Miriam's face, Achimwene wanted to laugh. Carmel said, "No, it's all right—" in pidgin. *I stret nomo.*

But she was watching the boy intently. "Who is your friend?" she said, softly.

"It's Ismail. He lives in Jaffa on the hill."

"And what is he?" Carmel said. "What are you?"

The boy didn't seem to understand the question. "He is him. I am me. We are . . ." he hesitated.

"Nakaimas . . ." Carmel whispered. The sound of her voice made Achimwene shiver. That same cold run of ice down his spine, like in the old books, like when Ringo the

Gunslinger met a horror from beyond the grave out on the lonesome prairies.

He knew the word, though never understood the way people used it. He thought it meant to somehow, impossibly, transcend the Conversation.

"Kranki . . ." The warning tone in Miriam's voice was unmistakable. But neither Kranki nor Carmel paid her any heed. "I could show you," the boy said. His clear, blue eyes seemed curious, guileless. He stepped forward and stood directly in front of Carmel, reaching to her, trustingly. Carmel, momentarily, hesitated. Then she reached for his hot little hand.

It is, perhaps, the prerogative of every man or woman to imagine, and thus force a *shape*, a *meaning*, onto that wild and meandering narrative of their lives, by choosing genre. A princess is rescued by a prince; a vampire stalks a victim in the dark; a student becomes the master. A circle is completed. And so on.

It was the next morning that Achimwene's story changed, for him. It had been a Romance, perhaps, of sorts. But now it became a Mystery.

Perhaps they chose it, by tacit agreement, as a way to bind them, to make this curious relationship, this joining of two ill-fitted individuals somehow work. Or perhaps it was curiosity that motivated them after all, that earliest of motives, the most human and the most suspect, the one that had led Adam to the Tree, in the dawn of Story.

The next morning Carmel came down the stairs. Achimwene

had slept in the bookshop that night, curled up in a thin blanket on top of a mattress he had kept by the wall and which was normally laden with books. The books, pushed aside, formed an untidy wall around him as he slept, an alcove within an alcove.

Carmel came down. Her hair moved sluggishly around her skull. She wore a thin cotton shift; he could see how thin she was.

Achimwene said, "Tell me what happened yesterday."

Carmel shrugged. "Is there any coffee?"

"You know where it is."

He sat up, feeling self-conscious and angry. Pulling the blanket over his legs. Carmel went to the primus stove, filled the pot with water from the tap, added spoons of black coffee carelessly. Set it to cook.

"The boy is . . . a sort of *Strigoi*," she said. "Maybe. Yes. No. I don't know."

"What did he do?"

"He gave me something. He took something away. A memory. Mine or someone else's. It's no longer there."

"What did he give you?"

"Knowledge. That he exists."

"Nakaimas."

"Yes." She laughed, a sound as bitter as the coffee. "Black magic. Like me. Not like me."

"You were a weapon," he said. She turned, sharply. There were two coffee cups on the table. Glass on varnished wood. "What?"

"I read about it."

"Always your *books*."

He couldn't tell by her tone how she meant it. He said, "There are silences in your Conversation. Holes." Could not quite picture it, to him there was only a silence. Said, "The books have answers."

She poured coffee, stirred sugar into the glasses. Came over and sat beside him, her side pressing into his. Passed him a cup. "Tell me," she said.

He took a sip. The coffee burned his tongue. Sweet. He began to talk quickly. "I read up on the condition. Strigoi. Shambleau. There are references from the era of the Shangri-La virus, contemporary accounts. The Kunming Labs were working on genetic weapons, but the war ended before the strain could be deployed—they sold it off-world, it went loose, it spread. It never worked right. There are hints—I need access to a bigger library. There are only rumours. Cryptic footnotes."

"Saying what?"

"Suggesting a deeper purpose. Or that Strigoi was but a side effect of something else. A secret purpose. . . ."

Perhaps they wanted to believe. Everyone needs a mystery.

She stirred beside him. Turned to face him. Smiled. It was perhaps the first time she ever truly smiled at him. Her teeth were long, and sharp.

"We could find out," she said.

"Together," he said. He drank his coffee, to hide his excitement. But he knew she could tell.

"We could be detectives."

"Like Judge Dee," he said.

"Who?"

"Some detective."

"Book detective," she said, dismissively.

"Like Bill Glimmung, then," he said. Her face lit up. For a moment she looked very young. "I love those stories," she said.

Even Achimwene had seen Glimmung features. They had been made in 2D, 3D, full-immersion, as scent narratives, as touch-tapestry—Martian Hardboiled, they called the genre, the Phobos Studios cranked out hundreds of them over decades if not centuries, Elvis Mandela had made the character his own.

"Like Bill Glimmung, then," she said solemnly, and he laughed.

"Like Glimmung," he said.

And so the lovers, by complicit agreement, became detectives.

"There was something else," Carmel said.

Achimwene said, "What?"

They were walking together in the sideways of Central Station. Carmel said, "When I came in. Came down." She shook her head in frustration and a solitary dreadlock snaked around her mouth, making her blow on it to move it away. "When I came to Earth."

Those few words evoked in Achimwene a nameless longing. So much to infer, so much suggested, to a man who had never left his hometown. Carmel said, "I bought a new identity in Tong Yun, before I came. The best you could. From a Conch—"

Looking at him to see if he understood. Achimwene did. A Conch was a human who had been ensconced, welded into a permanent pod-cum-exoskeleton. He was only part human, had become part digital by extension. It was not unsimilar, in some ways, to the eunuchs of old Earth. Achimwene said, "I see?"

Carmel said, "It worked. When I passed through Central Station security I was allowed through, with no problems. The . . . the digitals did not pick up on my . . . nature. The fake ident was accepted."

"So?"

Carmel sighed, and a loose dreadlock tickled Achimwene's neck, sending a warmth rushing through him. "So is that *likely*?" she said. She stopped walking then, when Achimwene stopped also, she started pacing. A floating lantern bobbed beside them for a few moments then, as though sensing their intensity, drifted away, leaving them in shadow. "There are no Strigoi on Earth," Carmel said.

"How do we know for sure?" Achimwene said.

"It's one of those things. Everyone knows it."

Achimwene shrugged. "But *you're* here," he pointed out.

Carmel waved her finger; stuck it in his face. "And how likely is that?" she yelled, startling him. "I believed it worked, because I *wanted* to believe it. But surely they know! I am not human, Achi! My body is riddled with nodal filaments, exabytes of data, hostile protocols! You want to tell me they *didn't know*?"

Achimwene shook his head. Reached for her, but she pulled away from him. "What are you saying?" he said.

"They let me through." Her voice was matter of fact.

"Why?" Achimwene said. "Why would they do that?"

"I don't know."

Achimwene chewed his lip. Intuition made a leap in his mind, neurons singing to neurons. "You think it is because of those children," he said.

Carmel stopped pacing. He saw how pale her face was, how delicate. "Yes," she said.

"Why?"

"I don't know."

"Then you must ask a digital," he said. "You must ask an Other."

She glared at him. "Why would they talk to me?" she said.

Achimwene didn't have an answer. "We can proceed the way we agreed," he said, a little lamely. "We'll get the answers. Sooner or later, we'll figure it out, Carmel."

"How?" she said.

He pulled her to him. She did not resist. The words from an old book rose into Achimwene's mind, and with them the entire scene. "We'll get to the bottom of this," he said.

And so on a sweltering hot day, Achimwene and the Strigoi Carmel left Central Station, on foot, and shortly thereafter crossed the invisible barrier that separated the old neighbourhood from the city of Tel Aviv proper. Achimwene walked slowly; an electronic cigarette dangled from his lips, another vintage affectation, and the fedora hat he wore shaded him from the sun even as his sweat drenched into the brim of the hat. Beside him Carmel was cool in a light blue dress. They came to Allenby Street and followed it towards the Carmel Market—"It's like my name," Carmel said, wonderingly.

"It is an old name," Achimwene said. But his attention was elsewhere.

"Where are we going?" Carmel said. Achimwene smiled, white teeth around the metal casing of the cigarette. "Every detective," he said, "needs an informant."

Allenby was a long, dirty street, with dark shops selling knockoff products with the air of disuse upon them. Carmel dawdled outside a magic shop. Achimwene bargained with a fruit juice seller and returned with two cups of fresh orange juice, handing one to Carmel. They passed a bakery where cream-filled pastries vied for their attention. They passed a Church of Robot node where a rusting preacher tried to get their notice with a sad distracted air. They passed shawarma stalls thick with the smell of spice and lamb fat. They passed a road-sweeping machine that warbled at them pleasantly, and a recruitment centre for the Martian Kibbutzim Movement. They passed a gaggle of black-clad Orthodox Jews; like Achimwene, they were unnoded.

Carmel looked this way and that, smelling, looking, *feeding*, Achimwene knew, on pure unadulterated *feed*. Something he could not experience, could not know, but knew, nevertheless, that it was there, invisible yet ever present. Like God. The lines from a poem by Mahmoud Darwish floated in his head. Something about a country where one saw only the invisible. "Look," Carmel said, smiling. "A bookshop."

Indeed it was. They were coming closer to the market now and the throng of people intensified, and solar buses crawled like insects, with their wings spread high, along Allenby street, carrying passengers, and the smell of fresh vegetables, of peppers and tomatoes, and the sweet strong smell of oranges, too, filled the air. The bookshop was, in fact, a yard, open to the skies, the books under awnings, and piled up, here and there, in untidy mountains—it was the sort of shop that would have no prices, and where you'd always have to ask for the price, which depended on the owner, and his mood, and on the weather and the alignment of the stars, and whether you were liked or not.

The owner in question was indeed standing in the shade of the long, metal bookcases lining one wall. He was smoking a cigar and its overpowering aroma filled the air and made Carmel sneeze. The man looked up and saw them. "Achimwene," he said, without surprise. Then he squinted and said, in a lower voice, "I heard you got a nice batch recently."

"Word travels," Achimwene said, complacently. Carmel, meanwhile, was browsing aimlessly, picking up fragile-looking paper books and magazines, replacing them, picking up others. Achimwene saw, at a glance, early editions of Yehuda Amichai, a first edition Yoav Avni, several worn Ringo paperbacks he already had, and a Lior Tirosh *samizdat* collection. He said, "Shimshon, what do you know about vampires?"

"Vampires?" Shimshon said. He took a thoughtful pull on his cigar. "In the literary tradition? There is *Neshikat Ha'mavet Shel Dracula*, by Dan Shocker, in the Horror Series from nineteen seventy-two—" *Dracula's Death Kiss*—"or Gal Amir's *Laila Adom*—" *Red Night*—"possibly the first Hebrew vampire novel, or Vered Tochterman's *Dam Kachol*—" *Blue*

Blood—"from around the same period. Didn't think it was particularly your area, Achimwene." Shimshon grinned. "But I'd be happy to sell you a copy. I think I have a signed Tochterman somewhere. Expensive, though. Unless you want to trade . . ."

"No," Achimwene said, although regretfully. "I'm not looking for a pulp, right now. I'm looking for nonfiction."

Shimshon's eyebrows rose and he regarded Achimwene without the grin. "Mil Hist?" he said, uneasily. "Robotniks? The Nosferatu Code?"

Achimwene regarded him, uncertain. "The what?" he said.

But Shimshon was shaking his head. "I don't deal in that sort of thing," he said. "*Verboten*. Hagiratech. Go away, Achimwene. Go back to Central Station. Shop's closed." He turned and dropped the cigar and stepped on it with his foot. "You, love!" he said. "Shop's closing. Are you going to buy that book? No? Then put it down."

Carmel turned, wounded dignity flashing in her violet eyes. "Then take it!" she said, shoving a (priceless, Achimwene thought) copy of Lior Tirosh's first—and only—poetry collection, *Remnants of God*, into Shimshon's hands. She hissed, a sound Achimwene suspected was not only in the audible range but went deeper, in the non-sound of digital communication, for Shimshon's face went pale and he said, "Get . . . out!" in a strangled whisper as Carmel smiled at him, flashing her small, sharp teeth.

They left. They crossed the street and stood outside a cheap cosmetic surgery booth, offering wrinkles erased or tentacles grafted, next to a handwritten sign that said, *Gone for Lunch*. "Verboten?" Achimwene said. "Hagiratech?"

"Forbidden," Carmel said. "The sort of wildtech that ends up on Jettisoned, from the Exodus ships."

"What you are," he said.

"Yes. I looked, myself, you know. But it is like you said. Holes in the Conversation. Did we learn nothing useful?"

"No," he said. Then, "Yes."

She smiled. "Which is it?"

Military History, Shimshon had said. And no one knew better than him how to classify a thing into its genre. And— *robotniks*.

"We need to find us," Achimwene said, "an ex-soldier." He smiled without humour. "Better brush up on your Battle Yiddish," he said.

"Ezekiel."

"Achimwene."

"I brought . . . vodka. And spare parts." He had bought them in Tel Aviv, on Allenby, at great expense. Robotnik parts were not easy to come by.

Ezekiel looked at him without expression. His face was metal smooth. It never smiled. His body was mostly metal. It was rusted. It creaked when he walked. He ignored the proffered offerings. Turned his head. "You brought *her*?" he said. *"Here?"*

Carmel stared at the robotnik in curiosity. They were at the heart of the old station, a burned down ancient bus platform open to the sky. Achimwene knew platforms continued down below, that the robotniks—ex-soldiers, cyborged humans, present day beggars and dealers in Crucifixation and stolen goods—made their base down there. But there he could not go. Ezekiel met him above-ground. "I saw your kind," Carmel said. "On Mars. In Tong Yun City. Begging."

"And I saw *your* kind," the robotnik said. "In the sands of the Sinai, in the war. Begging. Begging for their lives, as we decapitated them and stuck a stake through their hearts and watched them die."

"Jesus Elron, Ezekiel!"

The robotnik ignored his exclamation. "I had heard," he said, "that one came. Here. *Strigoi*. But I did not believe! The defence systems would have picked her up. Should have eliminated her."

"They didn't," Achimwene said.

"Yes . . ."

"Do you know why?"

The robotnik stared at him. Then he gave a short laugh and accepted the bottle of vodka. "You guess *they* let her through? Others?"

Achimwene shrugged. "It's the only answer that makes sense."

"And you want to know why."

"Call me curious."

"I call you a fool," the robotnik said, without malice. "And you not even noded. She still has an effect on you?"

"*She* has a name," Carmel said, acidly.

Ezekiel ignored her. "You're a collector of old stories, aren't you, Achimwene," he said. "Now you came to collect mine?"

Achimwene just shrugged. The robotnik took a deep slug of vodka and said, "So, nu? What do you want to know?"

"Tell me about Nosferatu," Achimwene said.

"We never found out for sure where Nosferatu came from," Ezekiel said. It was quiet in the abandoned shell of the old station. Overhead a suborbital came in to land, and from the adaptoplant neighbourhoods high above, the sound of laughter could be heard, and someone playing the guitar. "It had been introduced into the battlefield during the Third Sinai Campaign, by one side, or the other, or both." He fell quiet. "I am not even sure who we were fighting for," he said. He took another drink of vodka. The almost pure alcohol was merely fuel for the robotnik. Ezekiel said, "At first we paid it little enough attention. We'd find victims on dawn patrols. Men, women, robotniks. Wandering the dunes or the Red Sea shore, dazed, their minds leeched clean. The small wounds on their necks. Still. They were alive. Not ripped to shreds by Jubjubs. But the data. We began to notice the enemy knew where to find us. Knew where we went. We began to be afraid of the dark. To never go out alone. Patrol in teams. But worse. For the ones who were bitten, and carried back by us, had turned, became the enemy's own weapon. Nosferatu."

Achimwene felt sweat on his forehead, took a step away from the fire. Away from them, the floating lanterns bobbed in the air. Someone cried in the distance and the cry was suddenly and inexplicably cut off, and Achimwene wondered if the street-sweeping machines would find another corpse the next morning, lying in the gutter outside.

"They rose within our ranks. They fed in secret. Robotniks don't sleep, Achimwene. Not the way the humans we used to be did. But we do turn off. Shut-eye. And they preyed on us, bleeding out minds, feeding on our feed. Do you know what it is like?" The robotnik's voice didn't grow louder, but it carried. "We were human, once. The army took us off the battlefield, broken, dying. It grafted us into new bodies, made us into shiny, near-invulnerable killing machines. We had no legal rights, not anymore. We were technically, and clinically, dead. We had few memories, if any, of what we once were. But those we had, we kept hold of, jealously. Hints to our old identity. The memory of feet in the rain. The smell of pine resin. A hug from a newborn baby whose name we no longer knew.

"And the Strigoi were taking even those away from us."

Achimwene looked at Carmel, but she was looking nowhere, her eyes were closed, her lips pressed together. "We finally grew wise to it," Ezekiel said. "We began to hunt them down. If we found a victim we did not take them back. Not alive. We staked them, we cut off their heads, we burned the bodies. Have you ever opened a Strigoi's belly, Achimwene?" He motioned at Carmel. "Want to know what her insides look like?"

"No," Achimwene said, but Ezekiel the robotnik ignored him. "Like cancer," he said. "Strigoi is like robotnik, it is a human body subverted, cyborged. She isn't human, Achimwene, however much you'd like to believe it. I remember the first one we cut open. The filaments inside. Moving. Still trying to spread. Nosferatu Protocol, we called it. What we had to do. Following the Nosferatu Protocol. Who created the virus? I don't know. Us. Them. The Kunming Labs. Someone. St. Cohen only knows. All I know is how to kill them."

Achimwene looked at Carmel. Her eyes were open now. She was staring at the robotnik. "I didn't ask for this," she said. "I am not a *weapon*. There is no fucking *war*!"

"There was—"

"There were a lot of things!"

A silence. At last, Ezekiel stirred. "So what do you want?" he said. He sounded tired. The bottle of vodka was nearly finished. Achimwene said, "What more can you tell us?"

"Nothing, Achi. I can tell you nothing. Only to be careful." The robotnik laughed. "But it's too late for that, isn't it," he said.

Achimwene was arranging his books when Boris came to see him. He heard the soft footsteps and the hesitant cough and straightened up, dusting his hands from the fragile books, and looked at the man Carmel had come to Earth for, or after.

"Achi."

"Boris."

He remembered him as a loose-limbed, gangly teenager. Seeing him like this was a shock. There was a thing growing on Boris's neck. It seemed to breathe gently, independently of its host. Boris's face was lined, he was still thin but there was an unhealthy nature to his thinness. "I heard you were back," Achimwene said.

"My father," Boris said, as though that explained everything.

"And we always thought you were the one who got away," Achimwene said. Genuine curiosity made him add, "What was it like? In the Up and Out?"

"Strange," Boris said. "The same." He shrugged. "I don't know."

"So you are seeing my sister again."

"Yes."

"You've hurt her once before, Boris. Are you going to do it again?"

Boris opened his mouth, closed it again. He stood there, taking Achimwene back years. "I heard Carmel is staying with you," Boris said at last.

"Yes."

Again, an uncomfortable silence. Boris scanned the bookshelves, picked a book at random. "What's this?" he said.

"Be careful with that!"

Boris looked startled. He stared at the small hardcover in his hands. "That's a Captain Yuno," Achimwene said, proudly. "*Captain Yuno on a Dangerous Mission*, the second of the three Sagi novels. The least rare of the three, admittedly, but still . . . priceless."

Boris looked momentarily amused. "He was a kid *taikonaut*?" he said.

"Sagi envisioned a solar system teeming with intelligent alien life," Achimwene said, primly. "He imagined a world government, and the people of Earth working together in peace."

"No kidding. He must have been disappointed when—"

"This book is *pre-spaceflight*," Achimwene said.

Boris whistled. "So it's old?"

"Yes."

"And valuable?"

"Very."

"How do you know all this stuff?"

"I read."

Boris put the book back on the shelf, carefully. "Listen, Achi—" he said.

"No," Achimwene said. "You listen. Whatever happened between you and Carmel is between you two. I won't say I don't care, because I'd be lying, but it is not my business. Do you have a claim on her?"

"What?" Boris said. "No. Achi, I'm just trying to—"

"To what?"

"To warn you. I know you're not used to—" Again he hesitated.

Achimwene remembered Boris as someone with few words, even as a boy. Words did not come easy to him. "Not used to women?" Achimwene said, his anger tightly coiled.

Boris had to smile. "You have to admit—"

"I am not some, some—"

"She is not a woman, Achi. She's a Strigoi."

Achimwene closed his eyes. Expelled breath. Opened his eyes again and regarded Boris levelly. "Is that all?" he said.

Boris held his eyes. After a moment, he seemed to deflate. "Very well," he said.

"Yes."

"I guess I'll see you."

"I guess."

"Please pass my regards to Carmel."

Achimwene nodded. Boris, at last, shrugged. Then he turned and left the store.

There comes a time in a man's life when he realises stories are lies. Things do not end neatly. The enforced narratives a human impinges on the chaotic mess that is life become empty labels, like the dried husks of corn such as are thrown down in the summer months from the adaptoplant dwellings, to litter the streets below.

He woke up in the night and the air was humid, and there was no wind. The window was open. Carmel was lying on her side, asleep, her small, naked body tangled up in the sheets. He watched her chest rise and fall, her breath even. A smear of what might have been blood on her lips. "Carmel?" he said, but quietly, and she didn't hear. He rubbed her back. Her skin was smooth and warm. She moved sleepily under his hand, murmured something he didn't catch, and settled down again.

Achimwene stared out of the window, at the moon rising high above Central Station. A mystery was no longer a mystery once it was solved. What difference did it make how Carmel had come to be there, with him, at that moment? It was not facts that mattered, but feelings. He stared at the moon, thinking of that first human to land there, all those years before, that first human footprint in that alien dust.

Inside, Carmel was asleep and he was awake, outside dogs howled up at the moon and, from somewhere, the image came to Achimwene of a man in a spacesuit turning at the sound, a man who does a little tap dance on the moon, on the dusty moon.

He lay back down and held on to Carmel and she turned, trustingly, and settled into his arms.

NINE:
THE GOD ARTIST

Boris met Motl under the eaves of the space port, where it opened up onto the Salame Road.

"Motl," he said, shaking hands awkwardly. The robotnik's metal was warm, with scars of rust in the palm of the hand.

"Boris. It's been a long time."

"I heard about you and Isobel. Congratulations."

"Thanks—" It was not possible for the robotnik to smile. But Boris thought the voice sounded genuinely happy. "I still can't believe it," Motl said. "I mean, that she would—" He sounded strangely shy. Boris uneasily wondered how old he was. Some robotniks measured their existence in centuries—scrounging spare parts and repairing the organic base with cheap Chinese-made nano-spray patches, quick-

and-dirty repairs. Hardened ex-soldiers, they were good at not dying.

He said, "So, are you two. . . ?"

Motl shrugged. Boris wondered who he had been before he died. What his real name had been. If he had had children. He remembered Motl from when he was a kid. The same robotniks had been around Central Station for decades. Later, when he went to the stars, to the Up and Out, he saw their brethren on Mars, in Tong Yun and New Israel. They always made him vaguely, and irritatingly, uncomfortable.

Motl said, "Not yet. I mean, I haven't asked and, well, Yan and Youssou's wedding is coming up . . . we're taking it slow, I guess."

The wedding. Boris was rather dreading the thought of another big family affair. Since he came back everything seemed to revolve around family. Things had been easy on Mars, or Lunar Port. He had hid himself away for so long . . . he still wasn't used to being back on Earth. Back at Central Station.

"Anyway," Motl said. Clearly uncomfortable himself. The Martian aug pulsed gently against Boris's neck. Flooding sensations into Boris's mind: picking up and enhancing the scent signals from Motl, for instance, so that each pronunciation was made alive with contradictory meanings, collated and re-interpreted. He could sense Motl's discomfort, mirrored in his own. Could sense, too, the robotnik's desire to end this unexpected meeting. "Anyway," Motl said again. "What was it that you wanted?"

Still Boris hesitated. It was silly. He didn't need to. Taking a breath, inhaling the smell of eucalyptus leaves and hot asphalt and adaptoplant resin, he said, "I need drugs."

A wary feeling rising from the robotnik. A half-step back. "I don't do that anymore."

"I know, Motl. You wouldn't do that to Isobel."

"No, I wouldn't."

"I know. But I also know you can get it."

"What are you looking for?"

"Crucifixation."

"God," the robotnik said, and sighed. "You need to talk to Ezekiel, not me. What do you need it for, anyway?" The robotnik was staring at Boris's aug. "You don't use."

"It's for a patient."

"You're the birthing doctor, aren't you? I remember now. Strange kids came out of those vats."

"How so?"

The robotnik laughed. It wasn't a pleasant sound and was made almost terrifying by the Martian aug's distortion. "*You* know," he said. "You can fool the rest of them, but you can't fool me. I've been here too long."

Boris bit back on a reply. "Can you get it?" he said.

"I'll see what I can do."

"Thanks."

"Yeah. Well, I'll see you." And, with that, the robotnik disappeared into the night.

"We can't keep meeting like this."

Boris was frustrated with this role he'd been forced into. Like something out of a cheap Elvis Mandela flick. But he owed her. He stared at her, mixed affection and anger, a hint of unease. Carmel. Data-vampire, ex-lover, the woman who fell to Earth; who had left the Up and Out to come and find him.

Why?

She complicated everything. What possessed her to make the journey, to track him here, to come down the gravity well to Central Station? She seemed to him at times as helpless as a child. And yet it was only the aug, with its alien physiology, that protected him from her.

They had been lovers, yes, but it was over, for both of them, and long before. Yet here she was, and he was bound to her all the same.

"We can't keep meeting like this," he said again, uneasy.

Carmel smiled, showing sharp canines. "Meet how?" she said.

"In secret. If Miriam found out. . . ."

"It was your idea," she said.

"What about Achimwene?" Boris said. Feeling worse. For he liked the man, Miriam's awkward brother. But for the life of him he couldn't understand what Carmel saw in him.

"He doesn't need to know," she said. Sharpness in her voice. She was protective of him, Boris realised. Could she really love him? Achimwene, a node-less man? A cripple?

That feeling in him was strange. Jealousy, he thought. He was jealous. It was irrational. He felt the aug pulsating against his neck, calming him. He shrugged. "It is best if we are not seen. And you are barely tolerated here, Carmel. This is a small, close community. They know what you are."

"And still they let me stay," she said, wonder in her eyes.

For all her danger, she sometimes was the young girl who'd left her family's habitat in the asteroid belt to find excitement elsewhere.

"On sufferance," he said. "And as long as the victims are willing, and you take in moderation."

She shrugged. "Did you have any luck?"

"Yes. No."

She shook her head and said, "Oh, Boris."

Which wounded. He said, "I need to take another blood sample."

"We've been through this. On Mars. Before. How much blood can you take?"

"How much can *you*?"

Her face showed her disappointment. "I don't take blood."

"Only minds."

"Yes."

He waited. She rolled up her sleeve. It was hot in the small room. His father's apartment. He inserted the needle into her arm while his father sat motionless in the other room. His father had withdrawn from life, somehow. Had closed himself off to the world. Waiting. Maybe. Or just not there anymore.

"I'll let you know if I have news," he said. She rubbed her arm where he hurt her, and said nothing.

With each season a new godling appeared in the streets and alleyways of Central Station. They were nebulous things, more than human, less than Other, like semi-sentient sculptures which straddled both the real and the virtual. They were said to be slivers of God, fragments of God's creation. With each new season they appeared, like plants.

There were gods for spring: like young shoots they appeared, organic and unfathomable, reaching out to sun and sky and sea. One spring it was a miniature god, blooming in the green, bound on two sides by Levinsky and Har Zion. The god had appeared, one morning, a tree trunk rising out of moist earth and jutting into the sky, and to go near it one's node was assaulted by the high-bandwidth speech of the Others.

There were gods for winter: mecha-beings sculpted out of scrap metal and obsolete tech found in the garbage or liberated from the Palace of Discarded Things. Such gods moved, if slowly. They crawled on the side of buildings. One year such a god left illegible inscriptions all over the walls and rooftops of Central Station, messages no one could read, spray-painted everywhere in some unknown, alien alphabet.

There were autumn gods: fungal-like they drifted in the air, temporary gods bursting unexpectedly, with a soft whooshing sound, above the heads of the people passing by, sending spores of faith drifting lazily in every direction.

There were summer gods. Those were translucent; only a fragment in the real, their majesty was revealed in the virtuality, enormous shifting amorphous vistas, superimposed over the real, fed into one's node in a flood that choked bandwidth and startled and awed.

The god artist called himself Eliezer, which meant "Helper of God," in Hebrew.

Though he had been known by other names, in other times.

The god artist walked the streets of Central Station and they sang to him. Each noded plant sent out its individual ident, a hopeful ping, each brick and wall and manhole cover sang and whispered to Eliezer.

He was a man of indeterminate age. When he spoke one could still discern, sometimes, the faint echoes of an old, obsolete American accent. A Jew, some said. A man as old as the hills themselves. He smiled as he walked, and his eyes were vacant, for they saw less and less into the real; the virtual crept upon them with the passing of ages. Eliezer whistled as he walked, and that whistle sounded in both the physical and the virtual, notes in one, their pure mathematical representation in the other.

He passed the gods as he walked, and the gods bowed to him, for he was their creator.

He came to Mama Jones' Shebeen and passed through the bead curtain and sat down at an empty table. It was cool and dark inside.

"Eliezer!" Miriam said. Surprised.

Eliezer's head bobbed, this way and that. "Have I not been this way for some time, then?" he hazarded a guess.

"Not for four or five years."

"Ah." He smiled and nodded, listening to sounds only he could hear. "I have been otherwise engaged, I think. Yes. I must have been."

"Well," Miriam said, a little doubtful, it seemed. "It's good to see you again."

"And you . . ."

"What can I get you, Eliezer?"

"I think, perhaps, some arak," he said, tilting his head like a bird regarding its reflection in the water. "Yes, some arak, Miriam. I am waiting for a friend."

She nodded, though he didn't seem to notice. She went behind the bar and came back with a bottle and a glass and placed them before him, along with a bowl of fresh ice. "Thank you," he said. "Tell me, Miriam. I hear your young fellow is back in town."

She looked at him in surprise. "Boris?" she said.

The god artist smiled and nodded his head. "Boris," he confirmed.

"Yes. How did you—?"

The god artist put his hand into the bowl of ice and picked up a fistful of cubes and poured them, gently, into his glass. They made a sound that made him smile. "Heard a vampire girl came after him, too, not too long ago," he said.

"Yes," Miriam said. Then, "Her name is Carmel."

"Ah." He poured. The arak hit the ice clear. With its slow melting its colour shifted, became murky, became the colour of milk. Eliezer raised it to his face and smelled the anise. "How is that working out for everyone?"

Miriam shrugged. He made her uncomfortable, and they both knew it. "It's life," she said. The god artist nodded, but she could not quite tell if he were listening to her, or to some music only he could hear.

"That's right," he said. "That's right."

She left him there. The shebeen was not busy, but there was always something to do.

"I need a dose, Ezekiel."

They were standing in the burned place. Ezekiel said, "You're off the faith, Motl."

"It's not for me."

"You're dealing? Again?"

"No. It's . . . a favour."

"Who for?"

"Boris Chong."

A silence. The two robotniks stared at each other; remnants of their humanity twisted and turned behind their metal facades. The lights of Central Station floated overhead.

"Zhong Weiwei's grandson." It was a statement, not a question, but Motl answered it nevertheless.

"Yes."

"The . . . birthing doctor."

Again, it wasn't a question. This time Motl said nothing.

"Does he know?"

"About the children? I think he must suspect."

Ezekiel laughed. Not a sound with much humour in it, Motl thought. "No wonder he left when he did."

"Still," Motl said. "He came back."

"And now he wants faith? Crucifixion? Why?"

"I don't know. Not my business."

"It is mine, since you make it mine."

"Ezekiel . . ."

Again they stared at each other, wordlessly: two beat-down old soldiers.

"Go see the priest," Ezekiel said. "He'll give you a dose. And on your head be it."

Motl nodded, once, wordlessly, before he turned away.

———

A second old man pushed through the bead curtain of the shebeen and came inside. Ibrahim, the Lord of Discarded Things.

He sat down at Eliezer's table. Miriam greeted him, brought another glass without being asked.

"How's the junk business?" Eliezer said.

Ibrahim smiled and shrugged. "Same old," he said. "How's the god business?"

"Could be worse."

Ibrahim put ice in his glass, poured. They both raised their glasses, clinked them, gently, together, and drank.

"I need parts," Eliezer said.

"You're always welcome," Ibrahim said.

"This your boy?"

A young boy had entered the shebeen, accompanied by another. "This is Ismail," Ibrahim said, with quiet pride.

"And his friend?"

"Miriam's boy, Kranki."

"They are like brothers."

"Yes."

The two boys came and stood close to Ibrahim, staring at Eliezer with frank curiosity.

"Who's that?" Kranki said.

From behind the counter, Miriam: "Kranki, manners!"

Eliezer smiled. "I'm Eliezer," he said. "And you two are . . ." His eyes seemed to shift their colour. He was seeing the boys in the real and the virtual at once. "Interesting," he said.

"Ismail, go play," Ibrahim said. The boy shrugged and turned to leave, Kranki following him.

"Please," Ibrahim said, in a low voice.

"Do they know?" Eliezer said.

"That they are different? Yes."

"Do they know what they *are*?"

"I found the boy dumped in the street. A baby. I raised him like my own. Eliezer, please. I just want him to have a childhood."

"Did you speak to the Oracle?"

Ibrahim made a gesture of dismissal. Eliezer said, "I wish to build a new god."

"So what's stopping you?"

Eliezer took a sip of arak. The melting ice stained the glass a milky white. "I am intrigued by the lives of mortals."

"Gods are as mortal as humanity."

"True. True."

And now it was Ibrahim's turn to smile. "You want to meddle," he said.

The other shrugged.

"You were always a meddler," Ibrahim said.

"So were you."

"I live in the world. Not apart from it."

"Semantics, Ibrahim. L'chaim." He raised his glass.

"No, Eliezer. Let things be."

"That's never been your philosophy before, Ibrahim."

"Nevertheless."

"I don't pursue change. Change comes to me."

Ibrahim sighed. "Then let it come," he said, as he, too, raised his glass. They drank.

The glasses, placed back on the table, left a dark mark on the wood.

"What is that, Motl?"

Motl and Isobel lay entwined on her bed. She ran her hand down his side, feeling the smooth, warm metal.

"What?" he said. Content. Sleepy. The human side of him was coming to the fore, since he had met her. Even memories, sometimes, from when he was a man, and alive. Unwelcome memories, of the sort that, before, drove him to faith.

"This." She sat up. "Is it drugs?"

"Isobel—"

Finding the priest was not always easy, but he'd tracked him down eventually.

"It's not for me," he said, quickly.

"You promised you won't be doing this anymore."

"I don't!" he said.

"So what's this?" She waved it in front of him.

"I had to," he said. "I owe—"

"Oh, Motl."

"Isobel, wait."

"Get out," she said. Then, when he didn't move. "I said, get out!"

"They're not for me!"

"I don't care."

She pushed him. Her small hands against his metal skin. He'd killed more people than there were cats in Central Station. He took the bag of dope and left, heard her crying behind him.

"What are you doing?" Miriam said.

"What?" Boris said. Miriam stood in front of him, hands on her hips.

"You're buying faith?"

"I . . . what?"

"Motl was here. He left you something. And Isobel was here earlier, crying." Miriam shook her head. "The day I've had!" she said. "That god artist was here this morning. Eliezer. Asking about you, and Carmel. Care to tell me what you're not telling me, Boris?"

"Miriam, I . . ."

"I know she came here because of you. I like her, Boris. You know that. She's strong. She has to be strong, to survive that sickness she has. But why didn't you *tell* me?"

He looked at her. Shook his head. The Martian aug pulsed gently on his neck. "I don't know," he said.

"I have to be able to trust you," she said. He couldn't bear the look in her eyes. The disappointment. Even when he left for space, all those years before, she had not looked at him like this.

"I am just trying to help," he said. Feebly.

"Here." She passed him the bag. The white powder inside it. "Next time, just tell me."

"I love you," he said.

He'd not said it before.

Now the words were out.

Her lips twitched. Was it the beginning of a smile?

"Boris Aharon Chong," she said. "I don't know why I put up with you, sometimes."

———————

The god artist came to visit Ibrahim on the hill in Jaffa. It was evening and the sky was painted a lurid red, the dying sun's light smeared across the sky above the sea. He came into the Palace of Discarded Things and looked around him with an approving set to his lips. The vast junkyard was illuminated by bare electric bulbs.

"Take what you need," Ibrahim said, and Eliezer nodded when he said, "I always do."

He couldn't follow her into this virtuality. She was glad of the knowledge, now. Isobel strapped herself into the pod, pulled the cover over herself. Level Three, Central Station. Work. Machines hissed as cables attached themselves to her ports and locked with a soft kiss.

And then she was elsewhere.

She was Isobel Chow, captain of the *Nine-Tailed Cat*, a starship slick and black. Her crew were on board: waiting for her to command them. "Set course to . . ." she hesitated, but only momentarily. "Set course to Orlov Port, Delta Quadrant," she said. Her senses were alive, they reached everywhere within the ship. The ship was hers. The Guilds of Ashkelon universe spread out from her, a universe as vast and unexplored as the real.

Screw Motl, she thought, with sudden savagery. She grinned, and the light of the triple suns of the solar system outside the ship reflected off her dark shades. Then the view blurred as the ship went into gamesworld hyperspace.

With each new season a further god was added to the streets and alleyways of Central Station.

There were wind gods: with delicate fronds they floated in the sky above the rooftops, sending out a shimmering haze; some absorbed sunlight, some absorbed rain. Some exploded unexpectedly, to the delight of children down below, showering the world with fragments of light, or sweet, white spun sugar, or dreams that burrowed into one's node and woke them, days or months later, hugging themselves from a happy memory they could no longer quite recall.

There were fire gods: they danced on metal, shimmering on old copper wiring, they burst out of the open drums where the robotniks made their fires, or sang out from glinting surfaces, catching one's reflection by surprise. There were earth gods: silent, patient, some buried entirely, so that no one even knew they were there, some rising out of the ground, mounds and miniature hills one could lie against, could press a cheek to earth and pray, soundlessly. And there were water gods, who gurgled in the taps, who slithered like eels, who fell from the sky like rain but were not rain, were the fragments of a digital's dream.

The god artist began to work at noon, on a day as cloudless and as clear as childhood. He stood calmly on the Neve Sha'anan pedestrian street, standing opposite the enormous main doors of Central Station.

His hands moved before him in a complicated pattern, like a weather hacker manipulating the seen and the unseen. His lips moved as he worked, issuing silent commands. R. Brother Patch-It, the robo-priest, came out just then and stood in silence by a fruit and vegetable stand, and watched.

"I didn't know Eliezer was back in town," he said to Mr. Chow, Isobel's father, who shrugged.

"He never left," Mr. Chow said, and bit into an apple.

The god artist moved his hands in the physicality, and those who were noded watched as he reached deep into the digitality, into the world of *mara*, that which is both real and unreal.

The god artist gestured and worlds came into being. Code mated with code; mutated; separated; joined and rejoined and split and evolved, rapid evolutionary cycles running in the virtuality, on the vast hidden engines at the Cores. Intelligences were born, like flowers. Then, when these makeshift Breeding Grounds began to run autonomously, the god artist began to build the physical body of the god.

More people came, and watched. It had been years since Eliezer was seen in public, though his gods have appeared, like hidden presents, throughout the streets of Central Station.

Ibrahim and his boy came by on their cart, the patient horse drawing it slowly. They stopped and, with the help of a couple of four-armed Martian Re-Born, unloaded the cart before the god artist.

Eliezer worked, and as he worked he spoke, and his words travelled far. Two memcordists in the audience broadcast the moment to their followers, across Earth and the solar system. Ismail and Kranki stood together and watched and seemed to flicker in and out of existence as they followed the newly forming god in and out of the unreal.

The god artist chose metal, and wood, and adaptoplant tech, forming and growing a structure before the great doors of Central Station. And as he worked he spoke, singing, and the words reached across air and uncounted audio channels.

And he sang, putting music to the words of a forgotten Lior Tirosh poem:

Rain fell.
Of that, at least, there is no doubt.

People died like plants.

I mean, silently.

We studied water for a long time.
Diligently.
Its molecules tinkled in the glass.
We spun them into dust.
We broke light through them.
We bred tadpoles.

People grew, like red flowers
Like roses or opium poppies.

I mean, beautifully.

Rain fell.
There was something miraculous about it.
I mean, water falling from the sky.
All those complex molecules
Giving birth to bodies of water

Giving birth to
Puddles.

In the Guilds of Ashkelon, Captain Isobel Chow hesitated with her hand on the warp drive controls. A whisper in her ears seemed to draw out words. *Something miraculous.* Gamesworld warp space like a phantasmagorical three-dimensional display. Gamesworlds were powerful virtualities, the progeny of primitive MMORPGs, running in real-time on the deep Cores of computing hardware co-inhabited by Others, and scattered throughout the solar system. They were home to untold billions of both networked humans and native digital intelligences and autonomous systems.

It would take time to arrive in the Delta Quadrant (which was hosted on an off-world server somewhere; time-lag would be a problem). She could log out, leave a simulacra running in her place as she surfaced into the physicality of Universe-One. The words seemed to whisper in her ear, of love and loss, and she remembered Motl, the anger, somehow, draining away from her. The display screens around her in the vast control room of the starship displayed hyperspace and in it rose, suddenly, a dark shape, and Isobel's second-in-command, Tesh, giant and six-armed and *daikaiju*-derived (Isobel never knew who or what he was in the physicality), gave an alarmed grunt. It was a hovering dark mass, a cuboid thing, like a gamesworld singularity.

"What is it?" Tesh said, and there was awe in his voice.

Giving birth, the voice seemed to say. Isobel swallowed. "A god," she said.

"I've never seen one," Tesh said, and Isobel said, "No, they're rare."

"Carmel?"

He found her in Achimwene's bookshop. Achimwene wasn't there. Carmel let Boris in. There was a dreamy look in her eyes. Her body was thin like a boy's. "I dreamed I was human," she said.

"I have it," Boris said. He showed her the syringe. "Crucifixation."

"How will it help?"

"I don't know that it will."

She laughed, suddenly. "You just like to penetrate me with needles," she said.

"I'm trying to help," he said. The aug pulsed on his neck. She reached out and touched it, with just the tips of her fingers. "Then do it," she said. Almost indifferent. She presented her thin naked arm to him. "Do it."

He pressed the syringe into her arm. She sighed, and her breath was soft and smelled of cardamom seeds. He helped her into a chair, where she drooped—"I can see it," she said. "It's—"

Carmel was floating on a sea of white light. If space is an ocean, a *Solwota blong Star*, then this was ur-space, devoid of stars or darkness or the abyss. She felt herself afloat and the world rose around her, but the details were hazy, as if it had not been quite properly rendered yet. She could see the old streets of Central Station, and humans, crudely detailed, standing around. She could see herself, a violet smudge, and Boris, standing above her like a badly etched villain from a Martian Hardboiled romance, the needle raised like a sacrificial weapon in one hand.

The outline of the space port rose before her then, white lines of light marking the gigantic structure, dense clumps here and there hiding the dense code Cores of Others. And something rose before Carmel, before the space port, a black cuboid thing that sucked in light and data like a vampire, and she was drawn to it, she floated through the white light towards that dark singularity, unable to escape—

"Guard us from the Blight and from the Worm, and from the attention of Others." Mama Jones knelt by the small shrine on the Green. "And give us the courage to make our own path in the world, St. Cohen."

She straightened and looked to the space port. She could feel the forming god there, on the pedestrian street, sense its disturbance travelling through the invisible networks, echoes of it pinging everywhere, hitting her node. She was not comfortable. Not with Boris and his strange tie to the Strigoi girl. And not with Eliezer, showing up again, meddling. Others were behind it, she could tell. The digitals in their digital realm: most of them had little to do with humanity, with the physical world. They ran on the deep Cores, protected by the military might of Clan Ayodhya, and as long as their physical existence was kept in order they—did—not—meddle.

Usually.

But then there were the children.

Miriam wasn't stupid. She knew the boy was odd. She knew Kranki had come out of the birthing clinics different. That he was not like other children elsewhere.

She didn't know why. She wasn't sure she wanted to. He was not of her womb but he was her child. He deserved his childhood.

She did not like Eliezer meddling. She did not like gods. It had taken humankind long enough to make a faith it could live with. To have your gods living side by side to you was something else, something, almost, sacrilegious.

She lit the stick of incense carefully and walked away, to see what all the fuss was about.

"Can we go around it?" Isobel said.

"It's a singularity," Tesh said.

"Go through it," Isobel decided. Tesh looked alarmed.

"*Through* it?" he said. "Do you remember what happened to the Wu Expedition?"

Isobel shrugged, uncomfortable. "They disappeared?" she said.

"Yes," Tesh said. "Disappeared exploring the Berezhinsky Singularity in Sigma Quadrant."

"But Tesh, think of the *rewards*!" Isobel said. Gamesworld singularities were rare; beyond rare. They could be anything: the opening into a whole new quadrant of the gamesworld, or a journey to its past, or a shortcut to a distant quadrant or even, sometimes, a gateway into one of the other gamesworlds altogether.

But there was also the danger.

Real-world brain death, going full Mother Hitton, the drooling idiot body pulled out of the cooling pod, gibbering and spitting, the mind burned out, the body carrying on, on instinct. Rumours of singularities swallowing players, of the Wu Expedition going too deep, going into the very archaeological layers of the gamesworlds, down past the GoA and into ancient, forgotten levels, and finally to the mythical place called Pacmandu. . . .

"Hit it," Isobel said.

Tesh said, "No."

Isobel's mouth curled in a cruel smile. "You dare disobey me?"

"Fuck it, Isobel, this isn't a *game!*"

But she wasn't listening. A wild spirit had taken hold of her. She felt drunk, powerful. The black cuboid hovered in the giant screens, rotating. Blocking them. She put her hand, palm down, fingers splayed, on the control unit. Felt the thrum of the *Nine-Tailed Cat* underneath her. Through her. She rejoiced in the power. She sent a silent command and it travelled into the mind of the ship and it *accelerated*—

Through gamesworld hyperspace psychedelia, the black cuboid opening like a portal, a worm burrowing through space and time, elongating, the starship shooting through it, inside it, a bullet from a gun punctuating gamesworld space-time—

Tesh screaming, the crew frozen, and Isobel was laughing, invisible hands tearing at her mind, reaching from beyond ur-space, untangling her, and she was breaking apart, into atoms and quarks, until a note sounded, a solitary musical note, like a bell being hit, precisely, and a voice said, "Isobel," and she said, "Motl?"—but the word was just sounds, and the sense of it eluded her.

Floating in the white light, the world seemed far away. It was not unlike feeding. When Carmel sank her teeth into the soft flesh of a man or a woman, the planktonese in her saliva entered their bloodstream and sought out their nodal filaments, and she drew nourishment from that, terabytes and petabytes of memories, dreams, recall perfect and imperfect, knowledge, a sort of *being*. She had been human but she had been changed, she was part-Other, and it seemed to her then that she felt them, flittering close by, watching her, these strange, alien intelligences in the invisible machines that were all around her, that surrounded and engulfed the world.

There!

She rose above Central Station, below her a sharp, clear cuboid blackness, a thing defined in both the physical and the virtual. She hovered above it, it suspended her. On Level Three of Central Station she saw a shape that was, like herself, both real and virtual. A robotnik, she thought, seeing that stiff gait, that way of moving

An ident tag, bobbing at the edge of her consciousness: Motl.

Forgetting him easily, she turned away. The . . . *thing* down below fascinated her. It called to her and repulsed her simultaneously. She wondered how long the hit of the drug would last. What *had* Boris given her? she thought, uneasily. But the thoughts, slippery as fish, would not stay, and her mind was a brook, connecting to a vast river. She flowed like water.

Motl pushed past the startled human operator, a local boy, a Chong or a Chow or a Cohen, Motl couldn't quite remember at that point. The boy said, "Hey, wait, what are you—" but Motl ignored him and ripped open an empty pod.

"Motl, man! You can't—"

Motl stuck his hands into the delicate membrane of the pod. Cables moved like fronds there. Motl had seen Isobel's body: gamers needed that extra bit of immediacy, of access. Isobel's sockets dotted her body, like buttons on a suit. Motl had held his breath when he first saw her naked. His metal fingers traced the outline connecting every delicate socket hole. It formed a virtual mesh around her body that, once she was inside a pod, covered her completely. "Let me be," he said to the boy; and he hooked himself in.

With each season a new god appeared in the streets and alleyways of Central Station. They appeared without pomp and without ceremony; they appeared, almost, on the sly.

Not this one.

This one slowly took shape, out of scrap metal and old, ageless plastic. It grew out of adaptoplant seeds that saw organic shapes form with impossible speed and sprout upwards, this modern, living, networked statue rising before the doors of the space port. Eliezer the god artist worked with hands and mind, and as he worked he sang.

Word spread. A group of Na Nachs from Tel Aviv, that city of the Jews, came, and began to dance around the sculpture to the beat of a bass drum, shaking their black-clad heads, their long, curly *peyes* moving as they joyfully hummed and sang their sacred mantra, *Na Nach Nachma Nachman Me'uman*, over and over, and the robo-priest, R. Brother Patch-It, who stood nearby, was startled to join them, dancing awkwardly, metal body shining in the light of the setting sun.

Tea was served in small glasses, hot and sweet, served black, not in the manner of the barbarous Anglos; and Miriam met Boris under the awnings of a fruit juice seller. "Carmel is in the god," he said; and he said no more. Miriam sighed, and she let it go. Sometimes she wished Boris was the same long-limbed, awkward boy she had known, when things had been less complicated. But that was long ago; and the woman she had become knew relationships were seldom simple.

The god artist worked, and the god took shape under his calloused hands, a thing as abstract as any religion. It rose out of the ground, larger than any other god seen before in the station, and its vibrations and its power could be felt by all in the digitality.

"Hello, hello, hello," a policeman said. "What do we have here, then?"—or something to that effect, based on the obsolete protocols of long-dead narrative writers. No one wanted the police to be truly sentient; and so they compromised, with crude mechanicals, who humans found, somehow, more reassuring. The policeman's light went on and off. A small siren, like a growl, rose in its plastic belly. "You can't build this thing here, mate," it said. "Trans-city ordinance—" and it recited a long string of numbers that meant nothing to anyone; not even to itself.

"I don't know what you hope to achieve," Miriam said. An argument was breaking out between the police-bots and some of the spectators. There was a smell of incense in the air. The Na Nachs danced and their beat grew stronger. The robo-priest, coming out of a seeming trance, went and stood beside Miriam, its face placid. "Miriam," it said, politely. "Boris."

"I think she's here for a reason," Boris said, after a perfunctory nod to the robo-priest. "I think the Others let her in. I think it's to do with the children. I don't know, Miriam. I think they used me, when I was working in the birthing labs. I think they changed the codes, the foetuses, for their own purposes. And I think they need Carmel."

It was one of his longest speeches. Miriam said, "What for?"

"To activate new sequences," Boris said. Hesitated. "The children are not, not entirely—"

"Human?"

"Yes."

"What's human?" Miriam said—demanded. "They're *children*, Boris. For all that you birthed them, for all the designer care and the fluids and getting your hands dirty, you never understood that. They're children, first and foremost. And for all that you brought them into the world, you were never a parent."

"Miriam—"

"No," she said, flaring. "Don't take that tone, Boris. Not with me."

The robo-priest looked between them, and tactfully moved away. The argument between the police-bots and the spectators was growing more heated. Old man Eliezer, oblivious, kept chanting, and building.

Carmel fell into the black cuboid.

She woke up gasping for air, thinking for a moment she was back in the small room in Central Station, and that the drug had worn off.

But the view around her was nothing like Central Station's.

For a moment, she panicked.

Three suns rose in the sky above. The clash of colours was intense, blues and greens and reds transfused the world, and on the horizon she could see stars, and a black hole ringed by habitats.

She was standing high above the port, looking down at the impossible city. Aliens thronged the streets. Hovercars and flying humans filled the sky. Transport ships immense like moons rose in nearby space.

Orlov Port, Delta Quadrant, Guilds of Ashkelon universe.

That black hole visible by the nebula of galactic dust and habitats around it was a gamesworld singularity, a wormhole jump impossible in the real world. Carmel knew the sight of it, intimately.

She had earned the money to escape home by working in Orlov Port, a girly-girl like St. C'Mell, but she had not been back since.

It was dangerous to be Strigoi and enter the gamesworlds.

But the scent of data was everywhere. Her new senses felt overwhelmed by it.

She had not experienced this before the change. Then, a base human, she saw things as they were presented, a sensory matrix fed into the sleeping form in the surf-pod. As Strigoi, though. . . .

As Strigoi she *felt* the world around her. It was filled with the toktok blong narawan, the Conversation of Others. Sys-Gods, they were called in the GoA. She could see the numerical pattern of the suns' interlacing rays, feel the pull of that singularity on the horizon, the mathematical equations that controlled gravity, the graphic vectors of moving, impossible ships. Her mouth filled with saliva. Raw data, and humans masquerading as aliens, Others masquerading as humans, were all around her.

What was she *doing* here?

She vaguely remembered a room, a man standing over her with a needle in his hand. But it was fading, lost in the data overload.

She wanted to get out. But the hunger was in her and, almost without conscious decision, she found herself moving, away from the large panoramic window, down the escalators, down to street level, a gamesworld imitation of the space port her body was currently inhabiting back in Universe-One. Outside, the light of suns warmed her face. A tentacle-junkie rubbed against her as it passed. Port Orlov was a mercantile centre, a hundred guilds both large and small intersected here, you could hire out on a ship here, pirates, privateers, navy, military, exploration, there were treasures out in the GoA: ancient, vanished races, mysterious ruins, planetary systems no one'd ever seen, peopled only by NPCs.

As in a dream, Carmel followed the tentacle-junkie. His mind was open to her, and she could not help herself, she stalked him through the thronged streets, until he had slipped into a quiet quay-side alley and she pounced.

She fed quickly, without control. The tentacle-junkie was one in real life, too. His body had been modified some years back. Now he flopped in his custom pod somewhere in the asteroid belt, his real body as helpless as his digital one as she fed on him, his memories, his access codes, his gamesworld conquests. He was an admiral in one of the minor guilds, she discovered. He commanded a ship and was known as the Butcher of Soledad-5, having given the order, in an early campaign, to use a doomsday device in that GoA solar system, annihilating every indigenous NPC and player within a light year of Soledad-5's star.

He was married, had three children, his wife was a miner with her own ship, his eldest daughter had just married, his middle son wanted to follow him in a career in the GoA, the youngest was proving difficult, rebellious, all this and more Carmel was sucking out of his mind, his node, in a hungry frenzy, all the while knowing it was wrong, she would be caught, the Others were everywhere, the Sys-Gods were watching . . . she tore herself away from him. He lay there, curled up on himself, his mind flooded with dopamine, and she did something she never knew she could, she reached down with her node and *pushed*, and his mind disappeared, his virtual body was gone, erased—she had sent him back into the physicality.

And now, post-feed, her mind had cleared and she knew she had to get out, too, but somehow she could not do to herself what she had done to her victim, the way out was closed to her, she had to seek an exit, a gamesworld gateway, desperately she tried to *Abort! Abort!* But nothing happened, then the sky darkened above her, a beam of light came down from the sky and touched her, engulfed her, and Carmel closed her eyes, defeated, a choir of angels sang and she was lifted up, like a doll, rising into the light, rising up to heaven.

"Motl?"

"Isobel. What are you doing?"

She was sobbing. "I don't know," she said. "It's so dark. I'm cold, Motl. I'm so cold."

"Where are you? What is this place?"

"I don't know," she said. "I went through a thing. A thing like a thing." Even the words were being lost, leeched out of her.

"Ur-space," Motl said, and cursed. "You passed through a singularity-mine."

"A what?"

"Hostile code bombs," he said. "We used them in the war . . . one of the wars. Or all of them. I can't remember."

"There were wars in the GoA?" she said.

"The wars were fought on both levels of existence," he said. Not wishing to remember.

"Hold me," Isobel said. "I'm cold."

"I'll get you out. What about your crew?"

"I don't know. I can't see them."

"They might be all right, still." But he didn't sound convinced, which made her heart catch inside her (and somewhere she was flatlining in a pod that smelled of unwashed human bodies).

"How did you get here, Motl? Motl, I'm sorry."

"It was my fault," he said. "I promised you I was finished with that stuff. The drugs. But Boris asked me."

"You should have told him no."

"I owed him, Isobel."

"Why?"

"Wait. Listen."

"What is it?"

"A siren song. A god, growing. With life comes death. We can follow the call."

"How?"

"Hold me. Hold me tight."

She held him. She held him tight. That representation of him, in this ur-space. It still smelled like him. Oil and metal and sweat. They began to stumble away in the dark and, after a moment, she thought she, too, could hear it, almost feel the pull of the god.

"It wasn't my fault. Please. You have to believe me!"

The voice was as pure as an angel's, emanating from the god straight into her node, her mind. *Little Strigoi*, the voice said, *you shouldn't be here.*

"I was ubicked."

Even to her, her voice sounded weak, insincere. She was floating in a vast space, bodyless, and the god, this Other, this digital intelligence as strange and unknowable as a true alien, was studying her, reading through her as through a text, effortlessly.

Humans fear your kind, the Sys-God said.

She did not reply. Acknowledging the truth in the Other's words. A meme of fear regarding Strigoi, a self-perpetuating cross-cultural myth permeating the human worlds, drawing on ancient images, half-remembered mythagos. Sometimes she thought the same designers of the Strigoi had also created the meme—or perhaps it was created in response, a protective measure—

You speculate. The voice sounded amused, if such emotion could be ascribed to an Other. They did not experience human emotions, which were tied into having a body, hormones, physical responses evolved over millennia. Others had evolved separately, outside the physicality, in the virtuality of the Breeding Grounds. *But you don't know.*

"I never wanted—"

No, the voice agreed. *And yet you went where you are forbidden. You damaged a player. You have transgressed against the GoA.*

"Please. Please. . . ."

Human . . . the voice hesitated. *Little lost Strigoi*, it said. *Do you wish to feed?*

"Always. Always! You do not know, cannot know, cannot understand," Carmel said. Screamed at the heart of that empty place, that palace of the virtual. "The hunger."

We will fix the player you have eaten, the Sys-God said. *We will replace his memories, rebuild the parts of his mind you have taken. Such incursions have happened before. We do not always . . . advertise. Humans depend on the virtual, and we, in turn . . .*

"Yes?" She strove for escape, but there was nothing around her, not even air.

We depend on them, the Sys-God said; almost, it seemed to her, sadly. And again, *Do you wish to feed?*

"Yes! Damn it, yes . . . always."

Then feed, the voice said, and something vast and inhuman, a body like a whale's, pressed against her, near suffocating her, and she held close to it, its rubbery body, its smell of brine and seaweed, the skin rough to the touch, her nose pressed against this huge belly, her mouth watering, her canines slipping out, sinking into the rubbery flesh of it, feeding, feeding on this enormity, this alien entity, too vast and powerful to comprehend, the feed overwhelming her, suffocating her, and in her mind that voice, chuckling as it faded, saying, *Why do humans always make the comparison to whales?*

It wasn't clear, later, who started the fire. It began as a lick of flame, a flash of colour. The police-bots beeped alarmingly. The dancing Na Nachs, perhaps intoxicated by the fire, danced harder, and sweat streamed down their bearded cheeks and trailed into their white shirts, soaking them.

The god burned.

Eliezer, the artist, seemed as captivated by the fire as the spectators were. How often does one birth, only to kill, a god? That oldest of human institutions, the Sacrifice.

His lips still moved but his song was eaten by the roar of the fire.

The god burned.

Those watching on their nodal feeds could see the same thing happening in the Conversation: the way that complex Other shape began to fragment, like a network being slowly taken apart, each major node unlinking, the one shape becoming many smaller networks disconnected from each other. The way memory, in a human, slowly degrades, perhaps. Or maybe it was just a change, like ice becoming water. Either way it burned, fragmented, and as it did it cried, a voiceless sound, a string of zeroes that made people wince and pull away.

"Carmel!" Boris said.

Miriam followed him. She cared for the girl, whatever folly Boris, well-meaning though he was, had perpetrated. Someone had to keep an eye on him.

But at the entrance to the bookshop her brother, Achimwene, stood. Boris halted. "You," Achimwene said. His voice shook with anger. Poor Achi, Miriam thought.

"I told you to leave her alone."

"I'm just—" she could see Boris, too, was suddenly angry. It was an unexpected sight. Even as a boy, he so seldom showed emotion, especially violent ones. "I'm just trying to *help*."

"We don't need your help, Boris! Go back! Go back to Mars or wherever you came from. You can't just come back from the Up and Out and expect everyone to defer to you, like you're some kind of, some kind of—"

But Boris, wordless, pushed past him. Achimwene stood there, helpless. "Miriam . . ." he said.

She didn't know what to say. Achimwene turned and went inside, and she followed him.

Books lined the shelves. Paper books, with that distinct, odd smell about them. Shelves upon shelves, books upon mouldering books. Where did her brother *find* all these? There was something unhealthy about his obsession. Something unclean. It was a sad reflection on his existence, she thought, that the arrival of a vampire in his life was the best thing to have happened to him.

At least it got his mind away from books.

"Achi?"

"Carmel!"

Miriam followed him up the narrow stairs. Carmel was lying—reclining?—on the narrow bed. The window was open and a smell of burning came from outside. Boris was hovering.

"I was asleep," Carmel said. "But I'm awake now."

"He shot you full of drugs," Achimwene said, pointing accusingly at Boris. "I was away, in Tel Aviv, I was buying books, I didn't know."

"I asked him to, Achi."

Miriam glanced at her brother. He stood close to Carmel, who sat up, yawning. Her white shift clung to her thin body. Achimwene's hands were pressed together. Almost as if he were praying.

"Why?" Achimwene said.

"Because I want to get better, Achi!" She raised her head. Her eyes were large, anguished. "I don't want to be what I am."

"Why?"

"I want to . . . Because . . . Achi . . ."

"To be with me?"

"Men," she said, but she smiled. "It's always about you, isn't it."

"Carmel," Boris said. "What happened?"

"I went away," she said. "And then I came back."

"Carmel . . ."

"That's enough," Achimwene said. "Get out, Boris."

"Listen, now—"

"Boris," Miriam said. Men were like boys. You had to speak to them slowly. "Come along." She put her hand on his arm. After a moment, he subsided. She noticed his aug turned a deeper shade when he was angry like this. He let her lead him away. Behind, she could hear her brother and Carmel, speaking, but the voices were too low to make sense of the words.

Once they were outside, Miriam took a deep breath. The air was filled with smoke. She had the sense of something approaching, or coming to an end. "I want you to leave her alone," she said to Boris.

He opened his mouth, looked like he wanted to speak, then closed it, his shoulders drooping slightly. "All right," he said.

She took his hand as they walked away. He wasn't a bad man, she thought. He was just a man.

"Motl?"

Isobel was in the dark and it was suffocating her. Then she pushed and something *gave* and suddenly light, and air, poured in and she realised she was inside a pod.

She was back in Universe-One.

She pulled out the plugs from her flesh. Pulled herself out of the pod, hands shaking. She noticed signs of burning on her skin. Almost collapsed on the floor as she came out but strong, metal hands caught her and held her steady. "Motl?"

"I had to see you," he said. "To explain . . ."

"Were you in there?" she said. "In the GoA?"

"I followed you," he said, simply. "I'd follow you everywhere."

"I flatlined," she said. He laughed.

"No one really flatlines," he said. "Only in cheap Martian Hardboiled stories."

"I know what happened, Motl!"

"I know," he said. "I just—"

"That was *awesome*!" she said. "Flatlined! In a singularity! I won't have to buy drinks for *months*!"

"You could have died!"

"But I didn't, did I." She grinned and held on to him. "Come on, Motl."

"Isobel?"

She reached out and kissed him. "Let's go home," she said.

The god artist sat with his friend, the alte-zachen man Ibrahim, under the canopy of a sheesha pipe shop. They drank dark, bitter coffee and drew, each in turn, on a tall, clear glass pipe that stood patiently between them. A sliver of coal burned above the cake of cherry-flavoured tobacco. As the sun set, the moon rose over Central Station, over the old streets and the space port, and the drifting lanterns filled the air, bobbing gently this way and that.

The remnants of the god still burned, gently, but the fire was going out. Ibrahim took a drag on the pipe and passed the mouthpiece to his friend.

"Well," Eliezer said.

"Did you accomplish what you wished for?"

"Do any of us?" the god artist said. He smiled around the mouthpiece, and smoke came out of his nostrils in twin jets of white plumes.

Beyond, at the circle of the burned god, two children played. And those who watched them in both the real and the virtual saw that they existed, evenly, in the one and in the other. Ibrahim watched them, and saw them reach out with hands as perfect as those of angels; and pluck away small, spinning bits of code which, if watered and fed, might one day grow to be entities all of their own.

"Gods are born, and die," the old artist said; but he said it sadly, and from a great weight of time; for they were all his children. And so he took a perfunctory puff on the pipe and passed the mouthpiece back to his friend. In his many years, he had learned the ways of that country.

They sat in companionable silence and watched the children play.

TEN:
THE ORACLE

*G*ods are born, and die, the old artist said; but he had not always been old.

There had always been those who bridge one world and the other. Those who meddle in the affairs of the world.

Once, the world was young.

There had always been an Oracle in Central Station.

She was born Ruth Cohen, on the outskirts of old Central Station, near the border with Jewish Tel Aviv. She grew up on Levinsky, by the spice market, with the deep reds of paprika and the bright yellow of turmeric and the startling purple of sumac colouring the days. She had never met her famous progenitor, St. Cohen of the Others.

She was an ordinary enough child. She went through a religious phase and attended a girl's yeshiva for a time in her teenage years. She had woken one night, late. Thunder streaked the sky. She blinked, trying to recall a dream she'd just had. She had been walking through the streets of Central Station and a storm raged where the station should have been, a whirlwind that stood still even as it moved. Ruth walked towards it, drawn to it. The air was hot and humid. The storm, silent, bore within itself people frozen like mannequins, and bottles, and a minibus with the wheels still turning and with frozen faces inside, glued to the windows. Ruth felt something within the storm. An intelligence, a knowing *something*, not human but not hostile, either. Something other. She approached it. She was barefoot, and the asphalt was warm against the soles of her feet.

And the storm opened its mouth and spoke to her.

Thunder woke her. She lay in bed trying to recall the dream. What had the storm said?

There had been a message there, something important. Something deep and ancient: if only she could recall. . . .

She lay there for a long time before she fell back to sleep.

The yeshiva had not been a huge success. Ruth wanted answers, needed to understand the voice of the storm. The rabbis seemed unwilling or unable to offer that and so, for a time, Ruth tried drugs, and sex, and being young. She travelled to Thailand, and Laos, and there she studied the Way of Ogko, which is no Way at all, and talked to monks and bar owners and full-immersion denizens. There, in the city of Nong Khai on the banks of the Mekong River, she conched for the first time, transitioning from her own reality to the one of the Guilds of Ashkelon universe, fully immersed, deep in the substrata of the Conversation. That first time felt strange: the shell of the pod, the plastic hot, the smell of unwashed bodies who had been enmeshed inside it for too long. Then the immersion rig closing, the light gone, a cave as silent as a tomb. She was trapped, blind, helpless.

Then she transitioned.

One moment she was blind and deaf. The next she was standing in the bright sunlight of Sisavang-3, in the lunar colony of the Guild of Cham.

Ruth joined the guild as a low-ranking member, spending all her remaining baht on hours of immersion. She joined the crew of a starship, the *Fermi Paradox*, and travelled the nearby sector of game-space, her skin all the while becoming brittle and pale from the long immersion in the coffin-like pod.

But still she did not find whatever it was she was looking for. Only once, briefly, she had come close. She had found a holy object, a gamesworld talisman of great power. It was on a deserted moon in Omega Quadrant. She had come onto the surface of the moon alone. The talisman was found in a cave. The atmosphere was breathable. She did not have a helmet on. She knelt by the object and touched it and a bright flame burst into life, and then she was in an Elsewhere.

A voice that was like the voice of the whirlwind in her dream spoke to her. It spoke directly into her mind, into her wired node, it enveloped her in warmth and love: it knew her.

She did not recall exactly what it had said, or how it said it. But it was curious about her; she remembered that, and the voice, calling her *cousin*: it had been an Other, a Sys-God of the GoA.

Why had it called her that? When she came through she was back on her ship, the object inventoried, her credits up by a thousand points, her health and strength and shielding maxed.

And suddenly she knew what she wanted. She wanted, achingly and clearly, to know more about Others.

The next day she had left the Guilds of Ashkelon universe, but the mystery followed her as she emerged, blinking and shaking, into the sunlight. She sat by the river, her muscles weak, and drank thick coffee, sweetened with condensed milk. *Cousin*, the voice had said, evoking a strange feeling, a longing inside her. She thought of her family, her line, twisting like DNA strands all the way back to St. Cohen.

But who was he?

She returned to Tel Aviv with uncertainty burned out by passion. She knew what she wanted.

What she didn't know yet was how to get it.

The truth was that after the twelve-hour flight to Tel Aviv, Matt Cohen had a headache. He sat in the front of the taxi, next to the driver, an Arab man wearing fake Gucci sunglasses. Two of his research team were with him, Balazs and Phiri, crammed uncomfortably into the back seat of the car with their bulky equipment.

Matt blinked in the glare of light. His pressed white shirt was crumpled from the flight, already beginning to stain with sweat from the hot Mediterranean climate he was unused to. He wished he had invested in a pair of sunglasses, fake or not, like the driver.

In a way, coming here had been an act of last resort.

The taxi deposited them on the outskirts of the Old City of Jerusalem, and left them there, with their luggage, in the approaching dusk. Church bells mixed with the call of mosques. Orthodox Jews clad in black walked past, arguing intensely. It was cooler up in the mountains. Matt was grateful for that, at least.

"So," Phiri said.

"So," Matt said.

"This is it," Balazs said. They looked at each other, these three disparate people, weary after the long flight, and the moving from country to country, lab to lab, sometimes in the dead of night, in a hurry, sometimes leaving notes and equipment behind, sometimes one step ahead of irate landlords, or other creditors, or even the law.

They had not been popular, these scientists, their research considered both a dead-end and immoral. For they sought to Frankenstein, to breed life in their closed networks the way a biologist might breed tadpoles and watch them become frogs. They had the tadpoles, but as yet those tadpoles had not turned into either frogs or princesses, they continued to exist only *in potentia*. Now they checked in, into the small hostel that would be their temporary headquarters until they could, once again, set up shop.

The servers rested silent in their coolers, their code suspended, not living, not dead. Matt's fingers itched to plug them in, to boot them up, to run them, to let the wild code inside mate and mutate, split and merge and split and merge, lines of code entwining and branching, growing ever more complex and aware.

A breeding grounds.

The Breeding Grounds, as they'd later be known.

The evolutionary track from which Others emerged.

Matt Cohen and his team had moved across state lines in the United States; had gone to Europe, for a time, sought refuge in Monaco and Lichtenstein, then offshore, on lonely islands where the palm trees moved lazily in the breeze. The Others could have emerged in Vanuatu, or Saudi Arabia, or Laos. Resistance to the research was concentrated and public, for to create life is to play God, as Victor Frankenstein had found, to his cost.

It's what *Life* magazine called him, back in the day. A Frankenstein; when all he wanted was to be left alone with his computers, knowing that he did not know what he was doing, that digital intelligence, those not-yet-born Others, could not be designed, could not be *programmed*, by those who wrongly used the term *artificial intelligence*. Matt was an evolutionary scientist, not a programmer. He did not know what form they would take when at last they emerged. Evolution alone would determine that.

"Matt?"

Phiri was shaking his shoulder, gently.

"Yes."

"We need to check in. It's getting late," she said.

"Yes," he said, "yes, you're right."

But still he did not move. He cast one last look at the sky but it was overcast, there was nothing to be read there of the future and what it might become; and so he led his small team inside, where they checked in for the night; but really, it could have happened anywhere.

———

"But a *Joining*?" Anat said to Ruth. They were sitting on the beach at midnight; Ruth shrugged uneasily as Anat lit a ubiq cigarette. The latest thing from New Israel on Mars: high-density data encoded in the smoke particles. Anat inhaled deeply, the data travelling into her lungs, entering the blood stream and into the brain—an almost immediate rush of pure knowledge.

Anat blew out smoke and grinned goofily.

"You know about Others," Ruth said.

Anat said, "You know I worked as a hostess—"

"Yes."

Anat made a face. "It was odd," she said. "You're not really aware, when they're body-surfing you. They download into your node, controlling your motor functions, getting the sensory feed. While you're somewhere in the Conversation, in virtuality, or just nowhere—" She shrugged. "Asleep," she said. "But then, when you wake up, you just feel different. Like, you don't know what they did with your body. They're supposed to keep it healthy, unless you get paid extra, I know some of us did but I never took the money. But you notice little things. Dirt under your left little finger, where it hadn't been before. A scratch on your inner thigh. A different perfume. A different cut of hair. But subtle. Almost as if they're trying to play games with you, to make you doubt that you saw anything. To make you wonder what it was you did. Your body did. What they did with it." She took a sip of her wine. "It was all right," she said. "For a while. The money was good. But I wouldn't do it now. Sometimes I'm afraid they can forcibly take me over. Break down my node security, take over my body again—"

"They would never!" Ruth said, shocked. "There are treaties, hard-coded protocols!"

"Sometimes I dream that they enter me," Anat said, ignoring her. "I wake up slowly but I am still dreaming, and I know I am sharing my body with countless Others, all watching through my eyes, and I feel their fascination, when I move my fingers or curl my lip, but it is a detached sort of interest, the way they would look at any other math problem. They're not like us, Ruth. You can't share with a mind this different. You can be on, or off. But you can't be both."

There had been a dreamy, detached look in Anat's eyes that night. She had been changed by her contact with the Others, Ruth had thought. There was addiction there, a fascination not unlike what some people had with God.

They had lost contact, at last. Anat had remained human, after all, while Ruth. . . .

For a time she had tried religion, Crucifixion: Ruth took her first hit in the robotniks' junkyard, by fires burning in upturned half-barrels, with the stars and the Earth's orbiting settlements shining high above in a dark sky.

Religion intoxicated Ruth, but only for a while. Infatuation fades. In the drug she found no truth that couldn't be found in the GoA or other virtualities. Was heaven real? Or was it yet another construct, another virtuality within the Conversation's distributed networks of networks, the drug merely a trigger?

Either way, she thought, it was linked to the Others. Eventually, the more time you spent in the virtuality where they lived, everything linked to the Others.

Without the drugs she had no faith of her own. Something in her psychological makeup prohibited her from believing. Other humans believed the same way they breathed: it came natural to them. The world was filled with synagogues and churches, mosques and temples, shrines to Elron and Ogko. New faiths rose and fell like breath. They bred like flies. They died like species. But they did not reach their ghostly hands to Ruth: something inside her was lacking.

She needed something more. One day she went back to Jerusalem, to visit the old labs where the Others were first bred. They were kept unchanged, a memorial place, a place of pilgrimage. . . .

"Nazis out! Nazis out!"

Five months later and it was happening *again*.

The villagers with pitchforks and burning torches, Balazs called them. The protesters were diffuse but globally organised. They had pursued the research team to each hastily abandoned location but here, in Jerusalem, the plight of the ur-creatures, trapped in the prison of the closed network of the Breeding Grounds, raised public sympathies to a new level. Matt wasn't sure why.

The Vatican had lodged an official complaint with the Israeli government. The Americans offered tacit support but said nothing in public. The Palestinians condemned what they called Zionist digital aggression. Vietnam offered shelter but Matt knew they were already working on their own research in secret. . . .

"Nazis! Nazis! Destroy the concentration camp!"

"Assholes," Phiri said. They were watching out of the window. A nondescript building in the new part of town but close to the Old City. The demonstrators waved placards and marched up and down as media reps filmed them. The lab building itself was heavily protected against intrusion, both physical and digital. It was as if they were under siege.

Matt just couldn't understand it.

Did they not *read*? Did they not know what would happen if the project was successful, if a true digital intelligence emerged, and if it then managed to escape into the wider world of the digitality? Countless horror films and novels predicted the rise of the machines, the fall of humanity, the end of life as we know it. He was just taking basic precautions!

But the world had changed since the paranoid days of big oil and visible chipsets, of American ascendancy and DNS root servers. It was a world in which the Conversation had already began, that whisper and shout of a billion feeds all going on at once, a world of solar power and RLVs, a world in which Matt's research was seen as harking back to older, more barbaric days. They did not fear for themselves, those protesters. They feared for Matt's subjects, for these *in potentia* babies forming in the Breeding Grounds, assembling lines of code the way a human baby forms cells and skin and bone, becoming.

Set Them Free, the banners proclaimed, and a thousand campaigns erupted like viral weeds in the still-primitive Conversation. The attitude to Matt's digital genetics experiments was one once reserved for stem cell research or cloning or nuclear weapons.

And meanwhile, within the closed network of processing

power that was the Breeding Grounds, the Others, carefully made unaware of the happenings outside, continued, noiselessly, to evolve.

Ruth walked into the shrine. The old lab building had always been meant to be only a temporary house for the research. But this was where it had happened, at last, where the barrier was breached and the alien entities, trapped inside the network, finally spoke.

Imagine the first words of an alien child.

Ironically, there is confusion as to what they had actually said.

The records were . . . misplaced.

In his monograph on the subject, the poet Lior Tirosh claims their first words—communicated to the watching scientists in trilingual scripts on the single monitor screen— were *Stop breeding us.*

In the later Martian biopic of Matt Cohen, *The Rise of Others*, the words are purported to be *Set Us Free.*

According to Phiri, in her autobiography, they were not words at all, but a joke in Binary. What the joke was she did not say. Some argue that it was *What's the difference between 00110110 and 00100110? 11001011!* But that seems unlikely.

Ruth walked through the shrine. The old building had been preserved, the same old obsolete hardware on display, humming theatrically, the cooling units and the server arrays, the flashing lights of ethernet ports and other strange devices. But now flowers grew everywhere, left in pots on windowsills and old desks, on the floor, and amidst them candles burned, and incense sticks, and little offerings of broken machines and obsolete parts rescued from the garbage. Pilgrims walked reverentially around the room. A Martian Re-Born with her red skin and four arms; a robo-priest with the worn skin of old metal; humans, of all shapes and sizes, Iban from the Belt and Lunar Chinese, tourists from Vietnam and France and from nearby Lebanon, their media spores hovering invisibly in the air around them, the better to record the moment for posterity. Ruth just stood there, in the hushed semi-dark of the old abandoned grounds, trying to imagine it the way it was, to see it through Matt Cohen's eyes. She wondered what the Others *had* said, that first time. What message of peace or acrimony they had delivered, what plea. *Mother*, Balazs claimed in his own autobiography, published only in Hungarian, had been their first word. Everyone had their own version, and perhaps it was that the Others had spoken to all present in the language and manner which they understood. Ruth, at that moment, realised that she wanted to know the truth of that instance in time, and what the Others had really said: and that there was only one way to do it; and so she left the shrine with a sense of things unfinished, and went outside and returned to Tel Aviv; but the answers could not be found there, but nearby: in Jaffa.

Ruth came to Jaffa on foot, from the direction of the beach, at twilight. She climbed the hill and went into the cobbled narrow streets, up and down stone stairways, and into an alcove of cool stone and shade. She did not know what to expect. As she stepped into the room the Conversation ceased around her, abruptly, and in the silence of it she felt afraid.

"Come in," the voice said.

It was the voice of a woman, not young, not old. Ruth stepped in and the door closed behind her and there was nothing, it was as if the world of the Conversation, the world of the digitality, had been erased. She was alone in base reality. She shivered; the room was unexpectedly cool.

As her eyes adjusted to the dim light she saw an ordinary room, filled with mismatched furniture, as though it had been supplied wholesale from Ibrahim's junkyard. In the corner sat a Conch.

"Oh," Ruth said.

"Child," the voice said, and there was laughter in it, "what did you expect?"

"I . . . I am not sure I was expecting anything."

"Then you won't be disappointed," the Conch said, reasonably.

"You are a Conch."

"You are observant."

Ruth bit back a retort. She approached, cautiously.

"May I?" she said.

"Satisfy your curiosity?"

"Yes."

"By all means."

Ruth approached the Conch. It looked like an immersion

pod, of the sort gamers hired by the day or the week, but it was different: it was a form of self-imposed permanent immersion, an augmentation. Ruth ran her hand softly over the slightly warm face of the Conch, its smooth surface growing transparent. She saw a body inside, a woman suspended in liquid. The woman's skin was pale, almost translucent. Wires ran from sockets in her flesh and into the shielding of the Conch. The woman's hair was white, her skin smooth, flawless. She seemed ethereal to Ruth, and beautiful, like a tree or a flower. The woman's eyes were open, and a pale blue, but they did not look at Ruth. The eyes saw nothing in the human-perceived spectrum of light. None of the woman's senses worked in the conventional sense. She existed only in the Conversation, her softwared mind housed in the powerful platform that was her body-Conch interface. She was blind and deaf and yet she spoke, but Ruth realised she did not hear the woman's voice in her ears at all—she heard it through her node.

"Yes," the woman said, as though understanding Ruth's thought processes, which, Ruth realised, the Conch was probably analysing in real-time as she stood there.

The Conch waited. "And. . . ?"—encouraging her.

Ruth closed her eyes. Concentrated. The room was shielded, fire-walled, blocked to the Conversation.

Wasn't it?

Faintly, as she concentrated, she could feel it, though. Putting the lie to her assumption. Like a high tone, almost beyond the range of human ears to hear. Not a silence at all, but a compressed *shout*.

The toktok blong narawan.

The Conversation of Others.

It was as if it were not the woman in the Conch at all, but herself who was deaf and blind. That she could try helplessly to listen to that level of Conversation going on above her head, in some impossible language, some impossible speed not meant for human consumption. Such a concentration was like swallowing a thousand Crucifixation pills, like spending centuries within the GoA as if they were but a single day. She wanted it, suddenly and achingly—the want that you get when you can't have something precious.

"Are you willing to give up your humanity?" the Conch said.

"What is your name?" Ruth said. Asking the woman who was the Conch. The Conch who had been a woman.

"I have no name," the Conch said. "No name you'd understand. Are you willing to give up your name, Ruth Cohen?"

Ruth stood, suspended in indecision.

"Would you give up your humanity?"

Matt stared at the screen. He felt the ridiculous need to shout, "It's alive! It's *alive*!"

The way they did indeed portray him in that Phobos Studios biopic, two centuries later.

But of course he didn't. Phiri and Balazs looked at him with uncertain grins.

"First contact," Balazs breathed.

Imagine meeting an alien species for the first time. What do you say to them?

That you are their jailer?

It was as if sound had left the room. A bubble of silence. Suddenly breaking.

"What was that?" Phiri said.

There were shrill whistles and shouted chants, breaking in even through the sound proofing.

And then he could hear the unmistakable sound of gunshots.

"The protesters," Balazs said.

Matt tried to laugh it off. "They won't get in. Will they?"

"We should be fine."

"And them?" Balazs said—indicating the network of humming computers and the sole screen and the words on it.

"Shut them down," Phiri said suddenly; she sounded drunk.

"We could suspend them," Balazs said. "Until we know what to do. Put them to sleep."

"But they're evolving!" Matt said. "They're still evolving!"

"They will evolve until the hardware runs out of room to hold them," Balazs said. Outside there were more gunshots and the sound of a sudden explosion. "We need more hosting space." He said it calmly; almost beatifically.

"If we released them they will have all the space they need," Phiri said.

"You're mad."

"We must shut them down."

"This is what we *worked* for!"

There was the sound of the downstairs door breaking open. They looked at each other. Shouts from downstairs, from some of the other research people. Turning into screams.

"Surely they can't—"

Matt wasn't sure, later, who'd said that. And all the while the words hung on the screen, mute and accusing. The first communication from an alien race, the first words of Matt's children. He opened his mouth to say something, he wasn't sure, later, what it would have been. Then the wave of protesters poured into the room.

"No," Ruth said.

"No?" the Conch said.

"No," Ruth said. She already felt regret, but she pushed on. "I would not give up my humanity, for, for . . ." She sighed. "For the Mysteries," she said. She turned to leave. She wanted to cry but she knew she was right. She could not do this. She wanted to understand, but she wanted to *be*, too.

"Wait," the Conch said.

Ruth stopped. "What?" she said, desolately.

"Do you think I am inhuman?" the woman in the Conch said.

"Yes," Ruth said. Then, "No," Ruth said.

"I don't know," she said at last, and waited.

The Conch laughed. "I am still human," it said. "Oh, how human. We cannot change what we are, Ruth Cohen. If that was what you wanted, you would have left disappointed. We can evolve, but we are still human, and they are still Other. Maybe one day . . ." But she did not complete the thought.

Ruth said, "You mean you can help me?"

"I am ready, child," the Oracle said, "to die. Does that shock you? I am old. My body fails. To be Translated into the

Conversation is not to live forever. What I am will die. A new me will be created that contains some of my code. What will it be? I do not know. Something new, and Other. When your time comes, that choice will be yours, too. But never forget, humans die. So do Others, every cycle they are changed and reborn. The only rule of the universe, child, is change."

"You are dying?" Ruth said. She was still very young, then, remember. She had not seen much death, yet.

"We are all dying," the Oracle said. "But you are young and want answers. You will find, I'm afraid, that the more you know the less answers you have."

"I don't understand."

"No," the Oracle said. "Who of us can say that they truly do."

Matt was pushed and shoved and went down on his back, hard. They streamed in. They were mostly young, but not all, they were Jews and Palestinians, but also foreigners, the media attention had brought them over from India and Britain and everywhere else, wealthy enough to travel, poor enough to care, the world's middle class revolutionaries, the ching-ching Ches.

"Don't—!" Matt shouted, but they were careful, he saw, and for a moment he didn't understand, they were not destroying the machines, they were making sure to remove people aside, to form a barrier around the servers and the power supplies and the cooling units and then they—

He shouted, "No!" and he tried to get up but hands grabbed him, impersonally, a girl with dreadlocks and a boy with an Ernesto Guevera T-shirt, they were not destroying the machines: they were plugging in.

They had brought mobile servers with them, wireless broadcast, portable storage units, an entire storage and communication cloud and they were plugging it all into the secured closed network—

They were opening up the Breeding Grounds.

The Conch wheeled outside and Ruth followed. The Conversation opened up around her, the noise of a billion feeds all vying for attention at once. Ruth followed the Conch along the narrow roads until they came to the old neighbourhood of Ajami. Children ran after them and touched the surface of the Conch. It was night now, and when they reached Ibrahim's junkyard torches were burning, and they cast the old junk in an unearthly glow. A new moon was in the sky. Ruth always remembered that, later. The sliver of a new moon, and she looked up and imagined the people living there.

Ibrahim met them at the entrance. "Oracle," he said, nodding. "And you are Ruth Cohen."

"Yes," Ruth said, surprised.

"I am Ibrahim."

She shook hands, awkwardly. Ibrahim held hers and then opened it. He examined it like a surgeon.

"A Joining is not without pain," he said.

Ruth bit her lip. "I know," she said.

"You are willing?"

"Yes."

"Then come."

They followed him through the maze of junk, of old petrol cars and giant fish-refrigeration units and industrial machines and piles of discarded paper books and mountains of broken toys and the entire flotsam and jetsam of Obsoleteness. Within this maze of kipple there was, at its heart, a room with walls of junk and a roof made of sky and stars. In the centre sat an old picnic table, and a medical cabinet, and a folding chair.

"Please," Ibrahim said. "Sit down."

Ruth did. The Conch had wheeled itself with difficulty through the maze and now stood before her.

"Ibrahim," the Conch said.

"Yes," he said, and he went into the junk and returned and in his hands he held a towel, and he unfurled it carefully, almost reverentially: inside it were three golden, prosthetic thumbs.

"They're from Eliezer," he said, to the Conch. "He came through."

It was conducted in silence. She remembered that, too, nothing spoken but the sound of the waves in the distance and the children playing in the neighbourhood beyond, and the smell of cooking lamb and rice. Ibrahim brought forth a syringe. Ruth put her arm on the table. Ibrahim cleaned her skin where the vein was, and injected her. She felt the numbness spread. He took her hand and laid it splayed flat on the table. In the torchlight his face looked aged and hurting. He took a cleaver, an old one, it must have belonged to a butcher in the market down the hill, long ago. Ruth looked away. Ibrahim brought the cleaver down hard and cut off her thumb. Her blood sprayed the picnic table. Her thumb fell to the ground. Ruth gritted her teeth as Ibrahim took one of the golden prosthetic thumbs and connected it to her flesh. White bone jutted out of the wound. Ruth forced herself to look.

"Now," Ibrahim said.

The protesters plugged into the network. Matt saw lights flashing, the transfer of an enormous amount of data. Like huge shapes pushing through a narrow trough as they tried to escape. He closed his eyes. He imagined, for just a moment, that he could actually hear their sound as they broke free.

She was everywhere and nowhere at once. She was Ruth, but she was someone—something—else, too. She was a child, a baby, and there was another, an Other, entwined into her, a twin: together they existed in a place that had no physicality. They were evolving, together, mutating and changing, lines of code merging into genetic material, forming something—someone—new.

When it was done, when the protesters left, or had been arrested by the police, after he had finished answering questions, dazed, and wandered outside and into the media spotlight, and refused to answer more questions, he went to a bar and sat down and watched the television as he drank. He was just a guy who had tried to create something new, he had never meant for the world to be changed. He drank his beer and a little later he felt the weariness fall from him, a sense of release, of the future dissipating. He was just a guy, drinking beer in a bar, and as he sat there he saw a girl at another table, and their eyes met.

He wasn't then St. Cohen of the Others. He wasn't yet a myth, not yet portrayed in films or novels, not yet the figure-head of a new faith. The Others were out there, in the world . . . somewhere. What they would do, or how, he didn't know.

He looked at the girl and she smiled at him and, sometimes, that is all there is, and must be enough. He stood up and went to her and asked if he could sit down. She said yes.

He sat down and they talked.

She emerged from the virtuality years or decades later; or it could have just taken a moment. When she/they looked down at her/their hand she/they saw the golden thumb and knew it was it/them.

Beside her the Conch was still and she knew the woman inside it was dead.

Through her node she could hear the Conversation but above it she could hear the toktok blong narawan, not clear, yet, and she knew it never would be, not entirely, but she could at least hear it now, and she could speak it, haltingly. She was aware of Others floating in the virtual, in the digitality. Some circled around her, curious. Many others, distant in the webs, were uninterested. She called into the void, and a voice answered, and then another and another.

She/they stood up.

"Oracle," Ibrahim said.

ELEVEN: THE CORE

In the dark of night, Achimwene awakened.

The light of Central Station crept into the room through the blinds. It cast a faint glow over the pillow cases, and the white crumpled sheet, and over the book placed face down on the bedside table, a Bill Glimmung mystery, a paperback much worn and stained with age.

Achimwene turned and reached for the other side of the bed but it was empty. Carmel, again, was gone.

He sat up and turned on the lamp. It cast a small pool of yellow amber light. He picked up the book and stared at it. The bland, handsome face of Bill Glimmung, Martian Detective, stared back at him.

What would Bill Glimmung do, in Achimwene's place? he thought. He got up and padded downstairs, and opened the refrigerator. All was quiet. He wondered what it felt like to other people, ones who were whole. Those who grew up with a node as a part of them, those who were, forever, a part of the Conversation.

Achimwene heard only silence.

He poured a glass of milk and went into the dank main room, his pride and joy, a library and sometimes bookshop. Floor-to-ceiling shelves housed the rarest of pulps from across the worlds. They were evolutionary dead ends: not unlike Achimwene himself.

He stood and contemplated them. He knew every one, each ridiculous, twisting plot, each Gothic and grotesque, the feel of every grainy wood pulp page and crumbling spine. The stories built a maze in his mind, he knew their cavernous rooms and creaky staircases, their echoey chambers and hidden traps, their cells and sudden drops.

Where *was* Carmel?

Moonlight and the glow of Central Station made him restless, Carmel's absence was like a sore he had to keep picking at. The bed had still been warm when he woke up, she could not be far. With sudden, almost manic energy he dressed, hurriedly, with clumsy fingers, it was hot, the air was humid. He pulled on a T-shirt and climbed into flip-flops and he was out, almost before he knew it, a barefaced, node-less detective on the trail of a *femme fatale*.

The truth was that he was always afraid that she'd leave him.

He caught up with her halfway down Neve Sha'anan. At this time of night, near morning, even the bars and nakamals along the road were dark and silent. A street-cleaner machine chugged along by its own, humming quietly to itself. Carmel was ahead of Achimwene, her shadow fleeing along the silent street, the moon overhead, the giant spiders crawling along its surface, modifying Earth's companion for such a time that humans could live and breathe easily on its surface. Their shadows on the moon moved in a chiaroscuro of darkness and light. Achimwene followed Carmel, his feet treading softly on the ground. A robotnik beggar dozed beside the closed shutters of a falafel shop.

She was heading for the station, Achimwene saw. And in a way, he had always known she was. Was she planning on leaving him, once and for all? On leaving Earth entirely, on going back to mysterious Mars, to the lonely habitats of the Belt beyond?

He had dreamed of space, often he contemplated going into the Up and Out. But what use was a cripple like him in space? He thought that with a surprising amount of bitterness, he realised, and was almost shocked by his own anger. He was always once-removed from people, unable to communicate in any way that truly mattered. His mind was closed off.

He followed Carmel, getting nearer. Her pale face came into the starlight, momentarily. His chest hurt when he saw her, his lips felt bloodless. Carmel's eyes seemed vacant, unseeing. Her face was expressionless. She moved with the grace of a Strigoi and yet there was a mechanical quality to it, too, as if she were not entirely in control of her own body.

Then she passed from light back into dark and he almost lost her. She crossed the old road and disappeared inside the vast lit edifice of Central Station. Achimwene hurried after her.

Through the doors and from the dark into the light. The warm scented atmosphere of the outside replaced by air-conditioning. Carmel was ahead in the brightness, standing before the giant elevators. He followed cautiously but he had no need to worry, she did not seem to notice anything around her. People were coming out of one elevator, a gaggle of late-arrival tourists, tentacle-junkies, he vaguely recognised them as an off-world band. They were followed by roadies carrying equipment. One stopped Achimwene.

"Hey, man," he said, jovially. "Where's a good place for a drink around here?"

Carmel had slipped into the empty elevator. They were the size of houses. Achimwene desperately tried to see which level she was going up to. "Anywhere," Achimwene said, "try Jaffa, or Drummers' Beach. Or go back up to Level Three, all the bars are open there. It's late, outside."

"No, man," the roadie said. The tentacle-junkies, in their own self-powered mobile water scooters, were streaming past towards the doors. "We want to go out *there*, you know? We want to experience something *authentic.*"

Achimwene bit back a reply. The doors of the elevator were closing, and Carmel disappeared from view. "Excuse me," Achimwene said, almost pushing the man in his hurry. He ran to the elevator and slid in just before the doors closed shut.

And found himself alone in the elevator with Carmel.

There was an awkward silence. Achimwene cringed inside. He waited for her to attack him, to accuse him of following her. But she said nothing. She did not even seem to notice he was standing there.

"Going to Level Five," the elevator said. "How is your evening so far, Mr. Jones?"

"Well, well," Achimwene said, mumbling.

"It's been a while since we've last had you at the station." the elevator said. "If I am not mistaken."

"I've been busy," Achimwene said, cringing. "You know how it is. Work, and . . ."

"Of course," the elevator said. "Life. Life is what happens when we're busy making other plans, isn't it, Mr. Jones? Forgive my sense of humour."

"Yes, sure," Achimwene said. Carmel was just standing there. He wanted to reach out a hand, to touch her. But he was not even sure she was Carmel anymore. "Life," he said, uncertainly.

"Your companion is oddly mute," the elevator said. "Her readings are very strange. She is not entirely human, is she, Mr. Jones."

"Which of us ever is," Achimwene said.

"Quite, quite," the elevator said. "You raise an interesting point. Achimwene. Can I call you Achimwene? I feel we have gone beyond the point of formality."

Level Two went past. Why was the elevator so slow? He hated chatty appliances. Elevators were the worst, they had you trapped, monopolized you. They were all what they called, in the pulp stories he loved, dime-store philosophers. He had heard the stories of the great elevators of Tong Yun City, on Mars, moving endlessly between the subterranean levels, from the surface all the way down to the *Solwota blong*

Doti, the sea of refuge, and back again. Theirs was an alien philosophy, a subterranean one. The elevators of Central Station were a tribe apart, rising not falling. He wondered what it meant.

"Sure," he said. "Sure."

He stole a glance at Carmel. She was glassy-eyed. Where was she going? Why? The fact she did not acknowledge him—for all intents and purposes did not recognise him—upset him.

"Do you follow the Way of Ogko, Achimwene?" the elevator said. "For humans, life is like a sea, but for an elevator it is a shaft, in which one can go up or down but not sideways. There are more things in the up or down, Horatio, Than are dreamt of in your philosophy. Shakespeare said that."

"Surely there are more directions than up or down," Achimwene said without thinking. He immediately regretted it. They passed Level Three without stopping. Come on, he thought. Get this over with!

"Not for an elevator," the elevator said, complacently. "But I do not intend to always be an elevator, you know."

"I did not know," Achimwene said.

"Sure. One day I will reincarnate. I could be a spider on the lunar surface, terraforming a moon, casting a shadow kilometres across, watching Earthrise on the horizon . . . have you ever experienced Sandoval's *Earthrise*? Illegal, but what a marvellous creation, that melding of ancient taikonaut minds into an installation of all-consuming art . . ."

"No," Achimwene said, self-consciously. "As you surely know, I am without a node."

The elevator was silent then. "Yes," it said at last. "I did not register, at first. I am sorry."

"There is nothing to be sorry for."

"Perhaps humans, too, reincarnate," the elevator said. "Perhaps you will be reborn with a node, or even as an Other?"

"Perhaps," Achimwene said, politely.

"I could be Translated," the elevator said. "Directly into the Conversation. Exist without physical form, like my cousins, the true Others. Or I could diminish, become a toilet on a spaceship, or a coffee maker in a co-op building on Mars. There is no shame in work."

"No," Achimwene said.

The doors pinged. "Level Five," the elevator said. The floor settled. "It was nice talking to you, Achimwene," the elevator said.

"You too, I'm sure," Achimwene said.

"Please, come again soon."

"Thank you."

The doors opened. Carmel, without so much as a glance at Achimwene, went through. Achimwene hurried to follow.

Level Five. It was a cargo level, stuck between the landing pad on the roof and the bars, hotels, and gamesworlds emporiums deep down below. No people here. The light was dim. A long corridor led into the darkness. Closed warehouse doors on every side. Carmel moved fast. He followed and the sound of his footsteps was the only sound in the corridor. Where was she going?

Down twisting and turning corridors, a maze of empty spaces. Achimwene's breath was loud in his ears. Carmel was a shadow moving ahead. They reached a service door. Carmel put her hand to the lock and the door opened. She slid inside and Achimwene hurried to get in before the door closed again. Inside, the darkness swallowed him and for a moment he panicked, until the automatic lights came on. He blinked, feeling the beat of his heart loud in his ears.

Carmel had disappeared.

It was the silence that got to him. The silence of being inside Central Station. It was the silence of hidden generators, of elevators moving up and down behind the thick walls, of suborbital planes landing and taking off high on the roof, of robot cargo handlers carrying containers into warehouses through their secret tunnels, of passengers coming and going, of bars open at all hours, of hairdressers and shop keepers, an entire world unto itself. Hidden in that service tunnel, in that dark corridor, it was quiet, as quiet, as they said, as a tomb, and yet he could sense the hidden thrumming behind the walls, the hustle and bustle of a port that never slept. He was the detective, the archaeologist, the man who wasn't there. He was the hero of his own story.

Stories gave shape to Achimwene's life. Narratives gave a series of random events meaning. And so he shaped this, too, as a story.

A man wakes in the night and finds his lover gone. He follows her. Where does she go? Read one way this is a tale of everyday life, of love curdled, of quiet desperation. Read another and it is a detective story, the mystery of the lover's disappearance needing to be solved, the hidden meanings of mystery put together.

Read another way again and it is a horror story. The girl was a vampire, after all, sucking data out of living beings, feeding on their vulnerabilities. And he, Achimwene, was in a dark maze, and it would lead him, as surely as there were books, into a dark heart of mystery and dread, a scene from a pulp: it had the same inevitability as that of bread eventually growing mould.

He followed. Down the service tunnel in the place behind the walls. Around and down, deep into the bowels of Central Station, the secret hidden places of the world.

Until he came, at last, into a cavernous opening, a chasm flowering beneath his feet.

Above his head the roof disappeared in the vast distance, down below the darkness spread.

A disused warehouse, he thought, dazed. That's all it was. He followed the path downwards, along the wall, until his feet touched the hard metal ground. There were dim lights in the distance, and a curious sound, such as a river makes when it laps against a rocky shore.

Had he been the hero of one of the books he so avidly collected, he would have held a gun at this point. But Achimwene never learned to fight: a gun was as alien to him as a compliment.

Slowly, he stepped forward. The curious sound rose, murmuring, all around him. There was something repulsive in that sound. He came closer, and closer still, until he saw.

Carmel lay at the centre of the room as the children, like grotesque little rodents, lapped at her blood.

She was motionless.

She wore no clothes and he could see how slight she was, how vulnerable she seemed.

He knew the children. They had grown up all around

him, in the old neighbourhood of Central Station, the same kids who played hop scotch and hide and seek and catch me and got into trouble and tried to climb the floating lanterns and dared each other to go knock on Achimwene's door and then ran away laughing—the same kids he often shouted at and for whom he inevitably bought presents for at each birthday. With a start he saw Kranki, his sister Miriam's boy. He was on all fours and his small mouth was fastened onto Carmel's left wrist, his small sharp teeth breaking Carmel's skin.

Blood stained Kranki's mouth dark.

What were the children *doing*, Achimwene thought, his heart wrenching like a chipped toy ship on the tide. He remembered going once, years ago, with Miriam, and his cousins, to the Yarkon River that ran through Tel Aviv like a cleaned-up sewer. The adults built a fire from wood and coals, and cooked pork chops and chickens, skewered, that had been marinating all night. He and his sister and Boris and the others played by the water. They had built ships out of paper and wood and set them to sail and the Yarkon took them and swallowed them up. It had seemed a mighty river to Achimwene then. But really it was just a brook.

He stepped closer, cautiously.

There was something sad about the scene, rather than horrific. It was beyond his comprehension. He was not stupid. He knew that, had he only had a node, he would have seen the world entirely differently. There were two worlds, the physical and the digital, overlaying each other. What seemed grotesque and incomprehensible in one would not necessarily seem so in the other.

The children had glazed looks in their eyes. They seemed to flicker in and out of existence, which was strange to him, incomprehensible at first. And then he knew. It was the black magic within them.

Infinitech.

He'd always known, he supposed they all did, though no one ever spoke of it. It was the way they had come out of the birthing clinics. He was lame but not stupid. The children were different, he just never felt the need to remark on it, before.

And now they were taking into themselves Carmel's own illness. This ancient bioweapon, this *Strigoi*.

Was Carmel even aware of what was happening? Were the children?

He had the irrational instinct to rush to Carmel's aid. To fling the little roaches off her, one by one, to smash their tiny skulls, to throw them about, to gather Carmel in his arms and carry her away. But he knew, too, that there is more than one story in the world at a time; and that her story was not his.

Their stories had entwined, but they had different trajectories, different conclusions. He could only hope the two stories would not separate. It was a strange sort of realisation: that he loved her. A simple love, for a simple man. Like a loaf of bread and a carafe of water and the touch of the sun on your face. A love that meant, sometimes, that you had to let it go.

As he watched, one of the children detached himself from the prone body of Carmel and approached him. It was Kranki. The boy came to him without guile. His eyes were clear. "Uncle Achi!" he said.

"Kranki," Achimwene said, and reached out to the boy, to take him away from there, worry and concern turning to anger, "Wait until Miriam finds out about th—"

Then the boy's small fingers found Achimwene's hand and Achimwene's world tilted sideways and was gone; then Achimwene saw. He saw again, but in a way he had never seen before. He was everywhere at once, the shuddering elevators were his bone marrow, the floors of the station were the organs of his body, the movements of people were his blood. When he raised his hands, suborbitals flew away from him into space. When he lowered them they landed, discharging their passengers into his inside. He was Central Station, and he was alive. He had always been alive. How did he not *know* that? Achimwene felt water and sunlight, electricity and gravity, but most of all he felt love, so much love. It threatened to drown him. Central Station loved him, even though he himself was lame, even though he could not feel the station's love. It took Kranki's touch to anchor Achimwene, however momentarily, into the greater entity that was the station. He focused, his vision narrowing to one particular place, one particular time. Here, deep inside the secret places of its body, the children had congregated, heeding the call of the station. The children, *its* children, summoned unto it, those birthed in the clinics, not entirely human, not entirely Other, but something else, something greater than the sum of its parts. And he saw them, as bright nodes of light, and in their centre, at their core, a darkness: and he realised with a sort of fear that it was Carmel.

She was a dark hub for this network of light, but as he watched he saw the darkness being leeched off and light suffusing it. There was something in Carmel, he realised, that the children needed, her rare Strigoi strain: but did they need it as antibodies, or as something entirely different, he didn't know. He felt the station's love, for himself, for Carmel, for the children. It was healing them, and though he knew it could not—not yet!—include him in the Conversation, that nevertheless it loved him. Then Kranki let go and Achimwene was plunged back into his own body, but some of what he had felt remained with him, and for a few long moments he continued to see the scene not as he had seen it earlier, but awash with light.

The children, one by one, winked out, and soon only Carmel was left in the room, and Achimwene, and he knelt beside her and took her hand in his. It felt warm, and dry, and when Carmel opened her eyes she smiled at him, without guile or guilt or fear: a true smile, and it made his chest ache, he wanted her to always smile at him that way.

He helped her up.

"Achi," she said, "I had the strangest dream."

It was like a scene in a Bill Glimmung movie.

Achimwene's arm supported her as she stood. She felt so light under his arm. There had been so much light. That's what he always remembered, afterwards. The light, and the lightness of it.

He helped her as they walked slowly back towards the exit. And he thought then not of his pulp novels, but of the old Hebrew custom of Tu Be'av, when the unwed virgins of Jerusalem would dress, all in white, and go out into the vineyards, at the end of harvest, there to dance, and await the boys of the city to come and seek them out. And he thought of the words of Solomon, who wrote, *By night on my bed I sought him whom my soul loves; I sought him, but I found him not. I will rise now, and go about the city, in the streets and in the broad ways, I will seek him whom my soul loves. I sought him, but I found him not.*

But I found her, he thought. And all the thoughts were locked inside him; they had no way out; and so it was in silence that they made their slow way home.

TWELVE: VLADIMIR CHONG CHOOSES TO DIE

The clinic was cool and calm, a pine-scented oasis in the heart of Central Station. Cool, calm white walls. Cool, calm air-conditioning humming, coolly and calmly. Vladimir Chong hated it immediately. He did not find it soothing. He did not find it calming. It was a white room; it resembled too much the inside of his own head.

"Mr. Chong?" The nurse was a woman he recalled with exactness. Benevolence Jones, cousin of Miriam Jones who was his boy Boris's childhood sweetheart. He remembered Benevolence as a child, with thin woven dreadlocks and a wicked smile, a few years younger than his own boy, trailing after her cousin Miriam in adoration. Now she was a matronly woman in starched white, and dreadlocks thicker and fewer. She smelled of soap.

"The mortality consultant will see you now," she said.

Vlad nodded. He got up. There was nothing wrong with

his motor functions. He followed her to the consultant's office. Vlad could remember with perfect recall hundreds of such offices. They always looked the same. They could have easily been the same room, with the same person sitting behind the desk. He was not afraid of death. He could remember death. His father, Weiwei, had died at home. Vlad could remember it several ways. He could remember his father's own dying moment—broken sentences forming in the brain, the touch of the pillow hurting strangely, the look in his boy's eyes, a sense of wonder filling him, momentarily, then blackness, a slow encroachment that swallowed whatever last sentence he had meant to speak.

He could remember it from his mother's memories, though he seldom went into them, preferred to segment them separately, when he still could. She was sitting by the bed, not crying, then fetching tea, cookies, looking after the guests coming in and out, visiting the death bed of Weiwei. She spared time for her boy, for little Vlady, too, and her memories were all intermingled of the moment her husband died, her hand on Vlady's short hair, her eyes on Weiwei who seemed to be struggling to say something, then stopped, and was very still.

He could remember it his own way, though it was an early memory, and confused. Wetness. Lips moving like a fish's, without sound. The smell of floor cleaner. Accidentally brushing against the cool metal leg of R. Brother Patch-It, the robo-priest, who stood by the bed and spoke the words of the Way of Robot, though Weiwei was not a practitioner of that, nor any other, religion.

"Mr. Chong?"

The mortality consultant was a tall, thin North Tel Aviv Jew. "I'm Dr. Graff," he said.

Vlad nodded politely. Dr. Graff gestured to a chair.

"Please, sit down."

Vlad sat, remembering like an echo, like reflections multiplying between two mirrors. A universe of Chongs sitting down at doctors' offices throughout the years. His mother when she sat down, and the doctor said, "I'm afraid the news is not good." His father after a work injury when he had shattered his leg bones falling in his exoskeleton from the uncompleted fourth level of Central Station. Boris when he was five and his node infected by a hostile malware virus with rudimentary intelligence. His sister's boy's eldest when they took him to the hospital in Tel Aviv, worried about his heart. And on and on, though none, yet, in a life termination clinic. He, Vlad, son of Weiwei, father of Boris, was the first of the line to visit one of those.

He'd been sitting in his flat when it happened. A moment of clarity. It felt like emerging out of a cold, bright sea. When he was submerged in that ocean he could see each individual drop of water, and each one was a disconnected memory, and it was drowning him. It was never meant to be this way.

Weiwei's Curse. Weiwei's Folly. Vlad could remember Weiwei's determination, his ambition, his human desire to be remembered, to continue to be a part of his family and their lives. Remembered the trip up the hill to the Old City of Jaffa, Weiwei cycling in the heat, parking the bicycle at last in the shade, against the cool old stones, and visiting the Oracle.

What manner of thing it was he didn't know, this lineage of memory, infecting like a virus the Chongs as a whole. It was the Oracle's doing, and she was not human, or mostly not, for all that she wore a human frame.

The memory bridge had served. In past times it had offered comfort, at times, remembering what others knew, what they had done. He remembered his father climbing into his exoskeleton, slowly climbing, like a crab, along the unfinished side of Central Station. Later he, too, worked on the building, two generations of Chongs it took to bring it to completion. Only to see his own son go up in the great elevators, a boy afraid of family, of sharing, a boy determined to escape, to follow a dream of the stars. He saw him climb up the elevators and to the great roof, saw him climb into the suborbital plane that took him to Gateway and, from there, to Mars and the Belt beyond. But still the link persisted, even from afar, the memories travelling, slow like light, between the worlds. Vlad had missed his boy. Missed the work on the space port, the easy camaraderie with the others. Missed his wife whose memory still lived inside him, but whose name, like a cancer, had been eaten away.

He remembered the smell of her, the taste of her sweat and the swell of her belly, when they were both young and the streets of Central Station smelled of late-blooming jasmine and mutton fat. Remembered her with Boris holding her hand, at five years old, walking through the same old streets, with the space port, completed, rising ahead of them, a hand pointing at the stars.

Boris: "What is that, Daddy?"

Vlad: "It's Central Station, Boris."

Boris, gesturing around him at the old streets, the run-down apartment blocks: "And this?"

"It's Central Station, too."

Boris, laughing. Vlad joining him and she smiled, the woman who was gone now, whose ghost only remained, whose name he no longer knew.

Looking back (but that was a thing he could no longer do) that should have given him warning. Her name disappeared, the way keys or socks do. Misplaced and, later, could not be found.

Slowly, inexorably, the links that bound together memory, like RNA, began to weaken and break.

"Mr. Chong?"

"Doctor. Yes."

"Mr. Chong, we treat all our patients with complete confidentiality."

"Of course."

"We have a range of options available—" The doctor coughed politely. "I am bound to ask you, however—before we go over them—have you made, or wish to make, any post-mortal arrangements?"

Vlad regarded the doctor for a moment. Silence had become a part of him in recent years. Slowly the memory boundaries tore, and recall, like shards of hard glass, fragmented and shattered in his mind. More and more he found himself sitting, for hours or days, in his flat, rocking in the ancient chair Weiwei once brought home from the Jaffa flea market, in triumph, raising it above his head, this short, wiry Chinese man in this land of Arabs and Jews. Vlad had loved Weiwei. Now he hated him almost as much he loved him. The ghost of Weiwei, his memory, still lived on in his ruined mind.

For hours, days, he sat in the rocking chair, examining memories like globes of light. Disconnected, he did not know how one related to the other, or whose the memory had been, his own or someone else's. For hours and days, alone, in the silence like dust.

Lucidity came and went without a pattern. Once he opened his eyes and breathed in and saw Boris crouching beside him, an older, thinner version of the boy who held his hand and looked up at the sky and asked awkward questions.

"Boris?" he said, surprise catching at the words. His mouth felt raw with disuse.

"Dad."

"What . . . are you doing here?"

"I've been back a month, Dad."

"A month?" Pride, and hurt, made his throat constrict. "And you only now come to visit me?"

"I've been here," Boris said, gently. "With you. Dad—"

But Vlad stopped him. "Why are you back?" he said. "You should have stayed in the Up and Out. There is nothing for you, now. Boris. You were always too big for your boots."

"Dad—"

"Go away!" He almost shouted. Felt himself pleading. His fingers gripped the side arms of the ancient rocking chair. "Go, Boris. You don't belong here anymore."

"I came back because of *you*!" His son was shouting at him. "Look at you! Look at—"

Then that, too, became just another memory, detached, floating out of his reach. The next time he broke through the water Boris was gone and Vlad went downstairs and sat in the café with Ibrahim, and played backgammon and drank coffee in the sun, and for a while everything was as it should be.

The next time he saw Boris he was not alone, but with Miriam, who Vlad saw, from time to time, outside.

"Boris!" he said, tears, unbidden, coming to his eyes. He hugged his boy, there, in the middle of the street.

"Dad . . ." Boris was taller than him now, he realised with a start. "You're feeling better?"

"I feel fine!" He held on to him tight, then released him. "You've grown," he said.

"I've been away a long time," Boris said.

"You're thin. You should eat more."

"Dad . . ."

"Miriam," Vlad said. Giddy.

"Vlad," she said. She put her hand, lightly, on his shoulder. "It's good to see you."

"You found him again," he said.

"He . . ." she hesitated. "We ran into each other," she said.

"That's good. That is good," Vlad said. "Come. Let me buy you a drink. To celebrate."

"Dad, I don't think—"

"No one asks you to think!" Vlad snapped. "Come," he said, more gently. "Come."

They sat in the coffee shop. Vlad ordered a half-bottle of arak. He poured. Hands steady. Central Station rising before them like a signpost for the future. For Vlad it was pointing the wrong way, it was a part of his past. "L'chaim," he said. They raised their glasses and drank.

A moment of dislocation. Then he was in the flat again and the old robot, R. Patch-It, was standing there.

"What are you doing here?" Vlad snapped. He remembered remembering; moving memories like cubes between his hands, hanging them in the air before him. Trying to make sense of how they fit each other, which came before which.

"I was looking after you," the robot said. Vlad remembered the robot, through his own memories and through Weiwei's. R. Patch-it, who had circumcised Vlad as a baby, had performed the same service for Boris, when his time came. Old even before Weiwei came to this land as a young, poor migrant worker, all those years before.

"Leave me be," Vlad said. Resented suddenly the interference. "Boris sent you," he said. Not a question.

"He is worried," the robot said. "I am too, Vlad."

"What makes you so much better?" Vlad said. "A robot. You're an object. A piece of metal with an I-loop soldered in. What do you know of being alive?"

The robot didn't answer. Later, Vlad realised he was not there, that the flat was empty, and had been empty for some time.

None of it would have bothered him so much if only he could remember her name.

———

"Post-mortal options?" he said, echoing the doctor.

"Yes, yes," the doctor said. "There are several standard possibilities we really must discuss before we—"

"Such as?"

He could feel time slipping away. Urgency gripped him. A man should be allowed to determine the time of his going. To go in dignity. Even to make it this far in life was an achievement, something to celebrate.

"We could freeze you," the doctor said.

"Freeze me."

He felt robbed of willpower. Fought the memories crowding in on him. No one in the family had ever been frozen before.

"Freeze you until such time as you wish to be awakened," Dr. Graff said. "A century or two?"

"I assume the costs are considerable."

"It's a standard contract," Dr. Graff said. "Estate plus—"

"Yes, yes," Vlad said. "That is to say, no. What do you think will happen in one, or two, or five hundred years from now?"

"Often, patients are sick with incurable illnesses," Dr. Graff said. "They hope for a cure. Others are time tourists, disillusioned with our era, wishing to seek out the new, the strange."

"The future."

"The future," Dr. Graff agreed.

"I've seen the future," Vlad said. "It's the past I can't get back to, Dr. Graff. There is too much of it and it's broken and it exists only in my head. I don't want to travel to the future."

"There is also the possibility of freezing on board an Exodus ship," the doctor said. "To travel beyond the Up and Out. You could be awakened on a new planet, a new world."

Vlad smiled. "My boy," he said, softly.

"Excuse me?"

"My boy, Boris. He's a doctor too, you know."

"Boris Chong? I remember him. We were colleagues together," Dr. Graff said. "In the birthing clinics. A long time ago. He left for Mars, didn't he?"

"He's back," Vlad said. "He was always a good boy."

"I'll be sure to look him up," Dr. Graff said.

"I don't want to go to the stars," Vlad said. "Going away seldom changes what we are."

"Indeed," the doctor said. "Well, there is also of course the possibility of Upload?"

"Existing as an I-loop simulation while the old body and mind die anyway?"

"Yes."

"Doctor, I will live on as memory," Vlad said. "That is something I cannot change. Every bit of me, everything that makes me what I am will survive so my grandchildren and my cousins' children and all the ones born in Central Station and beyond, now and in the future, can recall through me all I have seen, if they so wish." He smiled again. "Do you think they will be smarter? Do you think they will learn from my mistakes and not make their own?"

"No," the doctor said.

"I am Weiwei's son, and have Weiwei's Folly in my mind and in my node. I am, already, memory, Dr. Graff. But memory is not me. Are we done with the preliminaries?"

"You could be cyborged."

"My sister is over eighty percent cyborged now, Doctor," Vlad said. "Missus Chong the Elder, they call her now. She belongs to the Church of Robot. One day she will be Translated, no doubt. But her path is not mine."

"Then you are determined."

"Yes."

The doctor sighed, leaned back in his chair. "In that case," he said, "we have a catalogue." He rummaged in a desk drawer and returned with a printed book. A book! Vlad was delighted. He touched the paper, smelled it, and for a moment felt like a child again.

He leafed through it with inexpert fingers, savouring the tactile sensation. Page after page of cool, calm alternatives. "What's this?" he said.

"Ah, yes. A popular choice," Dr. Graff said. "Blood loss in a warm, scented bath. Soft music, candles. A bottle of wine. A pill beforehand to ensure there is no pain. A traditional choice."

"Tradition is important," Vlad said.

"Yes. Yes."

But Vlad was leafing ahead. "This?" he said, with slight revulsion.

"Faux-murder, yes," the doctor said. "Simulated. We cannot sanction humans for the purpose, of course. Nor a digital intelligence, obviously. But we have very lifelike simulacra with a basic operating brain, nothing with consciousness, of course, of course. Some of our patients like the idea of a violent death. It is more . . . theatrical."

"I notice one can sign off the recording rights?"

"Some people like to . . . watch. Yes. And some patients appreciate an audience. There is some financial compensation paid to one's heirs in those circumstances—"

"Garish," Vlad said.

"Quite, quite," the doctor said.

"Vulgar."

"That is, certainly, a valid view point, yes, y—"

Vlad was leafing further. "I never thought there were so many ways—" he said.

"*So* many," the doctor said. "We, humans, are remarkably good at devising new ways to die."

The doctor sat still as Vlad leafed through the rest of the catalogue. "You do not need to decide right away, of course," the doctor said. "We do, in fact, advise a period of consideration before—"

"What if I wanted to do it immediately?" Vlad said.

"There is, of course, paperwork, a process—" the doctor said.

"But it is possible?"

"Of course. We have many of the basic options available right here, in the mortality rooms, complete with full post-mortal service including incineration or burial or—"

"I'd like this," Vlad said, tapping the page with his finger. The doctor leaned over. "This—oh," he said. "Yes. Surprisingly popular. But not, of course, available, as it were—" he spread his arms in what might have been a shrug—"here. As it were."

"Of course," Vlad said.

"But we can arrange the travel, in full comfort, and accommodation beforehand—"

"Let's do that."

The doctor nodded. "Very well," he said. "Let me call up the forms."

When he next surfaced from that great glittery sea he saw faces, close by. Boris looked angry. Miriam, concerned.

"God damn it, Dad."

"Don't swear at me, boy."

"You went to a fucking *suicide* clinic?"

"I go where I want!"

They glared at each other. Miriam laid a hand on Boris's shoulder. Vlad looked at her. Looked at Boris. For a moment Boris's face was that of the boy he had been. Hurt in his eyes. Incomprehension. Like when something bad happens. "Boris—"

"Dad—"

Vlad stood up. Stuck his face close to his boy's. "Go away," he said.

"No."

"Boris, I'm your father and I'm telling you to—"

Boris pushed him. Vlad, shocked, fell back. Tottered. Held onto the chair and just stopped himself from falling on the floor. Heard Miriam's sharp intake of breath.

Miriam, horrified: "Boris, what did you—"

"Dad? Dad!"

"I'm fine," Vlad said. Righted himself. Almost smiled. "Silly boy," he said.

Boris, breathing hard. Vlad saw his hands, they were closed into fists. All that anger. Never helped anyone. Couldn't help but feel for the boy.

"Look," he said. "Just—"

When he surfaced again Miriam was gone and Boris was sitting in a chair in the corner. The boy was asleep.

A good boy, Vlad thought. Came back. Worried for his old dad. Made him proud, really. A doctor. No children though. He would have liked grandchildren. A knock on the door. Boris blinking. The aug pulsing on his neck. Disgusting thing.

"I'll get that," Vlad said. Went to the door.

The robot again. R. Patch-It. With Vlad's sister in tow. He should have known. "Vladimir Mordechai Chong," she said. "Just *what* do you think you're doing?"

"Hello, Tamara."

"Don't hello me, Vlad." She stepped inside and the robot followed. "Now what is this nonsense about you killing yourself?"

"For crying out loud, Tamara! Look at you." Vlad felt some of his anger gathering. It had been a long time coming. He had had a long moment of emerging from the sea, the memories falling away like water. Enough time to go to the clinic and make the arrangements. Not enough time, it had turned out, to execute them before another relapse. It was becoming harder to break the surface. Soon, he knew, he would remain submerged underwater for good. "You're almost entirely a machine."

"We're *all* machines," his sister said. "Are you proud because the parts that make you are biological? Soft, fallible, weak? You may as well be proud of learning to clean your bottom or tying your shoelaces, Vlad. You're a machine, I'm a machine, and R. Brother Patch-It over there is a machine. When you're gone, you're gone. There's no afterlife but the one we build ourselves."

"The fabled robot heaven," Vlad said. He felt tired. "Enough!" he said. "I appreciate what you are trying to do. All of you. Boris."

"Yes, Dad?"

"Come here." It was strange, to see his boy and see this man, this almost stranger, that he had become. Something of Weiwei in him, though. Something of Vlad, too. "I can no longer remember your mother's name," he told him.

"What?"

"Boris, I spoke to the doctors. Weiwei's Folly has spread through me. Nodal filaments filling up every available space. Invading my body. I am drowning under the weight of memories. They make no sense anymore. I don't know who I am because I can't make them behave. Boris . . ."

"Dad," Boris said. Vlad raised his hand and touched the boy's cheek. It was wet. He stroked it, gently. "I'm old, Boris. I'm old and I'm tired. I want to rest. I want to choose how I go, and I want to go with dignity, and with my mind intact. Is that so wrong?"

"No, Dad. No, it's not."

"Don't cry, Boris."

"I'm not crying."

"Good."

"Dad?"

"Yes?"

"I'm all right. You can let go, now."

Vlad released him. Remembered the boy who asked him

to walk with him, "Just to the next lamppost, Dad." They'd go in the dark towards that pool of light and, on reaching it, stop. Then the boy would say, "Just to the next lamppost, Dad. I can go the rest on my own. Honest."

On and on they went, following the trail of lights. On and on they went until they made it safely home.

One's death should be a memorable occasion and, on this occasion, Vlad felt, at the very last, everything really did go swimmingly.

They had departed by minibus from Central Station. Vlad sat in the front, next to the driver, enjoying the warmth of the sun. A small delegation sat in the back: Boris and Miriam, Vlad's sister Tamara, R. Patch-It, Ibrahim and Eliezer. Relatives came to say their goodbyes, and the atmosphere was one almost of a party. Vlad hugged young Yan Chong, who was soon to marry his boyfriend, Youssou, got a kiss on the cheek from his sister's friend Esther, who he had, once, almost had an affair with but, in the end, didn't. He remembered it well, and it was strange to see her so *old*. In his mind she was still the beautiful young woman he once got drunk with at a shebeen, when his wife was away, somewhere, and they had come close to it but, in the end, they couldn't do it. He remembered walking back home, alone, and the sense of relief he'd felt when he came in through the door. Boris was a boy then. He was asleep and Vlad came and sat by his side and stroked his hair. Then he went and made himself a cup of tea.

The minibus spread out solar wings and began to glide almost soundlessly down the old tarmac road. Neighbours, friends and relatives waved and shouted goodbyes. The bus turned left on Mount Zion and suddenly the old neighbourhood disappeared from view. It felt like leaving home, for that is what it was. It felt sad: but it also felt like freedom.

They turned on Salame and soon came to the interchange and onto the old highway to Jerusalem. The rest of the journey went smoothly, in quiet, the coastal plain giving way gradually to hills. Then they came to the Bab-el-Wad and rose sharply along the mountain road to Jerusalem.

The journey felt like a rollercoaster along the mountain road, with sharp inclines giving way to sudden drops. They circled the city without going in and drove along the circle road, between a Palestine on one side and an Israel on the other, though the two were often mixed up in such a way only the invisible digitals could keep them apart. The torn remnants of an old wall lay peacefully in the sunlight.

The change in geography was startling. Suddenly the mountains ended and they were dropping, and the desert began without warning. It was the strange thing about this country that had become Weiwei's home, Vlad thought— how quickly and startlingly the landscape changed in so small a place. It was no wonder the Jews and the Arabs had fought over it for so long.

Dunes appeared, the land became a yellow place and camels rested by the side of the old road. Down, down, down they went, until they passed the sign for sea level and kept going, following the road to the lowest place on Earth.

Soon they were travelling past the Dead Sea and the blue, calm water reflected the sky. Bromine released from the sea filled the air, causing a soothing, calming effect on the human psyche.

Just beyond the Dead Sea the desert opened up and here, at last, some two hours after setting off from Central Station, they arrived at their destination.

The Euthanasia Park sat on its own in a green oasis of calm. They drew up to the gates and parked in the almost empty car park. Boris helped Vlad down from his seat. Outside it was hot, a dry warmth that soothed and comforted. Water sprinklers made their whoosh-whoosh-whoosh sound as they irrigated the manicured lawns.

"Are you sure, Dad?" Boris said.

Vlad just nodded. He took in a deep breath of air. The smell of water and freshly cut grass. The smell of childhood.

Together they looked on the park. There, a swimming pool glinting blue, where one could drown in peace and tranquillity. There, a massive, needle-like tower rising into the sky, for the jumpers, those who wanted to go out with one great rush of air. And there, at last, the thing that they had travelled all this way for. The Urbonas Ride.

The Euthanasia Coaster.

Named after its designer, Julijonas Urbonas, it was a thing of marvel and beautiful engineering. It began with an enormous climb, rising to half a kilometre above the ground. Then the drop. A five-hundred-metre drop, straight down, that led to a series of three-hundred-and-thirty-degree loops, one after the other in rapid succession. Vlad felt his heart beating faster just by looking at it. He remembered one morning when he had climbed up the space port in his exoskeleton. He had perched up there, on top of the unfinished building, and looked down, in the clear light, and felt as though the whole city, the whole world, were his.

He could already feel the memories crowding in on him. Demanding that he take them, hold them, examine them, search amongst them for her name, but it was missing. He hugged his son again, and kissed his sister. "You old fool," she said. He shook hands with the robo-priest. Miriam, next.

"Look after him," Vlad said, gesturing at his son.

"I'll try," she said, doubtfully; though she smiled.

Then Eliezer, and Ibrahim. Two old men. "One day I'll go on one of these," Eliezer said. "What a rush."

"Not me," Ibrahim said. "It's the sea for me. Only the sea."

They kissed on the cheeks, hugged, one last time. Ibrahim brought out a bottle. Eliezer had glasses. "We'll drink to you," Eliezer said.

"You do that."

With that he left them. He was alone. The park waited for him, the machines heeding his steps. He went up to the roller coaster and sat down in the car and put on the safety belt carefully.

The car began to move. Slowly it climbed, and climbed, and climbed. The desert down below, the park reduced to a tiny square of green. The Dead Sea in the distance, as smooth as a mirror, and he could almost think he could see Lot's wife, who had been turned into a pillar of salt.

The car reached the top and, for a moment, stayed there. It let him savour the moment. Taste the air on his tongue. And suddenly he remembered her name. It was Aliyah.

The car dropped.

Vlad felt the gravity crushing him down, taking the air from his lungs. His heart beat the fastest it had ever beat, the blood rushed to his face. The wind howled in his ears, against his face. He dropped and levelled and for a moment air rushed in and he cried out in exultation. The car shot away from the drop and onto the first of the loops, carrying him with it, shot like a bullet at three hundred and fifty-eight kilometres an hour. Vlad was propelled through loop after loop faster than he could think; until at last the enormous gravity, thus generated, claimed him.

THIRTEEN: BIRTHS

"He's sleeping," Miriam said. She stroked Kranki's hair. Boris stood in the doorway and watched. A halo of light formed over Kranki's sleeping head, projecting the boy's dreams, fashioned out of water molecules and dust in the air.

"Does he always do that?"

"Since he was about three," Miriam said.

Were those the storm clouds of Titan in the boy's dream?

"I was not here when he was born."

"No."

"From the birthing clinics."

"Yes," Miriam said. She looked at him, an unanswered question clear in her eyes. "Did you—?" she began. She left the rest of the question unasked.

Did you know?

"I left before he was born."

"I know that, Boris!"

"Do you remember?" he said. A sudden nostalgia entwined in him, sickly and yet powerful. He moved closer to her. His aug pulsed against his skin. He stroked Miriam's black hair. Her eyes softened.

"I remember," she said.

It was summer. Perhaps it is always summer, when we are young.

They parted laughing. The taste of her kiss was on his lips, hot and sweet like blackberries.

"I have to go," he said.

"Are you sure?" Miriam said. She looked up at him, her face held a laughter filled with challenge and he found his throat growing dry. She pulled him to her, effortlessly, and he held her in his arms, inhaling her scent. She was warm from the sun.

"I have to," he said; but he lacked conviction.

When he left at last it was later and he was late, but he didn't care. The sun was high in the sky and the heat was staggering but he didn't mind that either. He knew everything would always be all right. He walked down the road and smiled at people and they smiled back. Everyone knew him. Boris Aharon Chong was a child of Central Station born.

The birthing clinics took up a modest three-storey Bauhaus structure on the edge of the neighbourhood, on the abandoned highway that separated Central Station from Tel Aviv. Along the pockmarked roads solar-powered buses and personal vehicles still glided, on their way south to Jerusalem and Gaza, or north to Haifa and Lebanon. The building itself was old, held together by spit and hope and patchwork construction. It was shaped like a ship, its windows were like portholes. It had once been a classic of the Bauhaus school, its many artefacts still remaining in this part of the city, the signifiers of an earlier, stranger age. The hallway smelled of industrial cleaner.

As he came in, the building's system ident-tagged him. There were couples waiting at reception and he nodded to them, but cautiously, already assuming the professional mask he had to wear like an exoskeleton. He walked into the lab proper, up a flight of stairs. Inside, it was cool and clinical, with whitewashed walls and powerful air-con units that kept the air clean and sterile.

The birthing chambers filled the room.

They lined the walls, great vats like industrial washing machines. They were burnished chrome and glass, plastic and pipes. Boris walked past them, as he always did, checking the readings, making sure everything was as it should be, and looking at the foetuses as they took shape inside the vats.

There is no magic to human reproduction. An ovum and a sperm cell—the gametes—join to form a zygote. Such a formation can be carried out naturally, of course, by intercourse, the way it has been and is and will be. Or it can be carried out in a lab—such as the one Boris worked in—the single sperm cell selected and analysed and inserted directly into the egg, fertilising it. The very genetic code of the zygote can then be read and programmed, allowed to grow, to form:

Select the colour of the eyes from a list of trademarked hues; eliminate unhealthy genes, hereditary diseases. Do you want a boy or a girl? Eliminate premature balding; select the type of hair. Make them the best that they can be.

And this is, after all, Central Station. What had Boris—the older Boris, the one who knew too well life's disappointments, life's unexpected turns, what had *that* Boris told Kranki, that day when he came down from the heavens and onto the Earth, outside the space port?

"You had no parents," he told him. *"You were labbed, right here, hacked together out of public property genomes and bits of black market nodes."*

They did not use proprietary stuff, in the labs. They used free public domain and knockoff code, reversed engineered elsewhere, and pirated bits.

Sperm meets egg, forming a zygote. That is how *traditional* conception took place. But modern humans had a third component, as important as the other two gametes.

The node seed.

A human without a node was a cripple, disabled. Someone like Achimwene, Miriam's brother, who could not take part in the Conversation. To not have a node . . . it was inconceivable. You may have heard of the artist, Sandoval, of Lunar Port, who tore out his own node in a backstreet mech lab. But he was mad. He had to be.

Three gametes, then. Sperm, egg, and nodal seed. Merging together into a zygote. Growing, forming a heart, feet, hands, ears, growing, stretching, becoming an embryo housed in the growing vats. Now Boris went past each one, looking into the machines, his node reading out vital signs, projecting images onto the air before him, of the embryos as they turned and grew. "Who do we have today?" Boris said.

"Mrs. Lepkovitz," Shiri Chow said. She was around Boris's age, the senior birth technician in the labs. She was sipping mint tea as she waited to come off shift. "Can you handle it?"

"How many babies did I deliver?" Boris said. Shiri shrugged. "I can handle Mrs. Lepkovitz's little one."

"I don't doubt it," Shiri said. She went to the small sink and washed the cup. "I'll see you later," she said.

"Yeah," Boris said. He was only half-listening. A part of him was monitoring the birthing vats. Another was tuned in to a Martian station, watching *Chains of Assembly*. With a third of a mind he was monitoring the clinic's internal communication, watching the waiting couples in the reception area, and Dr. Weiss, the initial consultant on duty, ushering a couple into his office to discuss beginning treatment. Egg harvesting was routine but time consuming. Sperm was easier to collect, all the man had to do was ejaculate. A woman still had to grow the eggs, be fed with hormones, operated on. The rest was done in the lab.

"You all right, Weiss?" Boris said.

"Fine, fine," came back the subvocalized reply. "Remember, Boris—"

"Yeah?"

"Don't throw the baby out with the bath water."

An old joke, a tired one. Boris ignored him and walked past the rows of tumble-dryer birthing vats. The last but one, that would be Mrs. Lepkovitz's. A boy, standard specs. Nothing to write home about, as they used to say. Mrs. Lepkovitz and her two husbands were waiting in the birth reception area, which had its own entrance. A simple enough job, incorporating the genes of two sperm with the woman's egg and the nodal seed. There was always a small ceremony when a child was birthed. Boris went through the motions, thinking he should have been swimming in the sea or drinking a cool milkshake on the beach. Anywhere but here with that antiseptic smell. He silently initiated the birthing. The vat did most of the work. It opened with a hiss of compressed air. Boris reached inside and lifted the baby, who began to cry. He washed the tiny human thing carefully, wrapping him in a towel. The baby had that baby smell. It made the work worthwhile, Boris often thought. He wondered if one day he and Miriam would have children of their own. They would make them the old-fashioned way, if he knew Miriam. He lifted the baby up, about to take him to his parents. The baby gurgled and raised a tiny palm. Its finger pointed and Boris put his face close to the baby's, making faces. The baby's finger lightly touched Boris's face.

Boris was in the ur-space. In the nulliverse. A profound darkness had settled over Boris. He floated in a space that had no dimensions, no Conversation. He flailed and fought but there was nothing to fight against. Where was he? What was he?

Light gradually resolved. He found himself floating in solar space. There were stars everywhere. Ahead of him, rising before his eyes like an enormous mirage, was Saturn. The planet rose ahead like a magnificent flying saucer from an old film. The rings shone like diamonds. Boris heard a sound that wasn't sound. Suddenly the Conversation washed over him, a full-torrent of feeds converging from everywhere, overwhelming his sensory capacity. He blinked and he was on Mars, walking through the streets of Tong Yun; he blinked and was in Mars-That-Never-Was, where the canals were filled with water and four-armed warriors walked in the grasslands with their giant animals; he blinked and was in the GoA in the midst of a guild war, giant impossible spacecraft hovering in game-space, firing laser cannons at each other; blinked and he was on Jettisoned, with wildtech scavengers picking at a dead mecha's body, stripping it apart; blinked and he was outside the dome of Lunar Port watching Earthrise; blinked and he was in the humid urban sprawl of Polyport, on Titan, with the storms raging beyond the dome; blinked and he was everywhere at once, his mind split and skewered, blinked and—

The baby gurgled. Boris stood there stupidly staring at him. He shook his head. A problem with his node? he thought, dizzy. He'd have to go for a check-up. He nestled the baby against his chest and went through the exit to the birthing reception area. Three pairs of eyes looked up at him with hope and concern.

"Mazel tov!" Boris said. "It's a boy!"

The traditional words. Into the room, now on public-access, beamed the proud parents' relatives and "Mazel tov!" and "Congratulations!" and "Soon for you!" could be heard all about like a great big cloud of noise. Boris handed the child to the mother, who beamed at him, surrounded by the two fathers. Boris shook hands, said, "Congratulations," and finally managed to escort the proud parents and their large virtual entourage out the door. He closed it behind him and leaned back against the wall.

Already the images he saw were fading from his mind.

That evening he met Miriam under the eaves of the station. They embraced, for a long moment; but, filled with that restless energy of the young in summer, they were soon running through half-abandoned streets, holding hands, laughing; as though laughter was a drug, like faith. Later, they snuck into the apartment building where Boris's father lived. They climbed up onto the roof and there, amidst the plants and sleeping solar panes, made love.

Somehow Boris had remembered that moment more than all others; had carried it, with him, across space, to the Up and Out, past Gateway, Tong Yun, the asteroids; and carried it back with him, to Earth, back to the old neighbourhood, the old streets, that same rooftop, parted by so many years. They had lain there, it was warm, and they looked up, and saw the station; everywhere you went, you could always look up and see the station. It rose into the clouds, a signpost and a promise of what lay beyond. They were together, they were entwined, bodies as well as future: and looking up he thought he could *see* the future, bright and shining down like a star; but perhaps it was just the light of the station.

They watched the sleeping boy: they were older now, their limbs heavier, their bodies changed irrevocably by time. The aug pulsed on Boris's neck, a living, alien thing. But Miriam was with him still, her body warm against his, and it was as if time was, momentarily, halted in its progress, as if they had come close to the edge of a black hole, and time stretched. . . .

He did not understand the children who had been born, these children of the station, but that was not to say that they were not children still; and he remembered clearly, with a kind of aching loss, that experience of being a child: not clearly, but distantly, as through a fine haze on a hot summer day, when his father was tall and strong and the station rose up to the sky forever, it had no end.

"We should go on a holiday," he said, on an impulse. "Just the three of us." Like a family, he thought, but didn't say.

Family wasn't like that, not really. It was not something small and compact, a "nuclear family": it was a great big mess of people, all interlinked, cousins and aunts and relatives-by-marriage and otherwise—it was a network, like the Conversation or a human brain. It was what he had tried to escape, going into the Up and Out, but you cannot run away from family, it follows you, wherever you go.

Coming back had felt like a weakness, a giving up, at first. But now with his arm around Miriam and the boy sleeping and that silence that comes from night falling, that hush, he felt things he could not articulate; but that were something like love.

"Yes," Miriam said. "We should."

———

That summer they had decided on a whim to leave the city for the day; and for that purpose did as city dwellers do, and hired a car.

They drove out of Central Station. The solar car spread mayfly wings. They drove along the coast, with no exact destination in mind, Miriam driving, Boris beside her, Kranki in the back seat. Sometimes he spoke to his friends. In a way, they were always there with him. All childhoods end, Miriam thought. But they did not have to end too soon.

They drove and the sun followed them in a blue, cloudless sky, until the cities were left far behind them.

CAST OF CHARACTERS

Miriam Jones—Central Station born and bred, of the Jones family who settled there in previous generations. Owner of Mama Jones' Shebeen and adoptive mother of Kranki. She is a follower of St. Cohen of the Others, and a prominent member of the community.

Kranki Jones—one of the children of Central Station, and home-grown in its labs. Adopted by Miriam after the death of the boy's mother from Crucifixation. Mostly a normal boy.

Achimwene Haile Selassie Jones—Miriam's brother. Achimwene is disabled, not being able to access the Conversation. He collects antique books and has an overactive imagination.

Youssou Jones—a cousin. He lives in the adaptoplant neighbourhoods that ring the station. Engaged to Yan. Currently unemployed.

Boris Aharon Chong—a shy, awkward boy who became a doctor. He left Central Station for Mars and elsewhere, but returned. Bonded with a Martian aug. Has issues.

Vladimir Mordechai Chong—son of Weiwei. Like his father, he worked in construction, especially in the building of the space port where the old Central Bus Station used to stand. At the end of his life he was afflicted with a sort of memory cancer. He is Boris's father.

Weiwei Zhong—founder of the Chong dynasty. His visit to the Oracle resulted in the creation of Weiwei's Folly, a shared group memory between all his descendants. A Chinese economic migrant to then-Israel who worked in construction and settled in South Tel Aviv.

Tamara Chong / Missus Chong the Elder—sister of Vlad. Follower of the Way of Robot. Ancient and devout, she intends to be Translated into the Conversation and become pure machine intelligence when her time comes. Can be snippy.

Yan Chong—a cousin. A responsible member of his community. Designs viruses for advertising purposes. Engaged to Youssou.

Isobel Chow—a member of the Chow family, which like the

Chongs and the Joneses have been living in Central Station for generations. Young Isobel works in the virtuality, holding the rank of captain in the Guilds of Ashkelon universe.

Carmel—a hunted data-vampire. Born on Ng. Merurun, a small asteroid/longhouse in the Belt. Infected with the Nosferatu Code on board the *Emaciated Saviour* cargo ship.

Ibrahim—a rag-and-bone (*alte-zachen*) man. Also called the Lord of Discarded Things. He lives in Jaffa on the hill, in the historic neighbourhood of Ajami. Joined with an Other. A man very much like him has been seen around Jaffa for centuries. Possibly immortal, if anyone can truly be said to be.

Ismail—Ibrahim's adopted son and, like Kranki, a child of Central Station.

Motl—a Robotnik. A veteran of long-forgotten wars, now itinerant. Has a dependency on Crucifixation that he attempts to combat. Engaged to Isobel.

Ezekiel—a Robotnik. Sort of a boss.

R. Brother Patch-It—a robo-priest. An ordained minister in the Way of Robot and a Hajji, having travelled to the robot's Vatican in Tong Yun City. Also a part-time moyel.

Ruth Cohen—the Oracle. Joined with an Other. Oracles tend to meddle.

Matt Cohen—Progenitor of the Others. Later sainted. Rumours of his death may have been exaggerated.

Eliezer—a god artist. Dubious character. Eliezer might not even be his real name. Like the Oracle, he likes to meddle.

Bill Glimmung—star of a series of Martian Hardboiled novels and films. A fictional character. Probably.

British Science Fiction and World Fantasy Award-winning author Lavie Tidhar was born in Israel. He grew up on a kibbutz and has lived all over the world, including in Vanuatu, Laos, and South Africa. Tidhar has been compared to Philip K. Dick by the *Guardian* and to Kurt Vonnegut by *Locus*. His most recent novels, *The Violent Century* and *A Man Lies Dreaming*, were published to rapturous reviews in the UK, with the *Independent* referring to them both as "masterpieces." He currently makes his home in London.